"I would very much like to kiss you right now. Is that okay?"

She froze. Who the hell asked permission for a kiss? She'd already given him a sexual green light for the week, so why make a big production number out of a little lip lock?

"Kai?"

Her throat too dry for speech, she rose up on her toes and touched her mouth to his. His lips were warm, softer than she'd expected, and brushed across hers like a breeze. It wasn't enough. She squeezed closer and his arms locked around her, almost lifting her off her feet. The kiss went from gentle to bruising in an instant, and his mouth devoured hers. The world slipped away, all thought of his sister and Joe swept out of her mind as he nibbled a path along her cheek to her earlobe and back.

Kai pulled away first, her breath coming hard and fast, her heart beating an irregular, unrecognizable pulse in her veins. Holy cannoli, Captain Hottie could kiss. He let her go reluctantly, his own breath noticeably uneven. Good. It would be embarrassing if he were unaffected.

"You're a dangerous woman," he said.

PRAISE FOR LAURA K. CURTIS

Twisted

"Sexy small town suspense, with finely drawn characters that will tug at your heart and keep you up at night turning pages."

—Dee Davis, bestselling author of the A-TAC series

"The writing is strong, the characters come to life, and it's a treat to have an interesting, complex female character who sends the message that she can solve her own mysteries and who doesn't exhibit TSTL behavior. Ethan is a well-drawn hero, but this is really Lucy's story, and she absolutely owns it."

—Sunita at Dear Author (DA Recommended Read)

Toying With His Affections

"In Toying with His Affections, Curtis turns the tried and true formula of "bad boy/good girl" on its head and the result is very entertaining. ⋯ this book has the whole package—an actual plot that surrounds the love story instead of just leaving the boy-meets-girl storyline to carry the book; characters who seem real and dimensional and capable of change; and sensual scenes that deliver heat without getting all clinical about it."

—Katherine Tomlinson

ALSO BY LAURA K. CURTIS

ROMANTIC SUSPENSE
Twisted
Lost
Echoes

CONTEMPORARY ROMANCE
Toying With His Affections

CRIME FICTION ANTHOLOGIES
"The Jaws of Life" in
Feeding Kate
"Only People Kill People" in
Murder, NY Style

GAMING THE SYSTEM

LAURA K. CURTIS

For Mary Kryah,
the hardest rocking chick I know.

ACKNOWLEDGEMENTS

There's an old adage in the writing world that instructs us to "write what we know." While I believe there's some value in writing the emotional truths with which you are intimately familiar, when it comes to plot I've always found it more fun to write what I enjoy researching. As such, I am deeply indebted to Siobhan Bouldin for sharing her experiences in a "goody" shop and allowing me to steal one outright for Kai.

My beta reader, Jackson D'Lynne, provided valuable insight. I told her I wanted her to give it to me straight, and she did…you can't ask for more than that! Isobel Carr helped me where my knowledge of print formatting fell apart—if you are holding this book in print, you have her to thank!

I also owe thanks to Heather Osborn, my editor, who corrected all my cringe-worthy mistakes (only some of which I can blame on Dragon's peculiar ideas of speech recognition). Without her assistance, you would not have wanted to read this book.

As always, my thanks to Jessica Faust, who wears many hats as my agent and all-around career shepherd and sanity-keeper.

And last but never least to my husband…he knows why.

CHAPTER 1

THE STRIP WAS BUSY BUT the shop was empty. If Kai didn't know Benny's business was cyclical, she might have worried. But while Vegas ran 24/7/365, most people weren't shopping for sex toys at eleven a.m. on a Wednesday unless there was a wedding in the works, and February was slow for those.

She wandered over to the condom wall to check what needed restocking. They'd had a pretty big group of twenty-somethings in the day before, and while they hadn't bought much, she would be less than surprised to find missing novelty condoms.

And once again, humanity lived down to her expectations.

"Those damned kids yesterday stole most of a row of glow-in-the-darks."

Joe looked over from wiping fingerprints off the counter—a never ending task even when business was off—and raised an eyebrow. "Most of those 'kids' were your age, you know."

"I still say Benny should have locks on the condom racks."

"I know. We all know. Just like you know it's not going to happen because that would stop some of our actual customers who are too embarrassed to ask for our help."

"Yeah, yeah. I might as well see what we need to reorder. I'll be in back. Holler if you need me."

"Sure thing."

No sooner had she pushed through the velvet curtain that separated the store from the stockroom than she heard the bell over the front door tinkle. She checked the security camera to be certain it wasn't one of her regulars or a large group Joe couldn't handle on his own.

The new customer was no threat to Joe, but she almost flipped the curtain back and walked out anyway. He was just that different from the norm. And just that good looking. Wavy, surfer-blond hair fell in a messy mop, brushing the tips of his ears and the back of his neck. A blue T-shirt emblazoned with a Maltese cross stretched over his broad chest. "CAPT" had been stitched at the hem of his left sleeve.

Well, hello, Captain Hottie. What brings you to Goody's Goodies?

Joe greeted him with a big smile and a slap on the back that would have staggered most men. Ah, a personal friend. That made more sense, because she didn't see Captain Hottie as the playful type, though if she'd learned anything working at Goody's, it was that you couldn't judge a kink by its cover. But it was more likely the man had met Joe through his other job as an MMA competitor…he sure had the muscles for it.

She finished doing inventory and went out into the store and reloaded the condom rack. Joe and his buddy had retreated to the hosiery corner, but she could still hear them.

"I'm sorry, man. You deserve better," Captain Hottie said.

"Shit happens." But the words rasped as if Joe were forcing them from his throat. What were they talking about? Despite having worked with Joe for close to a year, she knew almost nothing about his friends or family.

"I wish I had the balls to take one of these blowup dolls to the wedding as my date."

"The hell with that," Joe said. "You ought to take

Kai." Both men turned to look at her and she backed up a few steps.

"I have no idea what you're talking about, but whatever it is, count me out."

Captain Hottie's eyes made a quick pass over her and came back up to linger on the two hoops through her left eyebrow "My God," he said. "You're perfect. You have to say yes."

Her muscles tensed. "I don't *have* to do anything."

"No, of course you don't." He ran a hand through his hair, which made it stand up all over his head. *Too fucking adorable.* "I'm doing this all wrong."

He sucked in a deep breath, let it out slowly, and held out a hand. "Hi, my name is Luke Clarke, and Joe will attest that I'm not as much of a creep as I may have just come off."

She took his hand, unable to prevent the little laugh that popped out. "Kai Tyler. Any friend of Joe's, as they say…"

"Glad to hear that," Luke said, "because I have a proposition that only a friend could make."

"Really?"

"I want you to come to my sister's wedding with me."

"You… What?" No way was that actually what he'd said.

"My sister is getting married. I need a date—I won't bore you with the long and not very happy story about why—and you'd be perfect."

Kai looked him over, from his navy T-shirt with the Maltese cross to his clean jeans and black Italian leather loafers. "Precisely how am I the perfect date for you?"

"Because my parents will avoid you like the plague. They'll be so busy telling themselves that I couldn't possibly be serious about you that they'll leave me alone."

"Wait. You said you needed a date. Not a girlfriend."

"Yeah, I know." He shook his head and those golden

waves bounced around and caught the neon lights of the store. "I told you I was making a mess of things. Here's the deal—my sister Georgette is marrying the owner of the Oasis Springs resort. The whole shebang includes a weeklong extravaganza at the resort, during which time my parents will take every possible opportunity to try to convince me to marry a suitable woman and give up the life I have for the one they want me to have. They've done this before, but it's usually easy enough for me to avoid them."

"Can't you just go for the actual wedding and skip everything else?"

"No." He grimaced and glanced at Joe "I've never met Georgie's fiancé. I didn't realize they were so serious, or I would have made it a point to."

"What is she, sixteen? She needs your approval?"

"She's twenty-nine, and no she doesn't need my approval. For my own peace of mind, I have to be sure she's happy, that this is what she really wants."

"Why wouldn't it be?"

It was Joe who answered. "Luke's having a hard time believing that the same woman who dated me is marrying a man her parents might easily have hand-selected for her."

Kai studied him. Joe never talked about his personal life. She'd seen him fight once in an MMA competition and had met some of the guys he trained with, but she'd never known him to date.

She swung back to Luke. "And if she's not really happy? What then?"

"Then I'll get her out of it." Broad shoulders lifted in a careless shrug.

So damned confident. What must it be like to just assume you could make the world do what you wanted?

"What do you think, Joe? Should I go?"

He frowned. "Would I like to be sure Georgie is doing the right thing? Yes. And you've got plenty of vacation time coming. You've been working non-stop since Evie left, so you could use a break. But I've got to warn you, my interactions with the Clarke family have been less than pleasant."

"That's pretty much the sum of it," said Luke. "You'll stay at a very nice resort where the staff will treat you like a queen, but the wedding guests will treat you like a pariah. Keep my parents off my back and I'll pay you whatever you want."

"Pay me?"

"Well, yeah. I figured I'd be hiring you. You'll have to take a week off work anyway."

"Why don't you hire a paid escort from a service, then?"

His lips twitched. "A couple reasons. First, my parents would figure that out in a flat second. Second, strange as it sounds, I need someone I can trust, not someone looking for a payout."

"And you think you can trust me?"

"Joe says so."

Joe obviously trusted Luke, too, and she definitely needed a vacation. The idea of spending a week at a resort being pampered certainly appealed, and no matter how awful Captain Hottie's family was, she could deal with them; her own family had given her plenty of practice.

"When is it?"

"First week of March. The wedding is on Sunday the eighth, the festivities begin the evening of the first."

Two weeks. It didn't give her much time to get coverage, but both Celia and Louise had been asking for more shifts. Celia wanted to quit dancing, said it was wearing her out, but she needed a nest egg before she did. And Louise was new, but had a natural affinity for the work. "Let me see if I can organize people to work for me," she said to Luke. "I should know within a couple of days."

"We still haven't talked about money."

"I don't need payment. I'm salaried here. But you

will have to pay for the appropriate clothes and accessories I'll have to buy."

He frowned. "If I wanted someone to dress appropriately—"

"I understand that. But you don't want your family to think you picked me up off the street just to piss them off, either. I can't wear strategically torn T-shirts and miniskirts. I'll need to buy a white silk shirt to wear with my black leather pants. If it's just a little too sheer so my tats show through, well, at least it will look as if I tried."

One side of Captain Hottie's mouth kicked up, revealing a killer dimple. "My God. I think I'm in love." He pulled out a cell phone and a credit card and, once connected with customer service, arranged to overnight Kai a card on which she could charge whatever she wanted.

"You don't do things by halves, do you?" she asked.

"Why would I? It's inefficient and impractical. Speaking of which, practically speaking, I'll need to see you at least once before we head out to Oasis Springs so we can get our story straight. When we met, that kind of thing."

"I get off tomorrow night at six if you want to go out to eat." She watched him carefully, but he didn't hesitate even for a moment.

"That sounds good. Shall I pick you up here?"

"Sure."

Luke raised a hand to Joe. "You going to be working tomorrow?" Joe nodded. "See you then." He swung out of the store and Kai couldn't help watching him go. Damn, but the man was hot. He looked as good going as he did coming.

Once he disappeared from view, she walked over to Joe and poked a finger into his chest.

"So? Spill."

"What do you want to know?"

"Well, to start with, how did you meet the Clarkes?"

"I was living in California, working as a bouncer at a

nightclub. Georgie's friends brought her in for her twenty-first birthday. She got drunk, a little sick, and wandered outside where it was quieter. We talked until her friends came looking for her. After that she came back a lot. Her friends would party, she'd hang out with me."

"And Luke?"

"Oh, I met him a couple of years later, about a week after Georgie and I started officially dating. He stopped by the club one night to check me out. Georgie was pissed, but I'd do the same thing in his shoes. I told her so."

"And of course you passed muster." How could he not? Joe was the most honest and straightforward guy she'd ever met. The very definition of "what you see is what you get."

Joe shrugged. "Luke and I got on well enough, but he told me right off the bat that his folks wouldn't condone the relationship. And he was right."

"This isn't fucking Victorian England." In her anger, Kai temporarily forgot where she was. "Don't tell me she broke up with you just because her parents didn't approve."

"No. We made it last for a while. Even after I got the offer to train here and moved, she came to visit a couple of times. But we couldn't keep it together."

There was more to the story, Kai was sure of it—otherwise why would Luke have bothered to come into the shop to tell Joe about the wedding?—but she couldn't ask. Instead, she turned the conversation to Luke.

"So I gather Luke doesn't get along with his family?"

Before Joe could answer, however, the door swung open and three giggling women came in. They were planning a surprise bachelorette party—which sounded like hell on earth to Kai—and required a great deal of assistance. By the time they left, the moment for questions had passed.

LUKE LOOKED AT HIMSELF IN the mirror on the back of the bathroom door. He was dressed in his standard day off outfit of jeans and a Rockdale Fire Department T-shirt. Maybe he should change before picking up Kai. But he wasn't sure what he'd change into. What did one wear when going out with a woman who wore stilettos, fishnets, and eyebrow rings?

He was man enough to admit that she scared him just a little. He'd had second—and third, and fourth—thoughts from the moment he stepped out of Goody's Goodies. She looked like the type of woman who had experience way beyond his own, but there had been nothing hard or cold in her hazel eyes. What color was her hair under that shiny black and red dye? Her fair skin and pale eyes suggested blonde, but the dark wings of her brows, the right pierced with two tiny silver rings, argued for a darker color.

And pretty. The piercings, funky dye job, and heavy makeup couldn't hide the essential structure of her face. He'd never really understood the appeal of body modification, though he had a Maltese cross with his fire company's number tattooed on his shoulder. His ink signified acceptance into a group, much the way a uniform did. And it was high on his shoulder, where few would ever see it. People who put spiders or skulls or snakes on their bodies generally confused him. But Kai wore her body art almost like a dare, and he'd never been able to resist a dare.

He had nothing more appropriate to wear than what he had on, he decided at last. With a shrug, he pocketed his wallet and hotel room key, then headed out. In front of the hotel, a line of taxis waited. He didn't remember the address of the store, but he'd discovered the previous day that it didn't matter—the cabbies knew Goody's Goodies.

When he arrived at the shop, business was booming. A gorgeous woman with smoothly tanned skin and a tangle of long hair stood behind the counter helping three women with a huge variety of toys and some board games. Bachelorette party or bridal shower, he would guess. In the corner, Joe was helping a short guy whose red face shone like a beacon. And at the back, another man browsed a rack of brightly colored condoms. Who in hell wanted their dick to glow in the dark? Christ, what a job. Luke didn't think he could manage it himself, but Joe said he didn't mind the weirdness that came with the territory. Benny Silver, who owned Goody's Goodie's—and was known nationwide as The Sex Toy King—provided Grade A medical insurance to his employees, and as an MMA fighter, that was Joe's top priority.

Kai was nowhere to be seen, but as soon as the woman behind the counter finished up with her customers, she joined him where he stood. "Can I help you with anything today?" Her voice had a lilt to it— Indian? Middle Eastern?—that explained the thickly lashed dark eyes and bronzed skin. Her smile was friendly but completely impersonal.

"No, thanks. I'm here to meet Kai. Is she around?"

The false smile faltered for a second, but then came back real and strong. "She's in the back. I'll go get her." She disappeared through a curtained doorway.

Joe finished up with his customer, who didn't buy anything, and checked on the other guy, who seemed content to be left alone in his condom contemplation, then came over to Luke.

"When's your next fight?" Luke asked. He'd attended more than one of Joe's bouts and figured it was only a matter of time before he garnered national attention. Faster on his feet than many in his division, he also had killer jiu jitsu moves and above average ground and pound.

"April. It's a big one. You should come out."

"I will. Drop me an email."

"Will do." Joe jerked his chin. "Your date's ready."

Christ, is she ever. Kai hadn't been kidding about the leather pants. Soft and supple, they cupped her butt and outlined shapely legs. But instead of a white silk shirt, she wore a red bustier under a black lace button-down. A silver serpent-shaped bracelet wrapped around her wrist and snaked its way up her forearm all the way to her elbow. Black, fuck-me-heeled, pointy-toed boots with laces all the way down the instep and shiny steel caps on the toes completed the outfit. The entire look personified the provocative and his body reacted in a predictable fashion.

Before he could make an utter ass of himself, however, the curtains opened again to reveal none other than Benny Silver, The Sex Toy King himself.

"Hello, my children," he gushed. The customer looked up from his condoms and rushed over to meet Benny.

"Dude," he said, hands shoved into jeans pockets, "you rock."

"Why, thank you," said Benny, walking the guy back to the condoms. "What are you searching for today? What are we missing that would make your day?"

"This is something to watch," Joe muttered. "Guy's been standing in that same spot for half an hour. Can't decide which one he wants. He'll leave here in ten minutes with a half a dozen different things."

Sure enough, within a couple of minutes of conversation too low for Luke to overhear, Benny had selected three types of condoms and then taken the guy over to a shelf of creams and lubricants. Then they moved to the counter and Benny sent the customer on his way with an entire bag full of things Luke doubted he'd have the nerve to use when he got home. Salesmanship at its very finest.

Benny returned to the group and rested assessing eyes on Luke. "Who have we here?"

"Oh, for crying out loud." Kai shoved Benny. "Luke, this is my boss, Benny Silver. Benny, this is Joe's friend Luke, which you know perfectly well since we've already discussed me taking a week off."

Benny held out a hand and Luke shook it. The man's slightly aggressive grip combined with the shrewd examination in his gaze made Luke feel as if he were meeting his girlfriend's father. Which was ridiculous. Kai wasn't his girlfriend, and Benny wasn't her father.

"Pleasure to meet you," Luke said.

"So, where are you taking our girl tonight?"

"Benny! Stop it!"

So Kai was feeling it, too. If Benny wasn't deliberately putting on the overprotective dad act, Luke would eat his bunker gear.

"Well, I like Spago," Luke said. "But I'm easy. You know the area better than I do, so I'm happy to follow your lead." In a strange way, he found himself grateful for the inquisition. If he weren't around, he hoped someone would take an interest in Georgie's dates beyond their socioeconomic status. The approval on the faces of Kai's friends wasn't just because Spago was pricey, but also because it was both public and fashionable. His parents went there when his father's penchant for poker brought them to Vegas. Kai's friends liked that he was taking her to a respectable restaurant.

"Spago is great," said Kai. "Let's get out of here before Benny convinces himself I need a curfew."

She grabbed his hand and tugged, and he felt all the hairs along his arms stand on end. Damn. He needed to get his reaction to this woman under control or he'd never survive a week pretending to be her boyfriend.

OKAY, SO MAYBE TOUCHING CAPTAIN Hottie hadn't been such a great idea. His big hand was warm and rough and entirely too masculine. She let go the moment they were outside, but could still feel the imprint of his fingers on her own.

"Spago is in Caesar's, right?" she asked.

"Yes."

"Great. That's an easy walk." She set off toward Caesar's Palace and its fancy Forum shops and restaurants at a quick pace. But Captain Hottie—she really needed to start thinking of him as Luke—kept up effortlessly.

The maître d' seated them immediately, with barely so much as a flinch at her outfit.

"So," Kai said when they'd ordered drinks and were studying their menus, "tell me what I need to know about you."

"Well, I live in a small town in Northern California—Rockdale, which is near San Francisco—and I'm a landscape architect."

"I thought you were a firefighter?"

"Rockdale's department is strictly volunteer. But I'm trained and tested, and I've qualified as a smoke jumper, though I've never been called on for that. I do what I can to help out. One of the things I'd prefer not to talk to my folks about is the fact that I've taken the tests and I'm on the list for consideration for the San Francisco FD."

"How does that work? I've never lived anywhere where the firefighters were volunteers. I mean, what if no one was around when my house was burning down?"

"That doesn't happen. At least not like you're thinking. When an alarm goes off, we get a page, and texts on our cell phones. As we're heading for the firehouse—or not—we call into a system that records who's coming, who's delayed, who's going to meet the truck at the scene. If there's not enough response, the call goes out again, this time including another engine company. In off-hours life in a volly house is, well, let's just say a bit less pro-fessional than in a paid house, but when it comes to an actual fire, we get the job done."

Yeah, she could imagine. And though she never had

any desire to play damsel in distress, he could almost convince her to fake a swoon. Maybe she'd try it during the wedding week.

"What about you?" he asked. "Have you always lived in Vegas? We have to come up with a feasible way to have met."

"I spent a couple of years in LA. But I've been here ten years. I could say I was in your town visiting a friend, or you could say we met here."

"Here is better. As little as they like Rockdale, my family has visited and you might slip up."

"Are you here often?"

He grimaced. "No, actually. Not my style. But my parents don't know that and my sister won't care. She'll see right through the whole act anyway."

"Which brings up my next question." The waiter came by and they ordered before she continued. "I get that you want to look after your sister and in order to do that you need some time alone with her, so you want me to keep your parents away. That's the plan, right?"

"In a nutshell, yes."

"Then why not invite someone who fits in? Someone who could engage them in long conversations?"

He rubbed a hand across his face. "Let me start with some history. My mother's father was a banker. His father was a banker. She was raised to occupy herself with charity work—sit on committees, give away money, look good on a man's arm, stuff like that. She married a lawyer whose father and grandfather were both lawyers. When I popped out of the womb, they decided that I could choose either career—banker or lawyer. By starting along the lawyer path, I was supposed to bring the family to the political stage. And the banking…that would be a last resort, if it turned out I had no talent for the law. My father and grandfather had named their firm. It began as Clarke and Associates, then became Clarke and Clarke, and they were just waiting for me so they could become the Clarke family firm. When I didn't go to law school, they decided I could still manage a grassroots political campaign, and that's where they switched their focus."

"Yuck." Kai squinched up her nose. "I didn't really realize dynastic succession had such a firm hold in the modern world."

"Among the wealthy it does."

"'Wealthy.' The rich even have different words for themselves."

"It's an 'us versus them' thing. Let's say you win the lottery and after taxes you take home a hundred million dollars. Congratulations. You're rich. You can afford to live in my parents' neighborhood, wear all the best designers, eat at all the best restaurants. My parents would be perfectly happy to have you as a neighbor, but they'd never invite you to join their club. Because you're just rich, not wealthy. *Wealthy* goes back generations, and it's a designation of social class and behavior, as well as financial well-being.

"So, because of that, my job is unacceptable. Not only am I not contributing to our heritage on either side, but I dig in the dirt and in my spare time I run around with the fire department and dress in T-shirts. I have no sense of what's appropriate for my station in life. I haven't joined the town council, haven't run for mayor. That's the big push that's coming—to run for mayor of my dinky town so I can move up the political ladder."

"I can't imagine anything less appealing. And seriously, 'station in life'? That's a direct quote, right?"

His lips quirked. "How did you ever guess?"

She laughed.

"Look, I don't mean to insult you in any way, but if I brought a woman who looked appropriate to the wedding, all the work I've done to get my folks to give up on me as a lost cause would go down the drain. They'll think I'm growing up, and that will never do."

"You're a strange man, Luke Clarke."

He grinned, flashing that Captain Hottie dimple. "So

I've been told."

"Okay, then, where would a guy like you meet someone like me? They may not approve of you, but I doubt they'll believe you casually wandered into Goody's Goodies and fell in love."

"No, I suppose you're right. What do you do for fun? When you're not working?"

"The same things everyone else does, I guess. Read, hang out with friends, go to the movies. Celia—she's the one who is at the shop tonight—she and I like to watch really bad movies. You know, *The Piranha That Ate Florida*, that kind of thing."

"Oh, now, that's right up my alley. We can say we met at a B-movie festival. My family will have no problem believing that. We don't need too many details, because I doubt they'll pry."

"How long have we been seeing each other? I mean, it has to have been a while if you're inviting me to your sister's wedding."

HOW LONG? IT WAS A damn good question, and one he hadn't considered.

"I got the invitation about six weeks ago and RSVP'd for two."

She stared at him. "So it's been almost two months, and you've done nothing about it until now?"

He shrugged. "I figured I'd just show up without anyone. That way no one would have time to set me up, and I could claim to be too upset by my recent breakup to talk about it."

Kai took a tiny stylus and her phone out of her purse and began typing. "Okay. So we should have been together at least a little while when you replied to the invitation. So shall we say…September? Does that work for you? Would they have any reason to know you weren't here then?"

"No. That's fine. Were you working at Goody's back then?"

"Yes. I've been with Benny for almost three years."

"And before that?"

Something dark flitted behind Kai's heavily lined and shadowed eyes. Or maybe it was merely a flicker of candlelight, because a moment later she laughed. "What does any girl with halfway decent legs and a notable lack of other skills do in Vegas? I was a cocktail waitress. And before you ask, at a casino, not at a strip joint. The money isn't as good, but the job is less…how shall I put it? Demanding."

"And you don't find working at Goody's Goodies demanding?"

"Not really, but only because Benny's a great boss. There's a lot to be said for job with a salary and benefits. I had great weeks as a waitress, but I had really lousy ones, too. Especially since I have a tendency to say exactly what's on my mind. Which, now that I think about it, should turn you off this whole plan."

"You're telling me you're a hard-ass?"

"It's more that I'm a smartass. Your family will probably try to have you committed if they think you've fallen for me." She smiled as she said it, but the expression never touched her eyes.

"It can't be that bad. Tell me what you're apt to say."

"Well, there was the time I told a group of college boys what butt plugs were for."

He choked on his wine. He wasn't sure he knew what butt plugs were for himself, but he sure as hell wouldn't ask a woman. That's why God invented Google. "That was your conversation starter?"

"No. They came into the store and they were trying to embarrass me with the question."

"How do you know they weren't just naive? Sheltered?" *Normal.*

Those dark-rimmed eyes filled with pity and she shook her head. "Because if a guy is really curious, he doesn't bring his friends. If he can't find out what he wants to know on the net, he slinks in by himself and asks Joe or Benny or Adam. These guys were all cock-of-the-walk. Plucked a couple of our bigger ones off the shelf and said 'hey, what are these things for, anyway?'"

"And you said?"

"I said 'they're just what they sound like. Plugs. So when you go to a bar and have sex with each other in the bathroom, you don't have to leak in your tighty-whities on your way home.'"

He lost it. For a full minute, he couldn't even breathe for laughing and he knew everyone in the restaurant was staring at them. It only made him laugh harder.

"What I wouldn't give to hear you say that at my sister's rehearsal dinner."

"You're not serious."

"No, unfortunately, that's more than even I'm looking for. But it doesn't bother me. Joe wouldn't have recommended you if you couldn't handle yourself."

"Okay. I promise not to mention the down and dirty details of my job unless the situation calls for it."

"Fair enough. Do you like it? Aside from the roving groups of frat boys?" The idea of an adult boutique simultaneously fascinated and repelled him. What kind of people went into a store and discussed their sexual preferences and needs and even failures with strangers? And what kind of person listened to those people and advised them?

"I do. Most of our customers are happy—this is Vegas, so much of our business is bachelor and bachelorette related. The ones who come in for more personal reasons, well, I enjoy fixing them up, knowing that when they leave our shop they're going to have a better life."

"A better *sex* life."

"Sure. You don't think sexual gratification is important to overall well-being?"

Hell, yes. But that wasn't the impression he was

trying to make. "I suppose I've never really thought about it."

"That's because you've never had a problem finding a date. Or a release."

"You're very direct." He studied her. "I realize men are never supposed to ask, but I'll be expected to know. How old are you?"

"Twenty-seven. And you?"

Twenty-seven. Fuck. Georgie was twenty-nine, and she was getting married, but he had hoped Kai would say thirty. At least. At thirty-four, he was too old for a girl barely getting her life started. "So you, what, moved to Vegas to go to college?"

She stared at him blankly. "What makes you think I went to college?"

"Sorry. Guess it's my privilege showing. It was sort of a given when I was growing up that smart kids went to college."

Again, that flicker behind her eyes. "Yeah, well, I didn't. I did two years of community college while working at a big box store and continued that job until I was twenty-one, when I could serve drinks."

"How long have you been managing Goody's?"

"A few months. Our last manager, Evie, left to take care of her aunt. I was just supposed to fill in for her until she came back, but she fell in *love* and decided to stay in Tennessee."

"You don't approve?"

"I don't have an opinion one way or the other."

"Come on. There was enough derision on the word *love* to tar the entire Strip."

"Sorry." Again that false smile. "With luck it will all work out for her."

"But you don't believe it."

"If anyone can make it work, Evie can."

He wanted to ask about her parents, whether they'd loved each other, but didn't quite dare. It wasn't his business. But still...

"You know about Georgie. What about you? Any siblings?"

"No." She paused as if she were finished, but after a moment she continued. "My mother is the kind of woman who needs a man in her life. My father died when I was eight, and she remarried when I was thirteen, but my stepfather didn't want kids."

Including her. She didn't have to say it, Luke understood.

Before the silence could become awkward, the waiter brought their food and the conversation shifted to more neutral ground.

"So our relationship can have been mostly long distance," Luke said when they both finished eating and he was paying the bill. "With the occasional few days together here and there when we were both free."

"You do realize that if we tell people we've been primarily long distance, they'll expect us to be permanently attached at the hip."

Yeah. Because if he were dating Kai, he might never let her leave the bedroom. The thought must have shown on his face, because she laughed.

"Oh, yes. Hang on to that expression and you'll fool everyone. I wouldn't have pegged you for an actor."

What the hell. If they were going to be spending the week together, he might as well be honest. "It's not an act."

"Oh." The laughter died in her mobile face and her leaf-green gaze went brightly speculative. "Now *that* is interesting. In that case, you'd better pack your medical report when you come to pick me up."

Every nerve in his body fired. "Are you serious?"

She sighed. "Now you probably think I'm trashy." The light went out of her face and desperation to bring it back flooded his veins.

"I do not." He leaned over the table for emphasis. "You surprised me, that's all."

"I don't play games, Luke. We're going to be lying to

everyone else, we ought to be honest with each other. What's the difference between you saying you want me and me saying that it's mutual?"

"Nothing!" Christ, this whole dating thing was a mess. No wonder he didn't do it. It had become ridiculously complicated already and he and Kai weren't even really together. "I don't want you to think I expect—" Oh, crap, why had he even started? Kai tied his tongue as well as his guts into a thousand knots.

"If I had believed you expected sex in return for a week with miserable people at a nice hotel, I'd have shown you the door. And Joe would have shoved you through it."

The tension coiled in his chest relaxed and he laughed. "There is that."

KAI MADE IT HOME AT nine on the dot after only a small argument with Luke about how she would get there. He had that whole "raised as a gentleman" thing going on and didn't want her to take the bus, but it was ridiculous for him to take her home in a cab and then have to pay to come right back to the Strip.

"I always take the bus," she'd said. "It stops right outside my apartment complex."

"For my peace of mind, take a cab, okay? If anything happened to you…I wouldn't have a date for my sister's wedding." This last, and the rueful grin that accompanied it finally convinced her. He wasn't pushing her around, he was asking as a favor. It made a difference.

So standing beneath the portico of Caesar's where the cabs were lined up, she thanked Luke for dinner, took the twenty dollar bill he pressed into her hand for the cab, and gave him a quick, noncommittal kiss goodnight.

She couldn't resist turning in the seat to look out the back of the cab as it pulled away from the curb. Luke stood watching, his hands jammed into the pockets of his jeans.

That image remained even as she stood under the shower and washed the color from her hair. The water cascading down her body went from dark, muddy, stained with ruddy black, to a lighter tan, and eventually cleared. She rubbed conditioner into her hair left it in while she slathered makeup remover over her skin, then faced the shower's pounding water to let it rinse away both conditioner and makeup.

When she stepped out, she examined herself in the mirror. Usually, mirrors reflected tiny parts—the section of hair she was streaking, a bit of lip when she couldn't get her lip ring to close properly, the corner of an eye as she applied a sparkling sequin. This time, she allowed herself to see the whole without its mask.

Her wet, bleached hair clung to her head like a shaggy cap. Drab remnants of the black and red dye clung to the bleached yellow base. The liquid chalk she used for color would not wash out fully for several days. She hadn't seen her natural light-brown color—two shades paler than her chestnut eyebrows—in years.

Her skin was naturally pale, a perfect palette for striking makeup, but without it… What did Luke see when he looked at her? The black and red striped hair? The tightly laced corset? The heavily kohl-lined eyes? The bits and pieces she put on every morning and took off every night? This stranger she saw in the mirror was the one he'd meet at night during their week together.

She turned from her self-examination and pulled on a pair of pajamas.

Why should it matter what Luke Clarke thought of her? Aside from the obvious, of course—it had been a damned long time since she'd shared a bed with another human being and if her bare face, bleached hair, and cotton pajamas turned him off, it might be another long dry spell.

She sat cross-legged on her bed and pulled out a

sketchbook and her laptop. She knew what she wanted to wear to the wedding. It had been in her head for ages, but the materials she imagined—rich, floaty silks, velvet and brocade, were beyond her budget. With Luke's credit card, however, she could get what she needed. And she didn't even have to feel guilty because it would be so much cheaper than if she actually bought a dress. She just had to figure out the yardage.

Chapter 2

"Ｓo how was the big date last night?" Celia asked before Kai even got her jacket off.

Joe, who had opened with Celia, looked up from the clipboard on which he was writing inventory notes. "Thank God you're here. She's been bugging me all day about Luke."

"It wasn't a date, for crying out loud. It was an information-gathering session."

"To-may-to, to-mah-to," Celia said with a wave. "I wouldn't waste dinner with a man like that on information, unless it was to find out whether he was single, which we already know he is."

Joe clapped his hands over his ears. "La la la. Could you *please* stop talking about my friend like a piece of meat?"

"Why don't you go ahead and take lunch, Joe? Because I don't think Celia is planning to stop drooling anytime soon."

"Damn straight," said Celia. "I take my pleasure where I find it. My current book is stalled and I need to get in the mood before I can finish it. A little vicarious romance might be just the thing."

"It's not a romance. It's a week-long charade." Which bugged her more than it should. She'd been on the "fake it till you make it" plan for half her life. Seven days of playacting shouldn't be too difficult. Except that what she was playing—a woman in love—was so far beyond her experience as to be laughable.

Joe put away the clipboard and practically ran for the front door. On his way out, he let in a group of four women, which prevented Celia from continuing her interrogation.

The women spent almost forty minutes in the store, handcuffing each other with fuzzy cuffs, getting hands-on with the vibrators, and taste-testing lubes. One wandered into the clothing area and tried on a skirt.

"Why is this so expensive? I could get something similar online for a quarter of this price," she said when she saw the tag.

"Because that's handmade and unique," Kai replied. She'd learned to keep all defensiveness about her creations from her tone. The woman twirled in the ragged-hemmed miniskirt, watching as the plaid overskirt belled out to reveal the under layers of satin and lace, each cut to show tantalizing glimpses when she stood still.

"You totally need that, Cheryl," said one of her friends.

"Yeah, but it's a hundred and eighty dollars."

The other two women joined them and examined the skirt critically. Kai tried not to fidget as one of them, a tall, impeccably dressed brunette, fingered the skirt and squinted at the stitching.

"Buy it, Cheryl," she said at last. "It will look amazing with your black silk tank." If Kai could have gotten away with it, she would have pumped her fist. As it was, she had to suppress a little victory smile. Benny took forty percent of anything she sold, but that still left plenty for her. And more important, the skirt had only been in the shop for two weeks. She'd been uncertain about the viability of the design, but the quick turnaround meant she could make more.

Before the women left, two guys came in, and then Joe came back from lunch and it was time for Celia to take off so she could get to the casino in time to dance in the afternoon show.

"I'll be back Monday," she told Kai on her way out, "and I expect to hear details. Don't think you're getting off so easily."

"Yeah, yeah."

"Did it go okay?" Joe asked once Celia had left. "No details. Please. Just… Are you still okay with going to the wedding now that you've spent some time with Luke? I don't want you to feel as if you have to do this. I sort of pressured you."

"It's fine. He's a nice guy." And wasn't *that* just a bland expression? But Joe didn't want to hear that she thought Luke was hot enough to melt an iceberg.

"He is," Joe agreed.

"You want to tell me what happened with his sister?"

"Not particularly."

"Gotcha." She could relate to that. She had years and years she didn't discuss, so she wasn't about to press about one failed relationship. "Well, don't worry. Everything went fine. I'm looking forward to staying with the rich and beautiful for a week, even if they're not happy to have me. I checked out the resort online. It's something else."

"You got that right." A quick grimace flitted across his face. Was Joe still in love with Georgie Clarke? Had he looked up Oasis Springs because she was marrying the owner? The website showed a beautiful but slightly fussy resort, not the kind of place she could imagine Joe enjoying.

Maybe that was the problem—Georgie liked the elegant lifestyle and Joe didn't. Couples had broken up for less.

"What's the matter?" Joe asked.

"Huh?"

"For a minute there you were wearing your whips and chains expression."

She laughed. "Nah. Just resting bitch face."

"You have no idea how much I wish I could be a fly

on the wall to watch you with the Clarkes and Dunleavys. Talk about setting a cat among the pigeons."

"Are you calling me catty?"

"If the shoe fits."

"Yeah, I guess I walked into that one."

THE WEEKEND PASSED, AS IT usually did, in a blur of customers and busywork. Kai worked ten hour days Saturday and Sunday and she was too tired to think about much beyond how their supply of condoms and pink peppermint penis pops were holding up.

But Monday, her day off, the fabric she'd ordered with rush shipping on Luke's fancy platinum credit card arrived. Its presence forced her to confront the idea of spending a week surrounded by strangers in a way that not even her friends' questions had. As her scissors shaped the fabric, she imagined wearing the outfit she was creating at Oasis Springs. It was a black and pink houndstooth riff on a Chanel suit with peekaboo cutouts, black lace inserts, and chains on the epaulets. What would Luke think? And his relatives? Was she biting off more than she could chew?

Since when have you ever let that stop you? She'd always lived by instinct. Sometimes, as when she'd moved to Vegas on a wing and a prayer, it had paid off. Other times, it had definitely not. Of course, she usually had only herself to worry about. If she screwed up at Oasis Springs, she could hurt Luke and Georgie, maybe even Joe, as well.

By the time she finished the jacket, the sun had set. Her back hurt and her whole body felt cramped from sitting at the sewing machine all day. Her neighborhood wasn't terrible, but she didn't like to run at night. She stretched, hearing her spine pop and crack, and looked out the window. The sky was dusty purple, inviting her out, but long shadows covered the sidewalks and only a few cars passed by on the street. She might be impulsive, but she wasn't reckless. She'd settle for a hot shower and a stretch routine tonight and save the run for the morning.

As she completed the stretch, she heard the ding of her cellphone's text alert. She winced. *Please don't be work.* But the text was from Luke, and the sight of his name on the screen gave her a little shock of pleasure.

> Be jealous. Right now I'm settling in to watch Gargantula.

What? She snatched up a packet of popcorn and tossed it into the microwave, then grabbed a beer from the fridge.

> Please tell me that's a movie about a gigantic tarantula.

> What else would it be?

> I've got popcorn on now. What channel?

Not that she really had to ask. Sure enough, at the same moment she got his response she found the movie herself. On the screen, hundreds of tiny spiders swarmed across a rocky landscape. Of course, in the way of all cheap CGI animation, they'd created only one spider, then reproduced it over and over, using the same equations. Every leg moved in the same fashion and at the same tempo. The microwave buzzed and she plucked out the bag and returned as a tank rolled into the picture and three men jumped out.

Her text alert dinged.

> Cue the evil military scientists who will create the gargantula.

> Why is it always evil military scientists, anyway?

> It's a dirty job, but somebody has to do it.

All alone in her apartment, Kai laughed. Over the next two hours, she laughed a great deal. Luke was a charming text companion and at the end of the movie, she told him so. She waited a long time for his reply. Was he embarrassed? Should she not have been so forthright? But at last he responded.

↯ And now we can honestly say we've seen a movie together. It was a pleasure. We will have to do it again sometime.

ON TUESDAY, KAI SURPRISED HERSELF by bringing up Luke's name when business slowed down.

"I watched *Gargantula* last night," she told Celia. "Did you record it?"

"No! I had no idea it was on. Was it was bad as it sounds? Gargantuan tarantulas?"

"It was exactly that bad." Kai grinned at her.

"I can't believe you didn't tell me so I could set my DVR."

"I didn't know myself. Luke texted and told me because we'd talked about bad B movies."

"*Really*?" The word lasted at least three seconds.

"It wasn't a big deal. Bad movies are the one and only thing we have in common, so he texted a few times during the movie to discuss its glorious badness. Nothing special."

"Uh-huh. That's called laying a foundation. Dollars to doughnuts he's hoping to seduce you while you're away together."

Kai's clothes pinched and she pulled at the neck of her scarlet-and-black-striped T-shirt.

"Oooh," said Celia. "He already has?"

"No, nothing like that." Why was she even having this conversation? Girl talk was so not her thing. She'd never had any practice talking to women, and her one good friend, the girl she'd bonded with during the worst days of her life, had deserted her.

Nowadays, when she did go out with female acquaintances, she kept conversations strictly impersonal. But this urge to talk about Luke, to feel his name on her tongue, was as overwhelming as it was novel.

"What, then?" asked Celia. "Because honest to God, Kai, I've never seen you blush until just now. I didn't even think you could. I've seen you wear things without a wince that they wouldn't even set me up in on stage!"

"Of course I can blush. But I don't see anything embarrassing about what I wear."

"You know I love the way you look. You're avoiding the question. What happened with Luke?"

"I might have told him I wouldn't mind sleeping with him."

"No way! Oh. My. God." Celia laughed. "I wish I had your nerve."

"Well, I wish I had your grace and figure, so I guess we're even."

"Nuh-uh. Because I wish I could design and sew like you."

"And I would love to be able to write books." They grinned at each other. "Aren't we a pair of envious wenches? But seriously, anyone can learn to sew. I'd be happy to teach you." What a strange thought, that she'd be able to teach a skill to another person. *You've come a long way, baby*, as the poster on her bedroom wall said. It was a copy of an old cigarette ad, and she'd bought it as much for the fashionable drawing of the woman as for the slogan, but over time the words had taken on extra meaning for her as she tried to live up to them.

Celia sighed. "In what time? If I'm not here, I'm dancing or writing. Though I'm beginning to think I should give up the idea of being a writer. No one wants my books."

"Don't give up! I mean it, Celia. Hell, your books almost make me believe in love, so you know they're good."

"Well, if you're going to fall, I must say, you've picked an excellent candidate in Luke."

"Don't get your hopes up. The whole idea is that he *won't* be a candidate." She explained the Clarkes' political aspirations for their son and her role at the wedding.

Celia waved a hand. "Don't worry about the reasons he invited you. Two things I've learned from a combination of life and romance novels—you can't see the future, and men are not their parents. I dated a guy for two years when I was younger and the whole last year I only stayed with him because I adored his mother and his little brother. He bored me to tears. And Luke's parents, while they're a trial to him, could be okay as people."

"Yeah…I don't think so. I don't want that life."

"It doesn't sound bad to me. Money, status, never having to worry about eviction from your crappy apartment. And then there's waking up to a guy who looks like Luke Clarke every morning."

"Well, there is that. But all those benefits come with tradeoffs and at this point in my life, I prefer to live on my own terms. Can you really see someone who looks like me fitting into that mold? Not just the fancy family, but even the small town firefighter wives crowd?"

Celia gave a one-shouldered shrug. "I don't see why not. And if you don't fit in, you can always seduce the other wives over to the dark side of sex toys and fashionistas."

"Yeah. 'Cause that would go over so very, very well."

"Hey, you don't know. Maybe the town Luke lives in is progressive."

Maybe it was. What did she know about California towns? She somehow doubted they were like the little town outside Texarkana where she'd lived before her father's death. After that, it had all been cities. Dallas, Los Angeles, Las Vegas, where no one blinked at the strange.

Still, as much as she'd been compelled to mention

Luke's name, she was glad that the rest of the day was too busy for Celia to nag her over the details of their arrangement.

KAI SPENT MOST OF THE day before Luke picked her up attempting to pack in something resembling a reasonable fashion. She'd had to borrow a suitcase from Celia because she didn't want to crush her clothes. The big, black, hard-sided case was a lot more stable than her assortment of duffels, but it was also unwieldy as hell.

Her makeup, hair accessories, temporary color, jewelry, and an assortment of Goody's very best "goodies"—on the off chance she really needed to shock someone by pulling out one of the store's products— went into a separate case.

Only when all that was done did she shower, dress in her favorite black bodysuit paired with a jagged-hemmed schoolgirl plaid skirt, chalk her hair with streaks to match the skirt, and make up her face for maximum effect with thick kohl on her eyes and bright red lipstick to match her hair. The finished product was utterly respectable and suitably shocking at the same time. No cleavage showed beneath the solid tank top of the bodysuit, but the lace sleeves and midriff hinted at scandal. The skirt was short enough to show most of her legs, but stopped short of revealing her lack of thigh gap. *Look out, Clarkes.*

Luke insisted on carrying her bags down to the car for her and she had to stop herself from laughing when she saw the Range Rover parked in her designated spot. Way too much car for the neighborhood, and he never should have left the sunroof open even long enough to come up to her apartment, but it was exactly what she would have pictured him driving if she'd been asked.

"I can close the sunroof," he offered as he stacked her luggage in the back. "It's about an hour to Oasis Springs, maybe a little more. It's out by Pahrump."

"No, this is great." She pulled a kerchief with a skull and crossbones pattern on it from her purse and tied it around her head.

He laughed. "Very Jackie O."

"Yeah. Not hardly."

He opened the passenger door and handed her inside. The touch of his skin against hers sent little tingles up her arm and on impulse she leaned up and kissed his cheek, savoring the roughness of his stubble. The textures of men were so different. He was scruffy and tough on the outside, but she could feel a fine line of tension running through him.

"It's going to be okay," she said as she settled into her seat. "You'll see."

"If it's not, you'll tell me, right? Seriously, Kai. When this started I was so freaked by the whole situation I was grateful to have any way out. When Joe suggested you, you seemed like a godsend. I didn't even consider how it might affect you." He touched her hand, drawing her gaze. "But I know you now. If they're horrible to you, you have to tell me."

No way, no how. She'd been fighting her own battles since the age of eight, she wasn't about to start leaning on someone else now. "Luke, it will be fine. I promise."

They didn't talk much on the way to Oasis Springs, but the silence was not uncomfortable, and when they pulled up in front of the resort, Kai found herself impressed, despite her intention to retain a world-weary and jaded appearance in front of Luke's rich—scratch that, *wealthy*—family. Massive columns supported a marble archway leading to the front door, which was at least ten feet tall. She'd seen it on the web when she'd researched the place, but she hadn't considered how the scale would affect her. An ache settled behind her eyes and she pressed a finger to the spot just above her eyebrow rings.

Luke slid an arm around her shoulders. "It's pretty

amazing, I have to admit. I was ready for a tacky fake palace, like the Strip hotels, but this is actually nice."

"A bit ostentatious."

"Says the woman whose hair color changes daily."

"Well, yeah. It takes one to know one."

He laughed as they entered the grand lobby, attracting the attention of a tall blonde woman standing near the concierge desk. She rushed over, eyes fixed on Luke, ignoring Kai.

"Luke, honey, how are you?"

"Hello, Aunt Marcia. I'm well, thanks. This is my girlfriend, Kai Tyler. Kai, my aunt, Marcia Clarke."

Kai held out a hand and the woman took it in a languid grip, her gaze fixed just slightly over Kai's shoulder. Kai opened her mouth to say something—she wasn't even sure what—but was interrupted by a shriek from across the lobby.

"Luke!" A petite blonde whirlwind threw herself at Luke and he let go of Kai to catch her.

"Hey, Sprout."

"I'm so glad you're here." She turned to Kai and a crease of confusion formed between her neatly plucked eyebrows. "And this is?"

"This is Kai. Kai, my sister Georgette. Georgie."

"Nice to finally meet you," Kai said, once again holding out her hand. "Luke has told me so much about you."

Georgie took her hand in a grip considerably stronger and tighter than Marcia's. "Really? Because, not to be rude, but he's never said word one about you."

"Georgie."

Hectic flags of color flew on Georgie's pale cheeks as she rounded on her brother. "What? I'm just being *honest*." Telling emphasis sharpened the final word into a blade.

"Maybe I should leave," Kai said.

"No!" Luke wrapped an arm around her waist. "Georgie, let us get checked in and then we can chat, okay?"

Her lips twisted and she glanced at her aunt, who was watching avidly. "Sure. No problem. I'll come up in fifteen minutes or so."

"Great." Luke dipped his head. "See you soon, Aunt Marcia."

THE PORTER RODE UP IN the elevator with them, eliminating the possibility of discussion. Not that Luke had an answer for the questions in Kai's eyes anyway. He hadn't bothered to inform Georgie about Kai's appear-ance because he was certain his sister would laugh at his latest tactic. Maybe he'd underestimated the stress the wedding was putting on her.

They'd been given a suite, and the porter put the suitcases into the bedroom. Luke sent him on his way with a generous tip, then paced the living area while Kai sank into one of the fluffy armchairs.

"I'm sorry," he said when the silence had stretched to the breaking point. "I didn't expect Georgie to pitch a fit. My parents, absolutely. But not my sister."

"We'll figure it out. Relax. It's not as if your sister hates your *real* girlfriend."

Which was true. He could take Kai home, drop her off, and come back. But he didn't want to. At all.

A knock at the door signaled Georgie's arrival. He took a deep breath and opened it, his stomach muscles clenching at the glint of tears in her eyes. But when she swung into the room and rounded on him, he realized she was angry, not hurt.

"Okay, now we're alone. You can tell me why you felt the need to invite *her*." Georgie flicked a glance at Kai so filled with venom he found himself stepping between them, as if his sister were some kind of poisonous snake. And as if Kai needed his protection.

"Honestly, Georgie, once I RSVP'd with the plus

one, I figured you'd be on tenterhooks waiting to see what I had planned. I thought you'd approve of the goth-punk look."

His sister crossed her arms over her chest, hands gripping her upper arms so tightly her knuckles whitened. "I do. But I don't appreciated *her*." Her eyes fixed on Kai. "Do you think I don't know who you are? You work with Joe."

Oh, hell. "I had no idea you'd ever been to see Joe at Goody's Goodies. I didn't mean to upset you."

"I can leave," Kai offered again, and Luke suppressed his immediate impulse to tell her to stay.

Georgie deflated. She sank down onto a corner of the couch. "How did you two meet?"

"We plan to tell the family we met at a movie festival. But actually, we met when I went to tell Joe you were getting married." He sat next to her. "I swear, Sprout, if I'd known you'd been to Goody's, I would have found someone else. But Joe didn't say anything." Luke had a hard time imagining Joe deliberately sending Kai to mess with Georgie's head, but anything was possible.

"I didn't go when he was there. I didn't want him to think I was checking up on him." Georgie rubbed the front of her forehead with two fingers. Their mother did the same thing when anxious or upset, but he'd never seen his sister do it. He put an arm around her shoulders.

"I never meant to hurt you, Sprout, I swear." And now that he had, he couldn't very well broach the subject of her fiancé and double-down on the bad behavior. It would have to wait.

Kai crouched in front of Georgie, her whiskey-brown eyes serious. "I won't be offended if you want me to go. I can say there was a sex toy emergency and leave. This is your wedding. You should be happy."

"You're really not here because of Joe?"

"No. But he is my friend. He knows I'm here and I won't lie to him."

Georgie stared at her for a long moment, and then her shoulders straightened. "No. Stay. My parents will hate you. It will be awesome."

The knot in Luke's chest loosened. "Won't it? Can you imagine mom trying to find a way to compliment Kai's clothes?"

"That's her M.O.," Georgie explained, patting the spot next to her on the sofa in invitation for Kai to sit. "She has like a computer in her brain. The first time she meets a woman, she always says something nice about their outfit. Then comes hair or eyes or figure, then she'll ask questions about your pets, your job, whatever she learned the first two times she met you."

"Holy crapoli."

Georgie grinned and Luke relaxed. "Yeah," he said. "She's a special breed. The technique has served her well. She has a reputation for being gracious and kind because she makes people feel important and good about them-selves."

"And there's nothing wrong with that," Georgie said. "Except that it's so practiced and calculated. I learned 'be nice' at her knee and I still try to be kind, but eventually I realized with her it's all an act. She doesn't actually *feel* anything."

"That's...sad," Kai said.

"I suppose it is," Luke admitted, "but we don't usually consider it so much sad as predictable and a pain in the butt."

"If I'm not nearby when you introduce them, you have to tell me what mom comes up with."

"I will."

"And your father?" Kai asked. "Should I expect any odd behavior from him?"

"He's a frustrated politician, which is why they've always pushed me to take that route. Whatever he says to your face will be excruciatingly polite and will in no way reflect his actual feelings."

"Lovely. Why didn't he run for office himself?"

"It wasn't *done*. Not in his family and not in my mother's. They were both extremely conservative. Plus, he didn't marry until he was thirty-one, and politics isn't a single man's game. Voters, especially thirty or forty years ago, wanted to see a nice, respectable wife and two kids standing on the platform with the candidate. Thus the push to marry me off."

"They want you to be happy, too," Georgie chided. "It's not entirely selfish."

"Not entirely, no. Just mostly."

Georgie rolled her eyes, then turned to Kai. "Don't believe above half of what he tells you. He's my brother and I love him, but he has a rather jaundiced view of the world in general and my parents in particular." She stood. "But I should go. Elaine, Sue and I are taking a Pilates class in a few minutes. Dinner is at seven at Antichi Sapori. You'll find all the details in the wedding packet they left on the desk."

"Yes, ma'am," Luke said, saluting his sister. She rolled her eyes again, flicked a glance at Kai, and let herself out.

FIRST CATASTROPHE AVERTED. KAI COULDN'T decide whether she was glad about that. She'd become damn good at role playing over the years, but the situation at Oasis Springs was more complex than she'd expected, more filled with potholes and potential tragedy.

"Shall we explore the hotel, find tonight's restaurant, generally make our presence known?" she asked, rising from the sofa.

"Yeah." In two long strides look stood before her. "Thank you."

"For what?"

"For staying calm. Keeping me calm."

"I aim to please." The words came out less flippant, more squeaky than she intended.

"You succeed." He stepped closer and laid one big hand along her cheek. His gas-flame blue eyes burned into hers. "I would very much like to kiss you right now. Is that okay?"

She froze. Who the hell asked permission for a kiss? She'd already given him a sexual green light for the week, so why make a big production number out of a little lip lock?

"Kai?"

Her throat too dry for speech, she rose up on her toes and touched her mouth to his. His lips were warm, softer than she'd expected, and brushed across hers like a breeze. It wasn't enough. She squeezed closer and his arms locked around her, almost lifting her off her feet. The kiss went from gentle to bruising in an instant, and his mouth devoured hers. The world slipped away, all thought of his sister and Joe swept out of her mind as he nibbled a path along her cheek to her earlobe and back.

Kai pulled away first, her breath coming hard and fast, her heart beating an irregular, unrecognizable pulse in her veins. Holy cannoli, Captain Hottie could kiss. He let her go reluctantly, his own breath noticeably uneven. Good. It would be embarrassing if he were unaffected.

"You're a dangerous woman," he said. He glanced at his watch. "We have a little over two hours until dinner. It's probably a good idea if we don't come back to the room between now and then."

He had a point. Much more and she'd forget dinner altogether, which would upset Georgie. She grabbed her red patent leather purse from the table and followed Luke to the door.

They shared the elevator down with a half a dozen chattering girls, all of whom were clearly related. They had costumed themselves for an event in poodle skirts and tight, short-sleeved sweater tops. Two of them sized Luke up, then checked out Kai. One giggled and whispered in the other's ear. Kai raised a single eyebrow and gave them her best sneer. They shuffled their feet and turned to face the doors.

When the doors opened, the girls rushed out. Kai and Luke followed more slowly. As they did, they almost bumped into a tall, handsome, dark-haired man pushing his way in. Luke slipped an arm around Kai's waist and pulled her hard against his body.

"Luke!" The man said with a smile almost blinding against his tan. "You made it."

"Of course. It's Georgie's wedding. With a little luck, the only one she'll ever have."

"Well, sure. But I figured you'd arrive at the last possible minute. Not before the festivities even start. And certainly not with such a lovely companion."

The hand resting on her hip squeezed. "Kai, this is my cousin Gil."

Nothing about that iron grip on her hip encouraged friendliness, so she kept her hand at her side and merely smiled. "Nice to meet you, Gil."

"Have you met the rest of the family yet?"

"Only a few. I met Marcia—is she your mother?"

"Good God, no. I'm on the other side of the family. Once you've met the entire crowd and you're ready to escape, come find me. I'll help you relax."

Luke's grip was going to leave a bruise. She turned slightly into him and wrapped her arms around his waist. In what she hoped was a suitably adoring voice, she said, "Luke helps me relax just fine, but thanks for the offer."

"Don't tell me you're dateless for the week," Luke said.

"Only for a few days. After all, Georgie has five bridesmaids, all of whom are arriving on Wednesday. But I'm certain none of them are as interesting as your friend here."

"Give me a break," Kai said before the rumble she could feel in Luke's chest erupted into a full-on explosion. "What on earth would you, with your fancy clothes and your perfect hair find so interesting about me? When I look at you I see a Versace shirt—the gold

on the collar doesn't do you any favors, by the way—
and Italian leather brogues. And even though your
slacks—and for God's sake, no one in my life wear
slacks—are your basic cotton twill, they're tailored and
they probably cost more than my monthly salary. Enjoy
the bridesmaids. They may find you fascinating. I
don't."

To her surprise, Gil laughed. "Oh, well done, cuz.
She'll provide endless entertainment."

"Fuck off, Gilly. We're not here for your
amusement."

"Of course you are. You invited her to piss off your
parents." He shrugged. "I'll enjoy watching that. Just
don't ask me to believe you're serious about each other."
He stepped into the waiting elevator and waved as the
doors shut between them.

Luke inhaled deeply, exhaled slowly. Kai gave him a
gentle squeeze before letting go. "Nice guy."

"We grew up together. His mother is my mother's
sister. Sharla. Since we're only six months apart, Gilly
and I ran with the same crowd. We competed a lot. And
since he's younger, I was kind of an ass to him. When I
got my driver's license, I taunted him. Likewise when I
could drink legally. But he's always been better looking,
so he retaliated by stealing my girlfriends. The problem
was, I didn't particularly care, which made him even
crazier."

"That's stunningly immature."

Luke smiled down at her. "We were kids. By the time
we graduated from college, the six month age gap was
meaningless."

"But you're still competing."

"He is. But then, he's also in the state legislature, so
as far as my parents or his are concerned, he's already
won."

"Ah."

They wandered through the massive lobby and
outside, where signs pointed through a grove of palm

trees to a gym and spa and a casino.

"Do you gamble?" Luke asked as they poked their heads into the casino where people plugged coins into slot machines and sat at tall tables playing blackjack.

"Not really. I like to be in control. If I'm bored, I might donate a twenty to the penny slots. Same price as going to the movies for about the same amount of time and entertainment. What about you?"

"I play poker with friends, but I've never understood the appeal of casino gambling. It's loud, uncomfortable, and expensive. You get your free drinks, but if I want Pappy or Four Roses, it's going to cost me an arm and a leg. Plus, I don't know the other players, don't know their weaknesses."

"And yet, your sister is marrying a casino owner. You'll have to curb your dislike."

"The family never refers to Oasis Springs as a casino. It's a *resort*."

"Gotcha. How did she and the guy meet?"

"Brad. That's his name. Brad Dunleavy. They met in college. He took several years off to intern at his father's gigantic resort in Santa Fe before going to hotel school, so he's older than she is by about five or six years. I remember her talking about him back in the day, but not in a romantic way. I guess they reconnected when she moved her business out here."

"Her business?" For some reason, Kai had pictured Georgie sitting around doing her nails. Which was ridiculous. Joe would never have been involved with a prima donna. "What does she do?"

"She's a wedding planner. When she came to Vegas originally, it was because of Joe. None of us thought she'd stick it out after they broke up, but she found a niche here. She specializes in putting together all-out extravaganzas in less than forty-eight hours. She can get you a chapel, a limo, space for as many friends and family as you want, hair, nails, suits, dresses, tuxes, flowers, catering, cake—the whole shebang quicker than most people can arrange an oil change."

"You're proud of her."

"Very."

"But you still doubt her ability to pick her own husband."

"It's not that." He lowered himself onto a strategically placed granite bench and tugged Kai down beside him. The sun was setting in pink surrender, the evening turning cool, but the stone seat retained the warmth of the day.

"I know you don't believe in love…"

"That's not precisely true. I just don't think I'm constitutionally equipped for it. You have to be…more open." Not hiding your entire life would be a good start. But that wasn't all, and Kai struggled to put words to her meaning. "More easygoing. More like my old manager, Evie. Love's not in my makeup."

"I'm not sure it's in mine, either. God knows, neither Georgie nor I learned it from our parents. But Georgie, she was head over heels for Joe. I'd never seen her so happy, and now that I have, I don't want her to settle for less. Maybe she really is crazy about this guy. But if they're so perfectly matched, why didn't they get together in college?"

"There could be a thousand reasons, not the least of which is that age and experience change people. Why did she break of up with Joe if she loved him so much?"

"I'm not sure she did. I have no idea what happened there, because as far as I can see, it made both of them miserable. But here's the thing—I've shirked my responsibilities to her for too long. I wanted to avoid my parents, so I didn't see her nearly enough. But marriage is a life changing decision. It's time for me to step up."

"That's very sweet. I bet you're exactly the type of guy who's made for love." And that, inexplicably, brought her near tears.

CHAPTER 3

THEY FOUND THE DESIGNATED DINNER restaurant down a corridor off the lobby. Luke took a deep breath before opening the door and ushering Kai inside. His aunt and cousin had provided clues to the family's likely reactions, but this was the true test. Kai stepped into the restaurant, then took his hand as if to reassure him. Which was ridiculous. This was his family; if anyone should be providing support, it was him. But Kai exuded a quiet strength. Did she lend it to everyone or just him? He squeezed her fingers as the maître d' showed them to the back room where the family was gathering.

Place cards had been laid on three tables of eight. If his sister had arranged them, Luke would be seated next to her. But chances were his mother had organized this little shindig, which meant he'd be subjected to her interrogation over dinner.

"Lucas," his mother called, as if conjured by his thought. "You're here!"

"I am."

"And this must be…is it pronounced Kay or Kai? Lucas sent me an email so I'd know what to put on the place cards, but I've never heard him say your name, so…"

"It's Kai, mother. Not Kay."

"Kai, then. And you must call me Julia." She gave Kai a quick but comprehensive onceover, from the top of her scarlet-streaked hair to the soles of her combat boots. "What a unique skirt. I don't think I've ever seen one like it."

"Probably because I made it."

"You *made* it?"

For once, Luke and his mother were on the same page. Who made their own clothes? That was damned impressive.

"My girl's got skills," he said, brushing his lips over the top of her head. Then he coughed to mask the fact that he was rubbing his mouth with his sleeve. He was not at all sure her hair color hadn't come off onto his face. He should have asked her whether he could touch it.

"I..." His mother's lips moved, but no sound emerged. Then she recovered. "Is that what you do? You're a seamstress?"

"I'm a designer. But no, like most artists, I have a day job to pay the bills. I sell sex toys. In fact, I'm the manager of Goody's Goodies' premiere location on the Strip in Vegas."

Julia stiffened and the look she threw at him promised retribution, but she kept her cool. "I see. Well, it appears to be time for us to sit down. Lucas, you and Kai are next to me." She marched off, leaving no doubt she expected to be followed.

But Luke hung back. Pulling Kai into a quick hug, he murmured in her ear. "You okay?"

She pressed a kiss to his neck. "I'm fine. Relax. I've got no dog in this fight, so she can't hurt me. Let's go meet the fiancé."

They made their way through the crowd, hurrying by anyone who tried to stop them, until they reached Georgie, who exclaimed in delight when she saw them.

"Kai! This is my cousin, Sue, and Brad's sister, Elaine."

"Sue is Gil's sister," Luke explained.

"Now, now," Sue teased, "let the poor girl form her

own opinion without prejudicing her, okay? I'm nowhere near as obnoxious as Gilly."

WELL, OF COURSE THESE TWO were the women Georgie had gone to meet for Pilates. Slim and blonde, they were exactly the kind she expected would deny themselves cake and carbs even at parties, and exercise when on vacation.

"Girls," said Julia before Kai could find out precisely how little she had in common with them, "please find your seats. We can all talk later."

A tall man with dirty blonde hair, a swimmer's build, and hazel eyes that invited the world to share an unspoken joke approached, bent down and kissed Georgie on the neck. Georgie blushed and introduced him.

"Great to meet you," Brad said loud enough for everyone—including Luke's mother—to hear. "Georgie's told me so much about you. I can't wait to hear stories about your job. I bet you meet even more interesting people selling adult toys than I do in the hotel trade."

"Any job where you deal directly with the public has its entertaining moments. I'm sure Luke has his fair share, too." She leaned into Luke, drawing him into the conversation.

"Oh, yes," Brad agreed. "I've heard a few of those from Georgie."

"I bet she and I see some of the same people. We do a brisk business in bachelorette parties, bridal showers, wedding reception gag gifts... It is Vegas, after all."

Luke's mother picked up her water glass and clinked her fork against the side before Brad could answer. "Please, everyone, take your seats. I'm sure you're all hungry."

"Of course, Julia." Brad gave Luke's mother a

winning smile. "Kai, I look forward to chatting with you later. Alas, we're not seated next to each other."

"Alas," Kai agreed with a laugh.

Julia had placed Kai between Brad's father—"The name's Warriner, but everyone calls me Walt"—and Luke. Walt's hair was thinner and grayer, but otherwise he and his son looked remarkably similar. Brad's mother, Marion, had contributed little to her son's genetic makeup, but the laugh lines around her eyes told of her influence on his personality.

Walt kept Kai occupied through all three courses of the dinner with questions about Goody's Goodies. He knew all about Benny's rise from a working class kid selling risqué toys at parties he organized out of his parents' garage to the multi-millionaire king of the adult toy industry. Walt didn't care what products Benny—or by extension Kai—sold, he just wanted to find out whether he could make use of any of the same tactics.

They were having coffee when Brad pulled out his cell phone, frowned, and excused himself to deal with a hotel emergency. Luke's attention sharpened on the man's back as he strode out of the restaurant, but Georgie, deep in conversation with her father, barely looked up.

Dinner broke up shortly thereafter and as the families milled about, Luke tried to corner his sister. Georgie, however, was performing her duties as hostess and bride-to-be, hopping from one group to the next, introducing people, making sure their rooms were acceptable, and showing off her ring to anyone who hadn't seen it.

"You should come to the spa with Sue, Elaine, and me tomorrow," she said to Kai. "We're getting massages. At noon."

"Oh, no. I don't think—"

"Go on," said Luke. "I promised you luxury, didn't I? And what's a luxurious vacation without a massage?"

"Well, if you put it that way." She glanced up at him

and he winked. The man really was too hot for his own good. *Down, girl.*

"Great! We'll see you at the spa a couple of minutes before noon, then." Georgie waved and ran off to chat with another group.

Luke gave up on getting Georgie alone and told Kai he wanted to call it a night. In the elevator, nerves assailed her. When would he make his move? Would he? Or would he leave it up to her? Usually, she met a guy, they went out for dinner or drinks, and everyone knew precisely what would happen when she went back to his apartment. No muss, no fuss, no cuddling afterward, no waking up in strange beds. She hadn't been with the same guy long enough to invite him to her place, or even to find out what he smelled like in the morning, in five years.

Luke held the suite door open for her. "You want to see if there's anything on television?"

"Why don't you do that while I take a shower and change? I want to unpack, too. Most of my clothes are pretty wrinkle-proof, but I made a dress for the wedding that needs to be hung."

"I should do that, too." He stretched and Kai heard joints pop. He needed a massage more than she did.

She went into the bedroom to hang up her dress and put the rest of her clothes away. Luke did the same and it felt terribly domestic. *Yeah, right. If it were true domesticity, you'd be putting the clothes away and he'd be off somewhere with friends.* Her hangers at home were a motley collection of velveteen-covered plastic that held sleeveless dresses on by friction and chunky ones she'd found at thrift shops that didn't ruin the shoulders of her nicer shirts and jackets. By contrast, the hotel had supplied beautiful oak and cherry hangers polished to a high shine. Twice she adjusted her dress and twice it slipped off.

"Here," Luke said, hauling her suitcase off the luggage butler that the porter had laid it on. "Drape it over this. Tomorrow we can ask the concierge for a hanger that will work. There's a dry cleaner in the hotel, so they'll have something."

"A man of many talents," Kai teased. She carefully laid the dress over the stand and plucked her big cosmetics bag along with her pajamas off the bed. "Okay. Shower time. Next time I see you, I will be utterly transformed."

"Looking forward to it," Luke said, and the tone of his voice sent a tendril of heat through her belly.

The spacious bathroom was all grey-and-white marble, with fancy fixtures and thick, fluffy towels. A table stood by one of the two sinks, ready to hold her cosmetics bag. Turning on the shower was more of a production than she expected—a half dozen shower heads meant that she had a wide range of choice in force and direction of water as well as temperature. She settled on the overhead fixture, a rainfall type from which a sinfully wasteful amount of water cascaded, and scrubbed herself clean.

The bath sheet was twice the size of her towels at home, and she wrapped it around herself while she dried her hair, blowing it out without product. She put on her sailor-striped pajamas and braced herself. *Ready or not, here I come.*

Luke had left the bedroom when she let herself out and in the main room of the suite she could hear the television. As she stepped out, her feet silent on the thick carpet, he looked up and smiled that devastating smile.

"There you are."

"What, did I take too long?"

"No, not at all." He focused intently on her and a shiver ran up her spine. "I just wondered when I'd see the real you. Without the mask."

"Well, here I am." She forced a lightness she didn't entirely feel. "Chipmunk cheeks and all."

He laughed. "You so don't have chipmunk cheeks."

"I totally do. It was a running joke in school. Without

lovely cosmetic contouring, my face is basically a circle. Or even an oval on its side."

He rolled his eyes and patted the sofa next to him. "Look, I found *Godzilla*. Come watch while I get cleaned up."

"Oooh, the original?"

"Of course. Is there any other *Godzilla*?"

"Not in my book." She plopped herself down on the couch. "Too bad room service doesn't have popcorn."

"We just had dinner!"

"It's a movie. I'm a traditionalist. Movies are supposed to have popcorn."

"I'll keep that in mind." He stood. "Back in a couple of minutes."

Luke couldn't believe how different Kai looked stripped of her makeup. He wasn't naive enough to believe she was truly maskless, despite his words. His mother and his sister both wore masks that went far deeper than their skin, and his father's was so thick and strong Luke wasn't entirely certain there was anything behind it at all. But fresh from her shower, in striped pajamas with her hair still showing remnants of whatever temporary dyes she used on it, Kai seemed far younger. With her persona firmly in place, he'd initially guessed her to be close to his own age, but now she barely looked twenty-five.

He stayed in the shower long enough to let the steam soften the bristles of his stubble so he could clean it up. His mother hated when he got his "fisherman's beard," which was part of why he hadn't bothered to shave before dinner. Kai had accused him and Gilly of immaturity and he knew the little potshots at his mother proved her correct, but the spiteful behavior was a habit he couldn't seem to break. His mother brought out the worst in him. Hell, his whole family, with the exception of Georgie, brought out parts of his personality he'd prefer not to acknowledge.

He scraped the beard away, rinsed off, and toweled himself dry. He'd brought sweatpants to wear around the suite and, if necessary, to bed. At home, he slept in the nude, so he didn't own pajamas. And after Kai's comment the other night, he was hoping not to need them on the trip, but if she changed her mind about sex, he'd sleep in the sweats. Because no way could he sleep naked in a bed next to Kai Tyler without making love to her. She might think she had a fat face, but he was used to women's odd perceptions of themselves. As far as he could tell, she was damned near perfect and he wanted her with a ferocity he couldn't ever remember feeling in the past.

In sweats and one of his RFD T-shirts, he rejoined Kai. Her feet were tucked up and to the side in a position not unlike a lying foal. It couldn't possibly be good for her knees, but it left her bare feet exposed, which gave him an idea. He sat next to her and said, "So, do you intend to wear combat boots for the whole wedding party, or was that just for effect today?"

"I wore them because they went with the outfit. But I admit, after your descriptions of your family interactions, I thought I might need them. And honestly, talking to your mom and your cousin, I might have preferred to be wearing full body armor and carrying a 9 mil."

"Oh, come on. It's not that bad, is it?"

"No, not really. And I won't be wearing the boots most of the time."

"More of those spike heels you were wearing the other night?" He waggled his eyebrows, and she laughed.

"I did bring a couple of pairs of heels. I like variety."

He ran a finger down the sole of her foot and she shuddered. "Women and their shoes. I don't think any man really understands. I mean, don't get me wrong, I like to see them on you, but aren't they hideously uncomfortable? Those boots today didn't have heels, but they have to weigh a ton."

"A few pounds. Maybe four. Not more than that." She patted her thigh. "Good for the legs. I don't think I can really explain shoes. It's like clothes or makeup—you put them on, you feel like a different person. Taller, stronger, more confident. In their own way, stilettos are as much armor as combat boots."

He tugged her foot away from her body and she twisted around so that her back was to the arm of the couch, letting him pull her foot into his lap. He pressed his thumbs to the inside of the arch and she squirmed in a purely sexual way. His blood heated and he took a deep breath. *Not now. Slow down.* They only had a week, and some of that week they'd have to spend with his family, no matter how much he wanted to spend it locked in the bedroom. But she deserved better than for him to jump her every time they were alone together, regardless of how much he might want to.

He finished his rubdown of her foot, then switched to the other. She groaned.

"If you keep that up, we're not going to make it to the end of *Godzilla*."

"The hell with *Godzilla*."

She leaned up, folding her body in half, and pressed a kiss to his jaw. "Got a monster of your own that needs dealing with?"

"Jesus, woman. The things you say." But he laughed.

She reversed positions so that she was sitting in his lap, his erection pressing against her bottom through layers of cotton. Her mouth rose up and took possession of his. Unable to resist, he fisted a hand in her short hair and held her head in place. His other arm locked her body against him as her arms wound around his neck. He let his tongue dance with hers in a *pas de deux* that became every more frenetic. God, she tasted so damned good, all minty, hot, and sweet.

Her hands slipped down his body, then up beneath his T-shirt and she uttered a little frustrated murmur when the material bunched and refused to move.

"Bedroom," he muttered against her questing mouth.

She slipped off his lap and pulled him to his feet. The minute he was standing, he reached for her again and lifted her with one arm behind her back and the other behind her knees.

"Mmm. Nice muscles, Captain Hottie," she said, her fingers tangling in his hair.

He almost dropped her. "What did you just call me?"

"Oops." She buried her face against his neck and even through the sensual haze he could feel her skin's heat. She was blushing.

He carried her into the bedroom and placed her carefully on the bed. Her face was still bright red and he couldn't help laughing.

"Come on, now. Fess up. Did you just call me Captain Hottie?"

Her shoulders straightened and her back stiffened. "What if I did?"

"How'd you even know I'm captain of my company?"

"It was on your shirt. The first day you came into the store. Before I knew your name, I had to call you something in my head. So…"

"I like it." He pushed off the bed. "I have something for you. Well, for us." He grabbed his Dopp kit, unzipped it, and pulled out the medical report he'd slipped inside with a package of condoms.

"Oh, very nice," she said when she unfolded it. "I do like a man who can follow directions. I've got one, too. Top pocket of the suitcase."

He wanted to tell her that he trusted her, that he didn't need to see it, but he didn't want to look quite as eager as he felt. He plucked the paper from the suitcase and pretended to read it, though the words didn't penetrate his lust-fogged brain. When he laid it down, she crooked a finger at him.

"Now that we've been responsible adults, come on back over here."

He picked up the pack of condoms on his way, but she waved them off.

"Leave them. I'm on the pill and we've done the safety check. I want Captain Hottie in all his glory."

"I'd have that put on my next shirt if the guys would let me." He dropped to his knees next to her on the bed. "But I'd never live it down."

"Don't worry about living it down," Kai said. "Live it up." She grabbed a fistful of his shirt and pulled him down on top of her.

"Yes, ma'am."

KAI LUXURIATED IN THE WEIGHT of Luke's solid body pressing hers into the mattress. He was so tall and broad and strong and…present. Physically and emotionally, he was entirely present. It was a quality she found as appealing as all of his delicious muscles. Which, dammit, were still covered up. She pushed at the T-shirt and he pulled away long enough to drag it over his head, revealing a tanned body with, to her surprise, a tattoo high on his shoulder. A Maltese cross.

"Firefighter to the end?" she asked, tracing it with one finger.

He shrugged, his blue eyes hot on hers. "I'm a simple guy. It tells me who I am."

"In case you forget and think you're a politician?"

"Something like that." He plucked at the sleeve of her pajama top. "I know there's one here. And I saw something on your back when we went to Spago, but the shirt covered a lot of it. How many in total?"

"You'll have to count for yourself."

"Sounds like a plan." He dropped his head and kissed her again, hands slipping beneath the soft cotton of her top. He lifted her slightly, without any apparent effort, and drew the top over her head, then tossed it to the side. Rough fingers slid gently up her left arm, tracing the circle of the serpent around her wrist, then up her arm to where it wound around her shoulder.

"Coral snake," he said. "Pretty but deadly. Trying to tell people something?"

"That's me. Dangerous."

"Oh, you are. Let's see the back?"

She leaned forward to show him her fiery wings. They'd cost a fortune and taken forever and she was damned proud of them, but she knew they freaked some people out. Each feather licked like a flame, the bottoms tipped in pale blue and white softening to yellow and orange to a deep red lined with black at the top.

"That must have hurt like hell to do." He didn't sound turned off, just curious.

She shrugged. "Pain avoidance isn't the first thing I think about when considering a tattoo. Sometimes, what hurts is what's right."

She leaned back and his fingers continued their course down her body, lightly, delicately, like a blind man learning a face. They settled on her right hip, where tiny red and blue marks peeped out from her pajama bottoms. "Another?"

"Look and see."

He peeled down the waistband just far enough to see the flaming phoenix. "Nice."

"First tat I got. I was sixteen."

"Your parents let you do it?"

"Fake ID. Long story."

"Reinventing yourself out of the ashes?"

"Yeah. Teenagers don't have a lot of subtlety."

He slid down the bed and kissed the tattoo. "I like this incarnation. Lack of subtlety and all." He wiggled his eyebrows. "I'd like to see more of her."

Kai laughed. When had sex been so much fun? Most of her dates were intense, torrid weekends. Her two longer relationships had been filled with high highs and low lows but very little easy laughter. And Battery-Operated Bob, her steady for the last several years, had no sense of humor whatsoever.

She pressed her feet into the mattress, raised her hips, and stripped off the pajama pants. The laughter faded out of Luke's eyes as his gaze traveled over her naked body.

"God*damn*, woman."

"Oh, shut up."

"I will not." He pressed a kiss to her abdomen where it pooched out just below her belly button and every muscle in her body tensed in anticipation. "How did I get so lucky?"

"You haven't gotten lucky yet," she muttered, tangling her hands in his hair to drag him up her body for a kiss. "Get a move on."

He choked and smacked his lips against hers so fast she almost screamed in frustration. "Not on your life. Not rushing this." He traced her lips with one long finger, coming to rest on the spot where she'd removed her stud when she showered.

"There's no hole."

"The stud's magnetic," she explained. "I used to have actual piercings in my lip for the labret stud like the one I was wearing today, and the ring I sometimes wear on the side, but I had to take the jewelry out for work and the holes kept closing up. I thought about re-piercing when I went to work for Benny, but they make pretty good temporary jewelry now and I can move it around easily if I get bored."

He skimmed the finger down from her lip to her chin, then down her neck, following the path with his lips.

A shiver raced up her spine. She slid her fingers into Luke's hair and pulled his face to hers for a kiss. Tangling her tongue with his, she let her hands wander over the corded muscles of his back, the indentation of his spine and down beneath the waistband of his sweats to the very fine swell of his ass. He ground his body against her for a moment, then rolled to his side to strip off the last of his clothes. And then he was back and she could feel him against her. The scratch of his long legs along her freshly shaved ones, the press of his wide, muscular chest with its sprinkle of wiry hairs against her sensitized breasts, the blunt head of his heavy erection at her hot, wet center. She raised her knees and tilted her hips, but he ignored the invitation, shifting down her body to press heated kisses in a tightening spiral over one breast while his long, clever fingers toyed with the other.

ANY SECOND, LUKE WOULD LOSE control and take what he—what they both, if her little whimpers and wiggles were any indication—needed. But he'd never last once inside her, and he wanted their first time to be better than a quick minute, so he shoved aside his dick's demands as best he could. Instead, he focused on her reactions, intent on learning what gave her pleasure. When he pinched her nipple slightly, her body jerked against his, so he scraped the other with his teeth and she let out a gratifying little moan and twisted her hands in his hair, trying to drag him forcibly back up.

He ignored the unspoken command and shifted his attention lower, outlining the little phoenix on her hip with the tip of his tongue. It should have a taste, or at least a texture. Such a significant, permanent decision shouldn't be hidden to all senses but one. From there, her hip bone called to him, a tiny cliff in the landscape of her body, and he swiped his tongue over the ridge before biting down on it gently. Again, she clutched at him and her legs tightened around him where he knelt between them. The woman liked a little pain with her pleasure. He could work with that. He moved further down the bed and pressed his thumbs into the creases of her thighs, pushing her legs wide.

"Luke."

"Shh. I'm having a moment." And God, he was. His heart was beating double time and he felt every pulse thick and heavy in his cock. He wanted to be inside her. *Now*. He clamped down on the desire, forced it back. *Soon*. But first, that little thatch of mocha curls, silken and slick, was waiting.

He bent his head and licked her slowly, tasting the heat of her passion on his tongue. She squirmed and gripped his hair hard enough to send little, pleasurable sparks of pain shooting through him. He sucked her clit into his mouth and she sobbed his name and the leash finally broke. He allowed himself one last taste, then surged up her body and took her mouth, his tongue pressing inside at the same time as his cock found her entrance. She wrapped her legs around him, her breath coming fast and hard, her heels on his ass urging him on, and he was lost. He tried to wait, to be sure she was with him, but there was no staving off the rush of pure pleasure that blindsided him.

When his senses returned, she was snuggled against his side.

"Thanks," she said, heavy-lidded eyes giving a slow, sensual blink that had his body considering a second round. She leaned halfway up on her elbow and kissed his jaw. "That was lovely."

Lovely. He didn't think anyone had ever said that to him before. And while he still wasn't sure she'd gotten off, she clearly didn't have any complaints. Which meant she'd give him a chance to do better next time. He fell asleep with that thought in the forefront of his mind.

CHAPTER 4

Kai woke alone. Not so different from her other dates, after all. Of course, this time she wasn't in her own bed. But alone was alone. She levered herself up and staggered into the bathroom. Wow. No wonder Luke didn't stick around. Dull, matted hair stood up in a halo on one side of her head but stuck flat to her scalp on the other. Sleep lines creased her pasty skin. Definitely time for a second shower.

She emerged from the steaming shower considerably refreshed. None of this was real, so it didn't matter if the sight of morning Kai sent Luke scurrying for the nearest exit. The impromptu spa appointment meant she'd have to get in and out of her clothes fast, so rather than an elaborate outfit, she settled on black leggings, a black shell, and a boldly striped purple and black jacket that nipped in to a single button at the waist and then fell in an A-line to her knees. After applying a deep purple gel to her hair, she added a few black chalk streaks. Makeup, a couple of necklaces, along with a chunky silver bracelet and matching ring, and she was ready to face the world.

When she left the bedroom, however, she found Luke pacing the suite's living area with his cell phone attached to his ear and reflexively raised a hand to check her hair. *Screw that.* He was just a guy.

"I know," Luke said into the phone. "Look, Cesar, I don't like it any better than you do. We've been over this." He listened for several seconds. "No. We've had that discussion. Just do the small wall. I told him that was all we'd get to today." He ran a hand through his hair, which was almost as uneven as her own had been. Of course, ragged and scruffy was rather endearing on him, unlike on her. He glanced over, caught sight of her, and the scowl marring his features relaxed into a smile. "Hey, Cesar, I have to go. This isn't the first time we've put in a piece we knew we'd have to take out, and it won't be the last. Remember, he's going to have to pay a premium when we redo the work and that will make it easier."

He clicked off, dropped the phone onto the coffee table, then crossed the room in long strides and pulled Kai into a hug. "Did I wake you? I'm sorry."

"No." Cold sweat broke out over her skin and her heart pounded. *What the hell?* She slipped out of his grasp. "No, it's fine. Trouble at work?"

"Yeah."

"What happened?"

"If you want to hear, let's order room service. I got all this unexpected exercise last night and I'm starving."

Kai's nerves settled and she laughed. That weird, affectionate hug had thrown her off, but innuendo she could cope with. "Deal."

Luke dug up the room service menu and called in their order, then drew Kai down onto the sofa next to him.

"I meant to ask you yesterday—your hair, can I touch it when it's all done up like that, or will I end up with dye all over my hands?"

"It runs if you get it wet, but as long as your hands are dry you should be okay. So, who's Cesar?"

"Huh? Oh, right. Cesar's my installer. The site manager for all the projects we do."

"And he has an issue with the current job?"

"You could say that. He doesn't want to do it."

"Charming. And that's exactly why I don't count on

anyone but myself."

"Nah. Cesar's reliable." But a frown line formed in his brow and a muscle bunched in his jaw. "And he's a genius when it comes to masonry and soil. It's the client who's the problem."

She thought back to the bits of conversation she'd heard. "He doesn't know what he wants?"

"Most of our clients don't know what they want. Hell, I'd go as far as to say that in my experience very few people *do* know what they want.

"This guy is one of those 'master of the universe' types who can't be wrong, though. He wants to put in brick retaining walls, which will be ugly as hell with his landscape and architecture. But he heard about it from a guy with more money or a fancier car or something, so it *must* be right. I told him bluestone—which, by the way, is more expensive, and consequently more prestigious— would match the landscape better, but he wasn't interested.

"And what I didn't realize before we'd signed a contract is that he's also a bigot. He won't listen to anything Cesar says. Cesar wants to try to change his mind one last time before installation begins, but that might put his back up further and we'd never convince him to do the job right."

"Charming."

"Yeah. Cesar and I discussed this—we're going to do a small section first so the dude can see how bad it looks and change his own mind. We've done it before. But this guy pushes Cesar's buttons and he wants to be in and out, not do part of the job, then pull it out and do it all over again."

"I'm with Cesar, and I haven't even met the guy. Racism pushes my buttons and it isn't even part of my daily existence."

"Believe me, if I could figure out how to get out of this contract, I would. Usually, clients meet Cesar while we're discussing the project so he and I can see their reaction. We decide on clients together. But Cesar was visiting his parents in Guatemala when I took this job." Again that troubled frown. Luke wanted to be at home, running his business, watching over Cesar. Not here with her.

Damn. Hot, sweet, responsible, *and* socially conscious. Her next words popped out without thought. "How is it possible you're not married?"

He snorted. "Why, because glorified gardeners are such hot commodities?"

Her cheeks burned. "Sorry. Don't mind me. I haven't had my coffee yet."

As if on cue, there was a knock at the door. She vaulted to her feet and ran to let in the waiter with the breakfast cart. He rolled it over to the small counter that separated the kitchen area—containing a coffee pot, refrigerator, and toaster oven—from the living area. Luke came up behind her as the waiter laid out the food on the counter. She felt the heat of his body against her back. His arms surrounded her as he reached out and signed the bill and she had to steel herself against leaning backward. Damn the man, he was too easy to like.

WHY WAS KAI SO UNCOMFORTABLE? Every time he touched her, she practically jumped out of her skin, and she'd barely glanced at him as they'd eaten breakfast. A stress headache clawed through his skull from the conversation with Cesar. He hadn't been entirely honest with Kai, but she didn't need to hear about his business problems. She'd agreed to be his fake girlfriend for a spa vacation, not so she could listen to him whine.

But when he put a hand on her knee and she jerked back, his skull pounded and the pain gave his voice an edge. "Did I do something wrong?"

"What? No. Of course not. Why?"

"You seem…nervous."

She shrugged, but those dark eyes were watchful. "It's the situation. I…don't date much. I'm not used to playing house. I'm not used to playing anything, really. And in another hour, I have to go hang out with your cousin, your sister, and her fiancé's sister and pretend you and I are serious. I didn't expect your sister to require handling, not once you told me you were close. I thought I'd be able to sort of keep my distance from most everyone except your parents."

"Georgie knows the truth. She won't let the others badger you."

"I'm sorry if I'm freaking you out. I'll get myself under control."

"Don't worry about it. Honestly, I just wanted to be sure it wasn't me."

"No." She smiled, and her whole face changed, those cheeks she'd decried the night before turning her eyes into downward-tilting crescents. Goddamn, she was adorable. Which was an odd thing to think about a woman who wore her sexuality so openly, even aggressively. But there was no other word for her.

And her smile soothed his screaming head, so he returned it, leaning over to press a kiss to her syrup-glossed lips. The kiss went from sweet to hot in an instant and he slipped off his stool to stand between her legs, which wrapped around his waist. Her fingers slid through his hair and tugged and he slipped one arm around her waist to lock her in place while the other eased her off the stool and held her. Still fused, he carried her to the couch and eased them down with her kneeling astride his lap.

She pushed him back, separating them long enough to drag his shirt up and over his head.

"Fuck. Why did you put on clothes?"

"There aren't many." To demonstrate, she unbuttoned the single button holding the jacket closed and shucked it off, leaving her in only a black silky tank top and leggings.

"You're all clean." The protest sounded feeble, even to him, and she laughed.

"I don't mind getting dirty if you don't."

She ran her fingertips over his chest and goosebumps formed in their wake. Every nerve, every muscle in his body was alive. He swore.

"Not out here."

She was off the couch like a rocket, towing him along with her. In the bedroom she wriggled out of the pants and top. The sight of her in nothing but a little black bra and an even littler black thong ripped through him like a lightning bolt, leaving him sweaty and harder than he'd ever been in his life. She reached for the waistband of his sweats and her fingertips brushed the damp head of his cock. Letting him go for a moment, she brought her hand to her mouth, then licked her fingers, her eyes never leaving his.

He almost came on the spot.

In seconds, he was out of his sweats and on the bed. She was slower, but he could see the unsteadiness in her breathing when she stopped by the bed to strip off the last of her clothes. And then she was on top of him, and he was inside her, her soft heat surrounding him and sending the world spinning away.

He didn't come back down until they were both sweat-soaked and gasping. He staggered into the bathroom and grabbed a washcloth to clean her up. When he was done, she curled herself against him and mumbled something he didn't quite catch.

"What?"

"This has got to be better than a massage," she said only slightly louder.

A chuckle worked its way up through his exhausted muscles. "And I was planning on a run while you were at the spa. Not sure my legs will hold me up."

"Can I call your sister and tell her I changed my mind?"

BUT OF COURSE, SHE DIDN'T. The sun shone brightly as Kai stepped out of the hotel on the way to the spa building, and a light breeze brushed against her skin. She was running late, having had to redo her makeup after the morning's unexpected activities.

Georgie sat on a stone bench outside the spa under a large palm tree, tapping away on her cell phone. The minute she spotted Kai, she jumped to her feet and tucked the phone away.

"Elaine and Sue are already inside changing. You look great. Did you sleep well?"

Kai's cheeks heated. Damn, this blushing thing was getting out of hand. It was just *sex*. And she was pretty sure Georgie hadn't even been asking about that. Kai had no siblings, but she didn't think most sisters wanted to know about their brothers' sex lives.

"Yes, I did. I wish my apartment was half as nice as this resort."

Georgie grinned. "It is nice, isn't it? Wait until you see the lemon grove. That's where we're having the wedding. It's gorgeous."

Inside the spa, music played quietly over invisible speakers and a heavy, sky-blue area rug covered most of the marble floor. Buttery yellow-white walls reached up for miles to a vaulted ceiling. *This is what rich looks like. You* so *don't belong here.* Kai squelched the voice in her head.

Georgie went up to the large marble desk and spoke to the receptionist while Kai kept up her covert examination. A minute later, an attendant came and led them to the locker area and gave them each a thick, soft cotton robe.

Kai and Georgie changed quickly, then joined Elaine and Sue, who were bent over a long counter, examining a display of tiny, trial-sized nail polishes.

"We're trying to decide what colors we want for the wedding," Elaine said. "Are you coming to the big bridesmaid manicure thing on Saturday?"

"No, I'm not a bridesmaid, just a guest. I brought my own polish."

"Is it black?" Sue asked, a wink taking the sting from the question. "I'm not a bridesmaid either, and I'm going."

"No one has a manicure party without Sue," Georgie said with a laugh.

"Damned straight." Sue held out her fingers, showing off ten perfect French tips. "You don't think I keep these babies in this kind of shape by myself, do you?"

The attendant poked her head back into the room. "Are you ready ladies?"

She led them to two separate rooms across a short hall from one another. Each room held two padded tables with sheets folded up at one end.

"I set us up for doubles," Georgie explained. "I hope you don't mind. They had a double room open when I called this morning but not another single."

"Oh, no, not at all." Kai hung back slightly, however, watching out of the corner of her eye as Georgie took off her robe, lay on the table with her face in the little cradle attached to one end, and pulled a sheet up to her waist. *Okay, then*. Kai followed suit.

A minute later, a pair of muscular women entered, both dressed in yoga pants and dark T-shirts with embroidered Oasis Springs logos.

"Hello, Miss Clarke," said the brunette.

"Hi, Lisa." Georgie propped herself up on her forearms. "And how many times do I have to tell you to call me Georgie? Hi, Janice. This is my brother's girlfriend, Kai."

Kai craned her head around and waved a little. The two women smiled.

"Are you both ready?" Lisa asked.

"More than." Georgie lay her face back down into the

cradle, and her voice came out vaguely strangled. "This wedding business is stressful. I didn't think it would be, you know, for me. But now I totally understand why people are willing to pay me to organize all the details for them."

"Are you going to be able to keep the business if you move out here? Will you commute to an office in town?" Kai asked.

"Most of my business is done by phone. People who don't give themselves more than a week to plan a wedding are either already here and having too good a time to come into an office, or out of town, planning to make a quickie trip here for the wedding, and can't visit an office. They mostly find me on the web."

"So they call you and say 'I want to get married the day after tomorrow?'"

"Pretty much. And I say 'sure, I can do that.' And then freak out once I hang up."

Kai laughed. "Have you ever had one that didn't go off as expected?"

"Never, thank God. I mean, it will happen eventually, but I hope that when it does the bride is happy enough with her groom that she won't notice."

"What about your wedding? Did you set the whole thing up yourself, or hire help?"

"I did it. I didn't want a big deal, and since Brad owns this place, everything was easy. It was just a matter of finding a time everyone could come."

Kai wanted to pry, just a little, but they weren't alone. And even if the masseuses hadn't been there, she probably wouldn't have the nerve to ask what she really wanted to know. So she settled for asking whether Georgie was excited about the day.

"Oh, yes. Of course. I mean…it's a little different for me because Brad and I have known each other for years. And because weddings are my business, so I see them all the time. I am anxious to start our life together, but the wedding itself isn't such a big deal."

Janice pressed her palm onto a spot under Kai's shoulder blade that made her gasp and for a minute she couldn't speak.

"You're very tense," Janice said. "You should try to relax."

Georgie twisted slightly to look over at Kai. "I hope my family isn't stressing you out. They can be hard on Luke's girlfriends."

"Not at all. I'm just not a very relaxed person."

Georgie laughed. "No wonder you and Luke get along. He never takes a minute off."

Kai almost protested. Georgie knew the truth, she knew Kai and Luke's relationship was an act, so why was she pushing so hard? But again, the staff prevented her from speaking freely.

"He's taking a whole week for this vacation."

"Right. I guarantee you he doesn't go a day without a call to Cesar and the firehouse."

Kai didn't answer.

"He has already, right? I told you. Never a second's relaxation. *He* should get a massage."

It was Kai's turn to laugh. "He doesn't seem the type." But enough about Luke. For some reason, talking about him made her tense up in a way that had Janice grunting.

"So tell me about the plans for the next few days. I'm afraid I have to admit to not reading the whole itinerary."

WHEN KAI GOT BACK TO the room, she could hear the shower running. She plopped down on the sofa, put her feet up on the coffee table, and flipped on the news. As usual, it was all bad—authorities were investigating the deaths of three men found in the desert outside of Beatty, tourism was down, causing a constriction of the local Las Vegas economy, and California was on fire.

Luke came out of the bedroom with damp hair and

bare feet, wearing faded jeans and another of his ubiquitous RFD T-shirts. This one had no lettering on the sleeve and like the jeans, it was decidedly worn. He looked…normal. Like he probably did while digging around a yard.

"How was the massage?"

"You may have spoiled me for life." She stretched her arms over her head. "You don't have any other siblings getting married who might want me to spend the day at the spa with them, do you?"

"Afraid not. But feel free to go back while we're here."

Kai blinked. "You really do have too much money, don't you? You didn't even ask what it costs."

"I'm no Bill Gates or Warren Buffett, but I do okay." He sat beside her and dug a pair of boat shoes out from under the couch. "And I like to make my friends happy."

"Is that what we are? Friends?"

He took her hand, brought it to his mouth, and pressed a kiss into her palm. A gentle warmth spread outward from the spot. "I hope so."

"With benefits."

"The *best* benefits." He bit down lightly on the tip of one of her fingers and fire sparked deep in her belly.

Luke's phone buzzed with a text and he muttered a curse she couldn't quite hear. But when he picked it up and looked at the screen, his irritation vanished. "My sister wants to see me."

"When?"

"Now, apparently. She has time. We don't have any other commitments until the cocktail mixer at six. Will you be okay on your own?"

"Of course. Take the chance while you have it. Text me when you're done and I'll meet you."

"Thanks." He pulled her into a tight hug and she quelled the instinctive anxious reaction.

"No problem. I'm going to grab a bite to eat at the café."

They left the room together and while they waited for the elevator, Luke took her hand again. She glanced up at him, but he was lost in thought, likely trying to figure out how to broach the topic of Georgie's engagement. When she tried to slip her hand free, however, he tightened his grip and focused on her.

"This is one of my favorite benefits. We can negotiate terms on others, but I'm not giving up the hand holding."

Kai shook her head. "Strange, strange man. Where are you meeting Georgie?"

"Her room." They stepped onto the elevator and Luke pushed the buttons for both the third floor and the lobby. No one shared their ride, and when they stopped, Luke dropped a quick kiss on Kai's lips before heading down the hall toward his sister's room.

The first person Kai saw when she entered the restaurant was Gil. Leaning back in his chair, the remains of a meal in front of him, he was flirting with a young Hispanic waitress. When he spotted Kai, he dismissed the girl and beckoned Kai over.

"Join me."

"No, thanks. You look as if you're about to leave."

"It's not as if I'm busy. I can keep you company while you eat, since my cousin's deserted you."

"Luke is with Georgie."

"And you're alone."

She dug into her bag and pulled out her tablet. "I have a book. That's all the company I need."

"Oh, come on. Let me entertain you. I can tell you all the family's dirty laundry."

"I'm not really a fan of dirty laundry."

Gil tapped one long finger against his lips. He was handsome enough, and she was quite sure he could—and would—be a charming companion, but she needed some downtime.

"Your loss," Gil said.

She waved and walked across the restaurant to take a

seat at an empty table in the corner. The same waitress Gil had been chatting up came over with a menu and Kai ordered a BLT and an iced tea, then settled in to read.

She was deep in the history of the 1980s punk scene when the scrape of chair legs against the floor brought her back to the present. She looked up to find Julia Clarke sitting opposite her.

"Mrs. Clarke."

"Call me Julia."

"Julia. How are you doing today? Everything on track for the wedding?"

"I'm well, thank you. And you look very nice. Another of your designs?"

"It is, yes. Although in this case, I bought the jacket at a thrift shop because I liked the material, took it apart and remade it to fit my vision."

"I've been considering what you mentioned last night about artists and day jobs, and it occurs to me that we are in a position where we could help each other."

"We are?"

"Underneath all that glop, you have decent bone structure. And fashion design isn't the worst career choice for a politician's wife. Assuming, that is, you are serious about my son."

Kai ignored the question couched in a statement. "Luke doesn't want to go into politics."

"His father and I mismanaged that. We pushed too hard, so he ran the other way. But you could help explain to him that he'd be in a position to help a great many more people as governor than as a landscaper or even a firefighter."

"Luke likes his life the way it is."

"My dear girl, all men like their lives the way they are. None of them would change unless we women encouraged it. We'd have to whitewash your past a bit, but that's not so difficult."

You have no idea.

"Of course, I haven't had time to research your background, so I am trusting my instincts when I make this offer. If you have a criminal record, the deal will change. I can't allow Lucas to throw in his lot with a felon."

What a piece of work. But Kai kept her tone even. "Of course not."

"If you stay with my son, you quit your job. Clean up your act. Focus on designing. I will pay you three thous-and dollars every week that you and Luke are together for up to a year. By the end of that year I expect you to have convinced Lucas to take a more reasonable path. If you choose not to continue your relationship with my son, I'll write you a check right now for fifty thousand dollars to break up with him and never see him again."

Kai knew what Luke would recommend. Take the money. They weren't really dating, so why not let his mother think she'd gotten her way when they eventually "broke up." No harm, no foul, and his mother deserved to be taken for a ride for her behavior. Benny would give her the same advice, though coming from him it would be a simple business proposition.

But she couldn't. It was a matter of pride. Plus, the thought of Luke's parents believing they'd manipulated his life in such a way, even if it wasn't true, was untenable.

"I can't agree to that."

Julia leaned forward and lowered her voice. To hear her, Kai had to lean forward also.

"You think you'll get more from my son? Because you won't. You're an interesting diversion for Lucas, nothing more. My husband and I have learned our lesson. We will accept you, at which point Lucas will lose all interest and you will be left with nothing. If you accept my help, you'll have a career."

"But I won't have my self-respect. And I know when you look at me you don't see a person who values that, but I do."

"You sell dildos."

For a moment, the word *dildos* coming out of Julia Clarke's patrician lips set Kai so far aback she couldn't form a coherent thought.

"I do," she said when she recovered. "And I do it damned well. I make people happy. Improve their lives. It's not so different from fashion in that respect."

"You're making a mistake."

"It won't be my last, I'm sure. But it's mine to make."

Chapter 5

GEORGIE THREW HERSELF INTO LUKE'S arms the minute he got to her room. Accustomed to her impulsiveness, he caught her and spun her around as if she were still eight years old and obsessed with ballerinas.

"You guys had a good time at the spa?"

"Totally. It was fabulous." She rested a hand on his chest. "Luke, tell me you're serious about Kai."

"What?"

"She's awesome. So much cooler than most of your girlfriends."

"You figured this out from sharing one massage appointment?"

"She has a *life*, Luke. And she asked about mine. Not like, to impress you and show you how well she'd fit into the family, but because she really wanted to hear about my work."

"Is that what my girlfriends do? Pretend interest in you?"

Georgie rolled her eyes. "Of course it is."

And now that he thought about it, by the end of his relationship with Shelley, his last girlfriend, she'd been almost as bad as his mother about turning every story he told into a reason he should consider politics. He could easily imagine her faking interest in Georgie's business.

"I'm sorry, Sprout."

"It's not your fault. But now you've found someone

real. I don't want you to lose her."

"She's real, I'll give you that. But the relationship isn't. We're just friends." His throat tightened as he spoke. *Is that what we are?* He'd never had a friend like Kai.

"Are you sure?"

"Georgie, we just met a couple weeks ago."

"So?"

"*So* we hardly know each other."

"Well, get to know her, okay? Because from where I'm standing, she's way better than any of the others I've seen you with. And mom *hates* her." She grinned, a wicked sparkle in her eyes.

He laughed. "Devil. I'll take that into consideration. But this week is supposed to be about your relationship, not mine. Do I get to spend some time with Brad?"

"Of course! I was hoping that maybe after the cocktail party tonight we could get dinner. You and Kai and us."

"Double dating with my sister? That's odd even for our family, Sprout."

"It's not dating. You and Kai aren't dating and Brad and I are engaged. See? I just want you to have a chance to talk to him. Hang out. You'll like him."

"I'm sure I will if you do."

"Of course I do. I'm marrying him."

"I'll be honest, Sprout. This whole thing seems peculiar to me. I didn't even know you were going out with anyone until the invitation came."

"We were best friends in college. It just took a while to realize that we had more than that. That we really loved each other."

Was that how love worked? A sudden realization after years of friendship? He supposed it was possible. But it wasn't his sister's usual M.O. Of course, maybe the change was a sign of her growing up. It gave him a pang to think about her losing her exuberance and impulsive joy.

He studied her, but her face gave nothing away. Which set his nerves on edge in and of itself. She'd never tried to hide anything from him and it was disturbing to find out that she could.

"What do mom and dad think of him?"

"Well, they wish he had a more prestigious position, naturally. They're having a hard time with the fact that the hotel is here, not closer to them, and that it has a casino. You know how dad feels about gambling. They were pretty sure I'd give up on Vegas, even after I started my business."

"They miss you." Georgie's relationship with their parents had always been less complicated than his. They had fewer expectations of her. As long as she didn't embarrass them or drag the family name through the dirt, they left her alone.

"The grass is always greener," Georgie said. "Far from home, I'm the perfect daughter they wish lived nearer. Close at hand, I'm a nuisance."

"You are not." He slung an arm around her shoulders. "I wish you lived closer. I don't see enough of you."

"As I said to Kai this morning, you don't ever take any time off. If you did, we could hang out more." She frowned up at him. "Luke, do you ever think you're making a big mistake?"

"Every day. But are you talking about your wedding? Because it's not too late to back out."

"No, Brad and I are solid. I meant…well, I hate to even say it, but you honestly would be a good politician. Or I guess politician is the wrong word. Statesman. The 'rents have their sights set on the governor's mansion, and much as I have a hard time imagining you wearing a suit and tie every day, you'd be good at it. You're the most responsible person I know, and people trust you. They *like* you."

He ran a hand through his hair. "Yeah, but there's the suit and tie thing. And being nice to people all the time. And I don't actually *want* all that responsibility."

"Okay. So long as your resistance isn't just spite."

"Nah. I try not to let them control me quite that much. If I had any desire to run for office, I would."

"Okay, then."

WHEN LUKE TEXTED, KAI WAS still sitting in the café. After the meeting with his mother, her book couldn't keep her interest so she'd pulled out a sketch pad and was drawing out an idea that had come to her when she'd seen the band of poodle-skirted girls in the elevator.

Luke met her at her table and ordered himself a sandwich.

"How did your conversation with Georgie go?"

"She wants us to have dinner with them after the cocktail party tonight."

"That sounds good."

"I suppose."

She reached over the table and covered his hand with her own. "What's the matter? You don't like him? He seems like a good guy to me."

"It's not that."

"What, then?"

"You'd have to know Georgie. I always assumed that when she got married, she'd do it the same way she's done everything in her life—in a mad blaze of energy and passion. This whole thing is so *structured*." He laced his fingers through hers. "Did she talk about him at all this morning?"

"A little. Not much."

"Doesn't that seem strange to you? I mean, I haven't been to many weddings, but it seems as if the couple should always be thinking about each other, talking about each other. When Georgie had her first boyfriend, she wouldn't shut up about him. At twelve years old, she was suddenly fascinated by chess because he played it,

Same thing when she was dating Joe. I heard all about how his family came over from Cuba, she recounted every funny thing he'd ever said to her, and she learned all about MMA."

Kai remembered the taste of Luke's name in her mouth, the compulsion to discuss him with Celia. But surely that wasn't love.

"She's a grown woman, Luke. You have to trust that she knows what she wants."

He frowned. His head came up and he scanned the room. But before she could ask what he was looking for, an alarm blared. "Out," he said sharply. "Now. And take as many of these people with you as you can."

Then he was up and gone and she saw what he'd scented. Wisps of smoke curled from around the kitchen door, then puffed out in a gust as Luke pushed his way through. Over the sound of the alarm, someone screamed. Sprinklers popped on, drenching Kai as she urged the other patrons first into the lobby, then out onto the lawn.

The alarm continued to sound as the hotel emptied. The patrons of the café were immediately surrounded by curious guests begging for information. Georgie ran over and grabbed Kai by the shoulders.

"Have you seen Brad? Or Luke?"

"Luke went into the kitchen. To try to get everyone to leave, I think." But a nasty, bilious acid churned in her stomach and backed up into her throat.

They were joined by the whole Clarke family and, bit by bit, by the Dunleavy clan. At last, as fire engines and ambulances pulled up and men in protective gear pushed them back away from the building, Brad appeared. Soot and purple dust streaked his skin and his laughing eyes were grim. Georgie hugged him close and laid a hand on his blackened cheek.

"Thank God you're okay. Have you seen Luke?"

"Yeah. He's with the EMT's, but he'll be fine."

Kai was moving before he even finished the sentence,

pushing people out of her way as she ran for the ambulance. She heard Luke before she saw him, his voice hoarse and rasping, his words interrupted by wracking coughs. His beautiful blond hair was singed, tears leaked down his face, and he was coated with a combination of ash and purple powder.

"It was a grease fire. One of the kitchen staff tried to put it out with water."

Kai squeezed by the last person in her way. Luke sat on a gurney talking to a firefighter while an EMT tried to force him to put on an oxygen mask. His right arm was bandaged from palm to elbow, the right leg of his jeans was soaking wet where they'd cleaned him up, so she slipped around the gurney and came up on his left side to slide her arms around him and meld herself to his side. Luke wrapped his good arm around her and nuzzled the top of her head with his chin. The action brought the prickle of tears to her eyes. Or maybe it was just the scent of smoke on his clothing.

"Why were you in there so long? What were you thinking?"

"I was thinking that my sister would kill me if I let her fiancé's hotel burn down." He spoke lightly, but she could feel the strain in his body, and coughs punctuated his breaths.

"How badly are you hurt?"

"It's nothing, just a burn."

Kai addressed the EMT. "How bad?"

The woman looked from her to Luke and back. "He needs to go to the hospital. A doctor will make the determination."

"It's not that bad, sweetheart, I swear."

She ignored him. "Can I ride with him?"

"I'm not going to the hospital."

"It's your right to refuse," said the EMT, "but only a doctor can prescribe painkillers, and I promise you, once the shot I gave you wears off you *will* need them."

"I don't have to go in the damned bus to get painkillers."

"No." The EMT smiled. "But you'll get seen a whole lot faster if you do. Come on. Let us take you and your girlfriend. You'll be in and out in no time. And keep that arm up, please."

"Please, Luke. Do it for me."

Brad joined them and Luke snarled.

"What the hell, man? Don't you train your kitchen staff how to handle grease fires?"

"Of course I do! They're trained, drilled, all of it. But people aren't perfect and in a panic when they see fire, they still think water."

"Is everyone else okay?" Kai asked.

"Alvin got some bad burns." Brad jerked his chin at a second ambulance, where one EMT was closing the back doors. "But he's the only one."

"What happened?"

"I don't know exactly. I was hoping Luke could tell me."

"I wasn't there when it happened. But if Alvin is the one who got burned, it's likely he's the one who threw water at the grease. The Purple K hadn't started coming down yet. The heads went off just as I got there."

"Purple K?" Kai asked

"New restaurant stoves burn hot," Luke explained, "and the oils used are formulated not to smoke until they're far hotter than your basic corn oil. You don't want to throw water at even a humble home kitchen fire, but in a commercial kitchen it's much, much worse. Basically, the water doesn't put out the fire, it just breaks up the oil so you have bits of flame flying everywhere.

"So in commercial sprinkler systems for kitchens, they use a dry chemical rather than water. Purple K is a popular brand."

Which explained the strange purple dust all over him and Brad. And why they weren't soaked through. They must have gone out the back of the kitchen instead of through the lobby.

"And you breathed that shit—excuse my language—for entirely too long. Which is another reason you need to go to the hospital," the EMT said.

"We're going," Kai said. "*Now*. Brad, we'll catch up with you later."

"Tell my sister I'm okay," Luke said as the EMTs loaded his gurney into the back of the ambulance. Kai hurriedly gave Brad her cell number in case Georgie wanted to call while they were at the hospital and then climbed aboard. The woman who'd helped Luke strapped her into an awkward, harness-type seatbelt, and they pulled away from the hotel.

KAI DIDN'T EVEN CONSIDER HOW the hospital would affect her until it was too late. They pulled up to the ambulance entrance and the EMTs unloaded Luke, whose eyes had swollen a bit but who was breathing better. Kai followed them as they rolled him inside, through a maze of sterile corridors and directly into the emergency room itself.

It had been fourteen years since Kai had found herself in an ER, shaking, shocky, and wanting nothing more than to go home and crawl into bed. She fought the memories the way she'd been fighting them for years, but they reached out, tendrils creeping through her mind and strangling the deep breaths she used to try to calm herself.

She hadn't meant to hurt herself that night. She'd begun taking the occasional anti-anxiety pill from her mother's stash to calm down long before she reached her teens. But they made her tired, and after her mother slipped a disc, Kai discovered that taking an Oxy would help her get up and moving when she didn't want to. Alcohol smoothed out the ups and downs.

Kai had the system down to a science, but that day, the day her mother announced her engagement at an extravagant cocktail party, something went wrong. Kai had never been certain exactly what. Maybe her mother's new prescription was stronger. Maybe she'd had more to drink than she realized, because it had been so easy to swipe during the party.

Whatever the reason, the celebration had ended with Kai and her mother in the ER, her stepfather-to-be dealing with the guests. Declared a suicide risk, she went straight into an inpatient program and then—when the shit really hit the fan—to a private boarding school for troubled teens.

The sound of the curtain being drawn to their cubicle, the harsh fluorescent lights, the smell of industrial cleaner, the incessant beeping of unattended monitors…The past rushed over her and she was a child again, sick and dizzy, trapped and so damned cold.

Every nerve in her body screamed *run!* and she tried to obey, but she tripped and ended up in a pile on the floor. Far away, she could hear shouting, but she couldn't focus on it. Fear consumed her. She curled into a ball and scooted into the corner. If they couldn't see her, they couldn't take her away.

WHAT THE HELL HAD HAPPENED? KAI had been right beside him as he was wheeled into the ER. The nurse had told him to put on a gown, so he'd turned away for a minute to pull off his shirt and in that split second he'd heard a crash, and now Kai was huddled in the corner, arms around her knees, rocking and shivering. He dropped to the floor, calling over his shoulder for help.

"Kai?" He reached for her but she lashed out, her booted foot connecting with his bandaged arm. Pain streaked through his body and he cursed, fighting back the urge to yell at her. Behind him, medical personnel piled into the cubicle, but he ignored them.

"Kai, baby, look at me."

"I won't go." But she wasn't talking to him.

"No one's going to make you go anywhere. I promise."

"Delayed shock," said a voice in the background. Luke disagreed. He'd seen plenty of shock and this was more, deeper, but he didn't bother to argue. Focusing all his attention on Kai, he kept up a steady stream of quiet, soothing words, promising her she was safe, that no one would hurt her or take her away. Eventually, she raised her head and a frown creased her forehead.

"Luke?" She looked around. "What happened?"

"I was sort of hoping you'd tell me." He held out a hand and she let him pull her to her feet and into his arms. She burrowed into him like a kitten seeking warmth, and he held her tighter.

"We need to deal with your arm," said the nurse who'd first put them in the room.

Luke held out his right arm, anchoring Kai to him with his left. "Do what you've gotta do."

"Mr. Clarke…"

"Luke, I'm okay." Kai pulled away. "Sit down and let them do their jobs."

But she wasn't okay. Under her makeup, her skin was gray and tremors still shook her petite frame. How had he never noticed how small she was beneath that kick-ass attitude? He hopped up onto the hospital bed, but didn't let go of her hand.

By the time he was cleaned up and rebandaged, a little of the natural color had returned to Kai's face, but on the cab ride back to the resort her fingers still felt like ice in his. She was scared. Back in the ER, that had been pure, undiluted terror on her face, and the remnants still hung around her, a shroud dimming her usual radiance. His head throbbed in time with his arm.

"I'm sorry," Kai said.

"Sorry? What for?"

"You invited me to your sister's wedding to reduce the drama, not to increase it."

"That wasn't drama. That was…life, I suppose. Do you want to talk about it?"

She shook her head. "Not really. It's pathetic and even more than drama, it's melodrama. Better left in the past."

Whatever had scared her didn't seem very much in the past to him, but he had no right to pry. He leaned back on the vinyl bench seat and closed his eyes, draping his arm over her shoulders.

"No cocktails for you tonight," she said, curling into him. "The drugs that doctor gave you are too strong."

"Just imagine the damage I could do at the family mixer."

She laughed, and his headache eased. "I probably shouldn't tell you this in your weakened condition, but your mother tried to buy me off."

"She *what*?"

"She wanted to give me money to either clean up my act and convince you to see things her way or to cut and run. Either option was acceptable."

"Oh fuck."

"No, it was fun. I mean, once I got over the shock."

"It shouldn't surprise me. It really shouldn't. And yet…" He shook his head. "How can you consider that fun?"

"I've always enjoyed puzzles. I guess it's why I like sales. When a customer comes in, I have to figure out what will make them happy, and then I can provide it."

"Don't most people come in for something specific?"

"Sometimes. But it's like you said, very few people know what they really want. Some women say they're just looking to get off without a man's help, but in fact they've just come out of a bad relationship and they're looking for something that makes them feel feminine, worthwhile, attractive."

"That seems like a tall order for a sex toy."

"Exactly. What's required in that case is conversation and compliments, clothes and possibly perfume, and only then a toy. And it has to be the right toy."

"So my mother is like a sex toy shopper? I dare you to tell her that."

"Oh, sugar," she slanted a look up from beneath half-closed lids, "never dare me. I can't resist a dare."

THEY PULLED UP IN FRONT OF the resort a few minutes past five. Luke had texted Georgie to let her know he was okay and she'd told him that the fire had been safely contained, but still Kai found herself surprised that no signs of the chaos remained. The fire trucks were gone and no onlookers lingered. Why had she expected time to stand still while she was at the hospital? The flashback must have affected her more than she realized. Two years of therapy provided under court order by the people who'd screwed her over were supposed to have eliminated the shakes, sweats, and flashbacks. And they had, for a long time. But apparently some things never changed, including her inability to be normal.

And now Luke knew just how messed up she was. Not that that fact should bother her. After all, this was just a single week out of their lives. Once his sister was married, they would go their separate ways. She'd be the weird chick he took to the wedding, who turned out to be even weirder than he expected.

"Do you still want to go to the cocktail party?" Luke asked as they walked into the hotel. "I sort of have to, but I can make excuses if you're tired and want to stay in the room."

Well, yeah, she did want to stay in the room. Maybe for the rest of her life. But if she'd learned one thing from all that damned therapy, it was that locking herself away didn't help. If Luke was going to that cocktail party, she'd be at his side, playing faithful girlfriend.

"Are you sure you're up for it, Luke? Because I don't think anyone would blame you for skipping."

"No, I have to go. We have more relatives arriving tomorrow, and Wednesday the bridesmaids start showing up, so the longer I wait, the less I'll be able to watch Georgie and Brad together."

"Are we still going to dinner with them afterward?"

"I don't know. I have to ask Georgie. I expect Brad has a lot to deal with from the fire."

"Maybe you should just eat with her alone? I can claim exhaustion."

"No. I tried to go at her head-on this afternoon. It didn't work. I need to observe them for a while first. If she still wants to go without him, you should come too. After all, they're a puzzle, and you're good at puzzles."

"Luke, I have to ask you again, what are you going to do if you decide she's not really ready to marry this guy? I mean, she's an adult. It's not your decision to make."

"I know." He rubbed a hand through his smoky, purple-streaked hair. "I'll cross that bridge when—if—I come to it. She says she loves the guy. If she does, I won't have to worry, right?"

"Why are you so...invested in this?"

"It's not enough that she's my sister?"

"Maybe. I never had one."

"I don't want her to end up like our parents."

"There are no guarantees in life. You can't predict the future and you can't protect her forever."

They rode up to the room in silence. Kai tried to tell herself it was because a young couple shared the elevator with them, but she couldn't quite convince herself that the easy companionship that had marked their relationship from the moment they first went out to dinner remained.

You just have to keep pushing. You can't ever let anything be. And right on cue, more of her past reared its ugly, ugly head.

By the time they reached the room, the weight of silence had settled into Kai's bones and rubbed against her nerves. "You shower first," she said as Luke slipped his keycard into the lock. "I'm not going to wash my hair, so I don't need long."

"Sit with me for a minute first." He took a step toward the sofa, then looked down at himself, grimaced, and changed direction to take a seat at the counter. Kai followed.

He blew out a long breath. "I shouldn't have snapped at you. I'm not exactly rational when it comes to Georgie. She was thirteen when I went off to college. I was so happy to be free that I never stopped to think about how miserable her life would be once she was alone with our parents. I took summer classes so I had a reason to avoid going home for more than a few days at a time. I lost touch with her for years, until she was in college herself and called me one night, drunk and angry, telling me what a poor excuse for a brother I was."

"Oh, Luke." Kai's throat clogged. Responsibility was the backbone of Luke's personality. His sister's call would have devastated him.

"She was right. I'd been wrapped up in myself."

"You were a *kid*."

"I was her brother. I lived in that house too. I should have been there for her and I wasn't and I lost six years with her because of my selfishness. You tell me I can't protect her forever. My brain say's you're right, but my heart says I have to try."

"Whatever happened in the past, you're a good brother now. I'm sure Georgie appreciates your concern."

"Oh, I doubt it. She calls me an interfering old lady. But I can live with that."

Kai hopped off the stool and nudged his legs apart so she could stand between them and wrap her arms around his solid strength.

"I can explain to her that you're not a lady if you like."

Luke laughed and put two fingers under her chin to

tilt her face up to his for a kiss. "You're an amazing woman," he said. "Thank God I decided to go by the shop to tell Joe about Georgie's wedding."

"Trust me when I tell you I'm not so amazing. And coming by the shop *was* nice. The least I could do in return was to take an all-expenses-paid vacation with a hot guy who is very definitely *not* an old lady, whatever his sister says."

Luke closed his eyes and rested his forehead against hers. "Much as I would like to explore that statement further, I really, really need a shower."

"Yeah, you do." Kai eased away and he stood.

"Where's that thing I'm supposed to use to keep the bandage dry?"

Kai dug the heavy plastic wrap they'd picked up at the hospital pharmacy out of her bag and handed it over. Luke dropped a quick kiss on her lips as he took it, then disappeared into the bathroom.

Kai plopped down on the couch. Luke Clarke was bad for her equilibrium. He treated her as if she mattered, as if her thoughts and feelings were important to him, which was messed up. If he knew the truth, all that would change. Which, *dammit*, shouldn't bother her. She'd spent years working for emotional independence, overcoming her desperate need for approval and acceptance.

It's only a week. A week of good sex and luxury. And then back to her normal life, where no one asked questions or pretended she was more than a purveyor of dildos and underwear.

CHAPTER 6

A LTHOUGH LUKE CLEANED UP AS fast as he could, the combination of the plastic wrap on his arm and Purple K in his hair meant his shower took longer than it should have. The cocktail party was in full swing by the time he and Kai made their way downstairs to the private room behind the lounge. Gil stood just inside the door, flirting with two girls Luke didn't recognize.

"All hail the conquering hero," Gil said, raising a glass in Luke's direction. "Have you met Jenna and Cecily? They're Brad's cousins."

"Pleased to meet you," Luke said. "I didn't realize Brad's family was coming out this early."

The two women giggled in unison. Giggled. *Jesus.* Gilly's taste hadn't gotten any more discriminating over the years.

"Most of them won't be here until Friday, but Jenna and I wanted a vacation, so we came early."

"We're not working right now," Jenna added.

If you're not working, why do you need a vacation? The words almost slipped out; the painkillers were taking a toll on his self-control.

Kai laced her fingers through his. "Luke, sweetie, we should find your sister. She'll be worried about you."

"Of course." Damn, she was good, smoothly detaching him from the group before his irritation boiled over. He spotted Georgie talking to Walt in the corner, and he steered Kai in their direction.

"Luke!" Georgie broke off their conversation the minute she saw them. "Are you okay?"

"I'm fine. Nothing to worry about."

Georgie frowned. "I never really thought about your volunteer gig being dangerous. You've always made it sound as if it was mostly drinking beer with the guys and scolding people who put tinfoil in their microwaves. I don't like it."

"That's because the majority of my calls aren't even fires," he said. "Seriously. And when they are, I'm fully geared up and backed up by a bunch of other guys. I only got burned this time because I was stupid. I should never have gone in, and should certainly not have stayed and tried to put the damned thing out without proper gear. I'd ream any of my guys who did that."

"Still," said Walt, "it's a good thing you do. Volunteering like that."

Luke hated when people lauded him for doing what anyone would do if they could. What half the guys in Rockdale did. As a child, he'd dreamed of being a firefighter, but living in Berkeley it had never occurred to him that such things as volunteer firefighters existed. And as bad as his relationship with his parents got, he didn't consider fighting fires as a career until he'd already gotten a master's in landscape architecture. To him, volunteering was more than a duty, it was a reward unto itself.

"I enjoy it," he said. "We have a good group of guys. And as Georgie said, most of our calls are things like tinfoil in the microwave or a bad sensor head on an alarm system."

"Where's Brad?" Kai interjected, once again navigating around his discomfort.

"Dealing with the cleanup. He insists the café will be running again by Friday evening, even though it seems to me as though it would take ages to fix." She looked up at Luke. "What do you think?"

"It's his business. If he says it's possible, it's possible. Has the insurance adjuster been through yet?"

"Yes. Whole lot faster than the guy came out when a tree fell on my car, but Brad says they're very attuned to the needs of business owners."

"Then if he has a construction crew ready to go, he can do it. I didn't see how much damage the sprinkler system did to the restaurant, but the cafe isn't that elaborate. Drywall, mud, paint. They can worry about rehanging art and stuff after they open. If it were one of the fancier spaces, it would take longer."

"What about the kitchen?" Georgie asked.

"Commercial kitchen aren't like home kitchens. There aren't a million custom-made cabinets. Most of it is stainless steel racks, which will be fine. Replacing the appliances will be expensive but not time-consuming. Were you guys planning on using the cafe for any of the wedding events?"

"No, but that's the catering kitchen and we're catering a bunch of stuff."

"There are what, four restaurants here?" Kai asked.

"Yes. The Italian place, the steakhouse, the cafe, and the fusion restaurant and sushi bar."

"They'll manage, then," Kai said with a reassuring smile. "Trust me. I've lived in Vegas for ten years, and I've learned nothing shuts down a resort for long."

"Good," said Georgie. "That's good."

"Come on, Sprout. You can't really be worried. You can pull together an entire wedding in a weekend."

"No, I'm not really worried. But I don't want Brad tied up with repairs all week. I mean, I understand that he can't be here tonight or even guarantee dinner later, but we have events going all week. What if he can't make any of them?"

"Then he can't. No one will blame him. It's not ideal, but it's not a tragedy." Stress twisted between Luke's shoulders. Nerves like these were unusual for Georgie, who normally took everything in stride.

"You're right, of course. And that's exactly what I'd tell any of the brides I deal with. But it's different when it's your own wedding."

"I'm sure Brad feels the same way," Kai said. "He'll want to spend as much time with you as he can, so he'll make it work."

"I know. And I should stop freaking out and get back to doing the hostess thing."

"I think between them, your mother and your cousin Gil have that handled."

"Yeah," Luke said. "Mom has the men and Gilly has the women."

"My cousin Gil is a whore," Georgie explained to Walt. "I was actually hoping he be too busy to get here until the very last minute, but I should have known he'd never miss the opportunity for free food and booze and unattached women. But I couldn't avoid inviting him since my Aunt Sharla is my mother's favorite sister."

"You don't get to choose your family," Walt said. "My brother's girls don't have a complete brain between them. Sweet kids, but I tried to give them jobs at my hotel as a favor and they were utterly hopeless. And Eddie and Janice are both smart. You'd think their kids would be, too, but it just goes to show you can't ever tell how people will turn out." He laid a hand on Georgie's shoulder. "Luckily, my son found a good one."

"Aww, you're sweet," Georgie said. But because he was watching, Luke saw her twitch when Walt touched her. Wedding jitters, or something more?

"Are we still going to dinner even if Brad's busy?" Kai asked.

"If you guys are still up for it. I'll understand if you're not after the craziness this afternoon."

"No," said Luke, "we're fine. What did you have in mind?"

"We made a reservation at Grey's, the steakhouse, for seven-thirty. Brad will come by if and when he can."

"That sounds great." A waitress came by and he

ordered a scotch and soda. Kai glared at him, but didn't comment as she ordered herself a Coke.

"I'll be okay," he assured her. "I'll drink it slowly. And it's not as if I'm driving."

She smiled, but trouble still lurked behind her eyes. Was she really that concerned about a single drink on top of the single Percocet they'd given him at the hospital?

Before the waitress returned, they were joined by his parents. "Did you meet my husband at dinner last night?" Julia asked Kai. "John, this is Luke's friend Kai."

Not girlfriend. Not date. Luke didn't miss the distinction. But he'd made a point of introducing Kai to his father as his girlfriend the night before.

"It's good to see you again," Kai said politely. Much more politely than he would have. "Did you two have a good day? Aside from the fire, of course."

"Walt and I played golf," John said. "We were out on the course during the fire. I understand it wasn't terribly serious."

Luke felt Kai stiffen beside him. He considered stepping in before she exploded but the waitress brought their drinks. Luke took a sip of his, then almost spat it out when Kai, soda in hand, rounded on his father.

"You do realize that your son had to go to the hospital, right? And that one of the cafe employees is still there. And that the reason your daughter's fiancé is not at his own party is that his restaurant was destroyed. You got that? You might want to consider asking Luke how he is instead of assuming that because it didn't interrupt your golf game it wasn't a big deal."

"Obviously, Luke is fine," Julia said with a chilly smile. "He's standing right here."

Kai opened her mouth and Luke drew her into his arms and tight to his body. Not that he necessarily cared if she told his mother off, but he suspected she hadn't quite recovered from the ER incident. She seemed off-kilter, and despite her outlandish clothes he got the sense she didn't particularly like to draw attention to herself.

"Every fire is serious, Dad," Luke said. "It's worth remembering that if you ever have one. We're lucky this one wasn't worse."

"You couldn't have thought this one was," Julia said. "One of the guests told me you went to it rather than leaving."

"Yeah, well. No one ever accused me of being smart."

"My hero," Kai said. He was pretty sure the hint of mockery beneath the words was for his ears alone.

"Always," he replied, giving her his best smile.

WHEN THE COCKTAIL PARTY BROKE up, Kai breathed a sigh of pure relief. These people were too much like her mother's set. Smile to your face and slam the dagger in hilt-deep the instant you turned your back. After her father had died, they'd abandoned her mother as if widowhood were a communicable disease. It was a world she'd hoped to leave behind forever, and it brought back all her insecurities and the accompanying anger. When Luke had invited her to the wedding, she'd assumed that as he was part of that world, its denizens would treat him well and that her own emotional distance from the people and events would protect. Mistake. Rage boiled up from some deep, hidden spring, but she shoved it down. This was not her life, it was Luke's, and she had no right to shred it.

She and Luke hung back, waiting for the room to clear and Georgie to free herself from those wanting to chat with her. It took nearly twenty minutes and Georgie had to tell several people that she and Brad had private dinner reservations to keep them from tagging along.

"We should have eloped," she said once the host had seated them in a quiet corner of the restaurant.

"I'm sort of surprised you didn't," said Luke.

"Believe me, I thought about it. But mom would have insisted we have a proper ceremony afterward anyway. It wasn't worth fighting over."

"True enough."

A minute later Brad dropped into the fourth chair at the table with a groan. "Hi, guys." He lifted Georgie's hand and kissed it. "Sorry to have missed cocktails. I was going over plans with the G.C."

"G.C?" Kai asked.

"General contractor. His guys will be out at seven in the morning to begin the job, so we had to go over the contracts tonight."

"What a pain."

"Yeah, but it could have been so much worse. How's your arm doing, Luke?"

"Fine." Luke rattled the ice cubes in his glass. "One more of these and I won't feel it at all."

On cue, a waiter arrived and asked for their drink orders. Kai and Georgie were still working on their drinks from the cocktail party, but Luke and Brad ordered scotch and sodas. Kai stiffened. She couldn't help it. How much did Luke drink? How often did he combine alcohol and pain meds? *It's not your problem. He's not your problem.*

Luke laid a hand over hers. "Don't worry, baby. I have no intention of taking any more Percocet. My head hurts way worse from dealing with my family than my arm does from the burn."

"They gave you Percocet?" Georgie asked "You didn't say that when you texted! They must have thought your burn was pretty severe."

"No, it's the combination of the burn and a big bruise. I...fell on it as well." Oh shit, Kai thought, she'd kicked him. She hadn't even realized until just now it had happened, but instantly she relived the impact of her foot against his arm. He must be furious with her.

She stared at him as he dropped a kiss to her

forehead. "I'm okay, baby. I promise."

"I'm sorry."

He shook his head, then turned his attention to Brad. "Speaking of headaches, how's the family treating you?"

Brad's lips twisted. "About the way I expected. I've known Georgie a long time, so I was prepared for their behavior. And you, Kai? Enjoying your time on Lifestyles of the Rich and Dysfunctional?"

"Oh, sugar, this is practically *Leave It to Beaver* to me." Luke glanced sharply at her and Brad raised his eyebrows. *Oops. A bit too revealing there.* Time to backtrack. "What? I work on the Strip. Not exactly home of the functional family."

Brad and Georgie laughed, but Luke's eyes remained watchful. Well, what did she expect? Her self-control had taken a hit today and the crazy was leaking out around the edges of her calm facade.

"So tell me," said Georgie, "what's the most outrageous thing that's ever happened at Goody's?"

On solid ground once more, Kai entertained them through the rest of the meal with stories of frat boys, church ladies, and—her favorite—a woman who'd come into the shop looking for 'a replacement for her daughter's lousy boyfriend.'"

"Do you suppose she went home and handed her daughter the vibrator and said 'now you can ditch him?'" Georgie asked.

"I *so* wanted to ask her how she planned to broach that subject. She told me the guy didn't have a job and didn't help out around the house, so she assumed her daughter was in it for the sex."

"I'm trying to imagine saying that to a complete stranger. And failing."

"Oh, people confide all kinds of things when you work at Goody's. It's like being a bartender. Plus, I look as if I've heard it all before. It helps."

"I love your style," Georgie said. "And you do look rather unflappable. But I still don't think I'd tell you about my sex life."

"Kai makes her own clothes," Luke said, and the approval in his voice warmed her.

"Really?" This from Brad. "Have you considered a career in fashion? Starting your own boutique?"

"Hardly. I sell a few pieces in the shop, which is a nice supplement to my regular salary, but I have a fondness for life's little luxuries like a roof over my head, indoor plumbing, and electricity. Fashion design is not practical and it's extremely risky. Despite what my personal style suggests, I'm risk-averse."

"That's why you get investors. Structure the investment and alleviate the risk. I could find them for you if you're interested."

"You…why?"

"Brad's great-aunt was a designer in the 1950s," Georgie said.

"When women's fashion was a disaster." Brad shook his head. "She was the black sheep of the family. Never married, never did anything normal women were expected to do. But she was my favorite relative when I was a kid."

"I'm not sure what to say." Who the hell made an offer like that to a virtual stranger? He had no idea about her business capabilities.

"Don't say anything. It's just a thought. In case, down the line, you find selling sex toys isn't as fulfilling as you'd like."

"Who knew doing a favor for a friend would result in so many business opportunities?"

"So many?"

Slipping, Kai. Slipping. She turned to Luke. Would he mind her revealing the conversation with his mother?

"Julia offered her a chunk of change earlier."

"Now there's a shocker," said Georgie, taking a big slug of her drink. "Let me guess. You were supposed to clean up your act, become a proper lady, and convince Luke to go along with her plans."

"How did you know?"

"It worked with Luke's last girlfriend, so why wouldn't she do it again?"

Luke stared at his sister. "What?"

"Oh shit. I thought you knew."

"No. I mean, water under the bridge and all, but I had no idea. I'll be on the lookout next time."

Next time. The stark reminder that she and Luke were merely playacting shouldn't bother her. Wouldn't, were she in her normal headspace. She firmed her spine and caught Georgie studying her, her blue eyes—so like Luke's—filled with sympathy. What was that about?

"But she left you alone?" Luke asked Brad.

"Yeah. Not like money is going to have a lot of influence over me. But she tried to buy off Georgie's last boyfriend with a hundred thou."

Kai choked. A hundred thousand dollars. Twice what Julia had offered her. She must *really* have hated the idea of Georgie dating Joe.

"You never told me," Luke said.

"Yeah, well, Joe didn't take it And you were already angry enough with the parents. You didn't need the ammunition."

"Still think we're the Cleavers?" Luke asked Kai.

"Okay, I give. Maybe you're not a *completely* functional family."

WHAT WAS GOING THROUGH KAI'S mind? Her whiskey eyes were dark despite her smile, and emotions he could not identify rolled off her. She hadn't been herself since the hospital. Or maybe this darker, more troubled incarnation *was* her. Maybe the flirtatious and unflappable persona was put on. Could a person wear that comprehensive a mask in front of the whole world every day?

Dinner broke up relatively early, with a strain Luke couldn't help wondering whether or not he was imagining. Although he'd assured everyone he was fine, his arm throbbed and his eyes were gritty with exhaustion and adrenaline letdown. When he unlocked the suite door, the lights he'd left on pierced his skull.

"I need to crash," he said.

"Go for it." Kai sank onto the sofa and bent over, her slender form folding in half, to untie the scarlet laces of her tall black leather boots. A little kick of heat when through him at the sight and he knelt in front of her and brushed her fingers away.

"I thought you were crashing?"

"I am. But even a dead man would be unable to resist this invitation, and I'm not quite that far gone yet."

"I didn't invite anything." But she smirked as she said it.

"Oh, sure. Put it all on me."

"Men are so easy. I don't have to issue an invitation."

"Got me there. We are a pathetic lot in general." He peeled the leather off her, then ran his fingers over the indentations it left behind in her fair skin. "And women use that fact to their advantage."

Kai didn't speak while he removed her other boot, but when he rose to leave she laid a hand over his. "I'm sorry about your ex."

"Me too. In retrospect, I should have recognized the shift in personality the minute it happened. But it was smooth. Subtle."

"Hindsight is twenty-twenty. You trusted her."

"I did. I almost married her. Probably would have, if she hadn't started pushing me toward politics. It got so every time she opened her mouth, I heard my mother. Believe me, that will kill your libido."

She laughed. "Oh, I can imagine."

"I didn't tell her that though. I was as nice as I could be."

"I'm sure you were. You probably even felt guilty about it. At least now that you know your mother paid her, you can let go of the guilt."

That was true, and the memories of Shelley faded with the realization, but irritation rose to take its place. "I'm too fucking naive for politics. I don't know why my parents can't see that. I can do the little white social lies like 'oh, sorry, I just ate' instead of 'my God, your cooking sucks.' But big lies? That's the purview of politicians and I hate it."

She frowned and he wondered what she was thinking. At last she met his eyes. "They can't see it because they can't see *you*. Lots of people never look more than a few feet outside themselves. I've met more than my share."

Luke pondered her words while he brushed his teeth and changed into his sweats. *They can't see you.* Such a simple statement, but it explained so much. Had he been guilty of the same sin? He'd never suspected Shelley of being the type to deceive him for profit. Even the fact that she'd been an actress hadn't caused him to watch her more closely. What did that say about him?

He crawled into bed, the revelations and questions circling his brain keeping him awake despite the exhaustion dragging at his body. He heard Kai come in and go through her own ablutions, felt the shift of the mattress and drag of the sheets as she slipped into bed. In the darkness he reached out and drew her close so that her head rested in the hollow of his shoulder. His restless thoughts calmed and at last sleep carried him away.

He woke to the sound of strangled screams and Kai thrashing next to him, lashing out at invisible demons. He tried to restrain her, but she only fought harder and though her eyes were open, he was certain she didn't see him.

"Kai! Wake up!"

She scrambled away from him, still caught in her nightmare. Her body stiffened and for a moment she looked like a woman he'd once dragged out a fire who was having a seizure. He leaped from the bed, prepared to catch her if she fell, but then she clapped a hand over her mouth and bolted for the bathroom. He hesitated for only a second before following. He found her cross-legged on the floor, head resting on one arm she had crooked across the toilet seat.

"Go away, Luke."

"No." He settled next to her. "Friends don't let friends puke alone."

She laughed, but her lips trembled and tears clung to her lashes. "If I promise not to throw up, will you leave me alone?"

"No." A dark and shadowed chasm lay before him. If he turned away, went back to the bedroom, he wouldn't fall. But Kai was crying, and that was untenable. He smoothed his hand down her back. "Talk to me."

Kai shook her head.

"Please, sweetheart, let me help."

"There's nothing to help. This is who I am. A mess. A certified lunatic let out of the asylum on a technicality."

"No, you're not."

"Oh, but I am." The bitterness almost made him flinch, but he controlled the reaction and maintained the slow, steady strokes of his fingers down her spine.

"Tell me."

WELL, HE'D PUT UP WITH her so far. Poor guy deserved the truth, or at least a safely excised portion thereof. "I'm not doing this here. I don't care how swanky this place is, it's still a damned bathroom. Give me a hand up."

Luke helped her to her feet and her stability surprised her. She led the way out into the main room of the suite and put a decaf pod of coffee into the machine just to give her hands something to do while she figured out how much of her story she wanted to tell.

"Do you want a cup?"

"Sure." Luke sat on the couch, giving her space, his

sky-blue eyes shuttered.

She passed him the first cup, then made a second for herself. The last drops spat out of the machine long before she could straighten out her tangled thoughts. What she wouldn't give for an Ativan or a Valium right now.

Instead, she gutted up and did what she had to, the same as she'd done most of her life. But she wouldn't, couldn't look at Luke while she told him, so she curled up in an armchair and took three slow sips of coffee before she began.

"When I was thirteen, I screwed up. I ended up on the suicide watch ward of an…institution. I wasn't suicidal when I went in, but I don't blame the docs who sent me there. I was a mess. Some doctors want to help people. I still believe that. But that kind didn't work at Pinecrest. The institution charged ridiculous fees and had a vested interest in keeping the beds full. I thought…I thought I would never get out."

He made an inarticulate sound. She might have thought it was pity, but there was too much rage in it. The force of that anger gave her the strength to go on.

"I had a friend. Her name was Michelle. She really was suicidal, and they should have been watching her, but they weren't. She hanged herself."

She closed her eyes, but the image of Chelle being rolled out on a gurney, the rattle of the wheels on the tiled floor, the pressure of the silence left in its wake filled her mind. Acid backed up in her throat.

"Oh shit. Kai—"

Her stomach rolled and she cut him off. "Let me finish. Chelle's uncle was a lawyer and he unleashed hell on them. First he sued, then he got the state involved, and eventually the place was shut down. We—the patients—we were allocated funds to get help elsewhere. I spent two years in therapy and in the end I came out…me. Most of the time, I have the crazy under control. It's been years since I had a nightmare. I was still having them off and on when I first moved to Vegas, but they faded. If I'd thought for a single second that I'd have one this week, I never would have agreed to this."

He stood and crossed to her, knelt in front of her, took her hands. "I'm very glad you did."

"You say that now. When I lose my mind completely at one of the big family get-togethers you won't feel nearly so charitable."

"It has nothing to do with charity. It doesn't matter how you got to be you, I just like the person you are now."

Of course, he didn't *know* the person she was now. Some days, she wasn't sure she knew herself. The only way to keep from being drugged into a stupor and get a little peace at Pinecrest had been to pretend to be what the doctors wanted you to be. That was where she'd develop-ed the devil-may-care attitude she donned every morning with her makeup. *Fake it till you make it* had become her motto and she wasn't at all sure she knew how to do anything else.

But that was a revelation for another day. Enough truth had been told tonight. Luke's hand rested on her thigh, and she tangled their fingers together. "Can we go back to bed now?"

"Of course." He rose in a graceful, fluid motion, completely in command of his body in a way she couldn't even imagine, much less hope to imitate.

She went into the bathroom to splash water on her face and gain back a modicum of control, and when she came out Luke had straightened out the sheets and was lying in the bed waiting for her. She would have curled up on her own side, but the minute she slid beneath the covers he reached over gand gathered her close. The heat of his body surrounded her and her muscles relaxed inch by inch until at last her eyes drifted shut.

LUKE FELT THE MOMENT KAI surrendered to sleep. He'd reined in his fury, his desire to press for details she wasn't ready to give, maintaining a calm, soothing manner for her sake. But the minute her body relaxed completely against his, he let the rein on his temper slip.

Who tossed away a thirteen-year-old kid like yesterday's trash? It didn't take a genius to figure out that the place she'd been couldn't have continued to neglect and abuse their patients if the patients' parents had taken any interest in their children's welfare. And he hadn't missed Kai's phrasing, either. *I wasn't suicidal when I went in.* Did that mean she was when she was released? Two additional years of therapy would seem to indicate she hadn't been ready to face the world when she came out of Pinecrest.

Why didn't that implied instability freak him out? It should. Cesar's mood swings and compulsive gambling had put their business at risk several times before Luke had been forced to give him an ultimatum. Since then— for five years now—Cesar had kept it together, but Luke still worried. Hell, half the reason he'd stuck with Shelley had been that she kept a level head most of the time. It was what he needed. What he craved after coping with Cesar's ups and downs. So he'd stuck it out with Shelley even when he wasn't particularly thrilled with the relationship. Which made him a selfish asshole, now that he thought about it.

True to that lazy, selfish persona, he'd invited Kai to Oasis Springs for his own convenience. When she'd brought up the possibility of sex during their first real conversation, he'd figured he'd scored a jackpot. Later on, however, Kai's easy acceptance of a sexual relationship with a virtual stranger, a relationship that came with a built-in expiration date, had come to trouble him. It didn't fit his self-image. Partially, that was why he'd texted her the night *Gargantula* was on television. Yes, he'd known she'd get a kick out of it, but he also wanted to connect with her, to prove at some level that there was more to their relationship than a week of sex. *Now you probably think I'm trashy.* He'd denied her words at the time, but wrestled with his reaction for several nights, at last coming to the conclusion that—embarrassing as it was—Kai's attitude intimidated him. Maybe even scared him. The guys would laugh themselves sick if he told them his concerns about measuring up to the men in her past. Or even to the multitude of devices lining the shelves at Goody's Goodies.

You really are an ass. Talk about not looking outside of yourself. But he was paying attention now, and the pieces of the puzzle Kai had let slip were coming together into an ugly whole. Dead father. Mother more interested in finding a new man than taking care of her child. Institutionalized at thirteen. Two years of therapy and then—not coincidentally—a tattoo of a phoenix rising from its own ashes. When had she gotten the snake, he wondered. And did she see herself as poisonous?

Another of her comments slipped through his head. *I don't count on anyone but myself.*

He'd blown it off, as he had anything else serious she'd said. Because that was the kind of asshole he was, but also because he was worried about Cesar and hadn't wanted to talk about it. If Cesar went back down the rabbit hole, he'd destroy their business. And while Luke would survive financially, Cesar would not. And Cesar had taken Luke on when Luke got out of school, had found him business, had taught him the truth about soil composition and responsible landscaping, the reality outside of textbooks, so he wasn't about to let the man sink now.

He tried to see Kai's face, but it was buried in his neck. If she were awake, he'd look into her whiskey eyes and swear that she could always count on him, which, no doubt, she'd take as a joke. After all, they barely knew each other. But irrational as the idea was, he wanted to be the one to prove to her that people wouldn't always let her down.

And what about when she lets you *down?* He shut off the niggling voice. He didn't depend on Kai. Didn't need her. She couldn't disappoint him because he had no expectations. How had she put it? *I have no dog in this fight.* Which hinted at another piece of the puzzle he wanted to discover—wherever she had grown up, it hadn't been L.A. or Vegas. So how and when had she ended up out west? And the real question… Why was it so important for him to know?

THE MORNING SUN FILTERING THROUGH the shades brought Kai awake to a lonely bed and a stunning sense of *deja vu.* Through the half-open bedroom door, she could see Luke pacing the suite, phone sandwiched between his shoulder and ear.

"No. That's not how it works. We've been over that."

She walked up beside him and he slipped his bandaged arm around her shoulders. "Look, Hudson, I understand that your wife has a party planned, but that doesn't change how long it's going to take to get the stone from my suppliers." He sighed. "No. I cannot come and discuss it with you. I am out of town this week. Cesar is perfectly capable of overseeing the changes. I would advise leaving the short wall as brick for the moment. Let me order bluestone for the others and we'll get those done before we take out the brick."

Tremors of frustration ran through Luke's body and the arm around her clenched tight, but he kept his voice admirably calm. The other man's shouting, however, reverberated from the phone, broadcasting into the room.

"Our contract says you'll have the work finished March twenty-fifth!"

"Our contract was for brick and mortar retaining

walls. They're quicker, easier, and cheaper than layered stone. I can go to any warehouse and get brick. Flagstone has to be carefully selected for size and shape. If you stick with brick, I will meet the deadline and the price I quoted you. If you want to change the materials, we'll need to revise the whole contract."

"And how are we supposed to do that if you're not available to meet? If you're out of town, how are you going to come up with new numbers?"

Luke sucked in a deep breath and let it out slowly. "We have the wall measurements already. I can start calling suppliers and Cesar can check what's available locally. Of course, since you're changing direction on the project, if you'd rather have someone else do the work, I'll understand. No harm, no foul."

"You trying to back out? What the kind of business are you running? I'll fucking ruin you! First you put up this fucking ugly wall, then you try to leave the project in the middle?"

"You signed off on that wall. We drew it. You saw the plans." Luke's voice had acquired a hard, unfamiliar edge. "If you don't like it, that's understandable. But that's why we make you sign off at every stage; so we're all on the same page."

Kai tapped him on the shoulder and when he looked down at her she mimed putting the phone on hold.

"Hang on a sec, Hudson." He put his hand over the phone.

"Do you want to keep this guy as a client?" Kai asked quietly.

"Not particularly, but he has a ridiculous amount of money and travels in the circles where we find our best work. He could make life difficult for us. So if the choice is between having to the do the job and having him actively try to stomp us into the dirt, I'll do the job."

"Then let me talk to him."

"I don't think—"

"Trust me. What's his name?"

"Hudson Barrowman."

Kai held out her hand and after a long hesitation, Luke passed her the phone. She took a deep breath, wriggled her shoulders, blinked a few times, and found the voice she needed, thick with southern honey.

"Mr. Barrowman? Hi there. I'm a friend of Luke's and I asked him to let me talk to you for a minute because I love him to death but he's never gonna understand why you're so upset about your wife's party."

"*And you do?*" Suspicion and sarcasm coated the words.

"I can guess. See, I bet when you contracted for brick walls, you planned what *you* liked. And you probably think that wall looks just fine. After all, you know your own taste, right?"

"*Of course I do.*"

"Well, exactly." She allowed herself a little trill of laughter. "So it came as a surprise to you when your wife didn't care for the aesthetic. But you're a good husband and you want to make her happy, even if your yard doesn't look quite the way you envisioned it."

"*Yes. Yes, that's it.*"

"So tell me about this party. Is it an outdoor affair?"

"*No. It's a dinner party. But we will have tables in our living room, which has French doors that open out onto the yard.*"

"How many retaining walls is Luke putting in for you?"

"*Six.*"

"And how many are visible through the French doors?"

There was a long pause during which Luke held up two fingers and mouthed *I can do that.*

"*Two,*" said Barrowman at last. "*But my wife is worried about what people will see as they come up the drive.*"

Luke shook his head.

"Well," Kai said in her most soothing and apologetic tone, "I doubt even my Luke can get them all done that fast. But, my goodness, surely all your friends have gone through renovations, too. They understand that delays happen. And it gives your wife an excuse to have a garden party over the summer to show off her fancy new walls, walls she *loves*."

"*You don't know my wife*," Barrowman said.

"No, but I know how much you're doing to make her happy, and I am certain that when you explain the situation to her and how you went from nothing to two walls now and the rest of the yard looking how she wants it later, she'll understand."

"*Maybe*."

"Let me give you back to Luke so you guys can work out the details." She passed the phone over, then went to brush her teeth.

When she came out, Luke was sitting on the edge of the bed jotting down notes on a pad of paper.

"That was unreal," he said. "You played him like a damned piano."

"He was easy."

"Not for me. I was about to bite his head off."

"You think of him as an obstacle, not a puzzle. He didn't want the brick walls once he saw them, but he needed a way to get you to change the design without admitting he'd been wrong in the first place. That's why he blamed the change on his wife. But making adjustments because his wife wanted them has the potential to make him look weak. It was much easier for him to say that to me, because a woman will praise him for acceding to his wife's desires. And then, in order to let go of his anger at you, he needed a concession from you."

"The two walls."

"Yes."

"If I'm going to get that done, I need to get him a new contract by tomorrow. I should take a quick trip home. Talking the changes through with Cesar is the only way I am going to make this work. He's…temperamental. Especially when it comes to Barrowman. And hand-delivering the contract to Barrowman will keep him calm, too."

"Georgie will understand. Can you catch a flight out of Vegas, then turn around and come back?"

"I can. I should. I probably will. Doesn't mean I want to."

"Yeah. As the song says, 'you can't always get what you want.'"

He slanted a look at her. "So tell me, where did little miss southern belle come from?"

"People—men in particular—have a hard time being rude to her."

"No doubt. But that doesn't answer the question." He patted the bed next to him and Kai sat down. "Where'd you learn how to do the sweet southern thing?"

"We lived in a small town in East Texas until I was nine, then moved to Dallas for six years before heading to California." There, that was suitably casual.

But Luke, being Luke, wanted more.

"Dallas to L.A. Must have been quite the culture shock."

She shrugged. "It wasn't so bad. They're both big cities. Going from a town of four thousand to Dallas…that was the biggie."

"I guess I can understand that." He laid a hand on her leg. "I have to admit, I think little southern Susie is a big turn-on."

"Really, Sugar?" She pursed her lips, blew him a kiss, then grinned. "She doesn't work nearly so well when you can see my hair and makeup. She's much more effective on the phone."

"Hmm. Suddenly, I see the appeal of phone sex." He slipped his arms around and planted a slow, sweet kiss on her lips. "If I catch a flight out this evening and come back tomorrow afternoon, will you be okay?"

"Of course." But a little stab of longing slid beneath her breastbone. She'd miss him, which broke her cardinal rule. No one should be so important that they couldn't leave without repercussions. Because ultimately they all did. And Luke would be on his way sooner rather than later. It was already Tuesday. They had five more days together before he headed back to California for good. If only he were her usual type, a hot body with few brains and even less empathy. But he wasn't. He was so much more and it was driving her crazy.

Well, crazier than usual. The moat and walls that kept the crazy at bay usually managed to keep people out, but they seemed ineffective against Luke.

LUKE HATED THE IDEA OF leaving Kai alone, even for twenty-four hours. What if he came back and she'd shored up all her defenses, put the public face back on? He was just beginning to get to know the woman beneath it. Or was he? Maybe she was playing him the same as she did Barrowman. Giving him what he wanted.

"Do you remember at Spago when we talked about acting for everyone else but being honest with each other?"

"Sure."

"That's still the deal, right?"

"What are you asking?"

"Have you been lying to me?"

"About what?"

Shit. "About anything."

She stood and walked over to the window without speaking.

"Kai."

"I'm trying to figure out how to answer that."

"It's a simple yes or no question."

"No, it's really not. We're having a good time and I

don't want to ruin that." She shook her head. "But I guess it's too late."

His stomach knotted. "I'd say so."

She wrapped her arms around her stomach and he resisted the urge to reach for her. "I need you to understand something. It sounds like a cliché, but it's the truth."

"Okay."

"This…what I did…it's not about you, it's about me."

"Hard to get more clichéd than that."

"I know. But it's also true."

"Okay, then."

"I may have…*exaggerated* my climax the other night."

The words took a few seconds to sink in. "You were faking?"

"I hate that expression. No, I was not faking. I like sex. I particularly liked sex with you. But for me sex is a journey. Orgasm is a destination, and not one I can get to with anyone else. Or without electronic assistance."

He gaped at her. That personal style, all that in your face sexuality, and she didn't come?

"Why didn't you tell me?" He joined her at the window, and when she didn't face him, covered her arms with his so that her back rested against his chest.

"I didn't tell you because it's not a problem for you to fix. I've told two men about it—you're the third—and neither of them reacted in helpful ways. Rick took it as an insult to his masculinity and broke up with me less than a week later with a few choice adjectives in his breakup speech. Darius, on the other hand, considered it a personal challenge and kept…working…long past the point where it was fun or even comfortable. Eventually, I gave up and let him think he'd succeeded. It made him happy, but it wore on me and the relationship didn't hold up."

She swallowed, and he felt the fine bones in her back

move against him like a bird's wings.

"Not long after we split up, I wandered into Goody's Goodies to pick up condoms. I'd been by before, but I'd never been in. I didn't have any intention of talking about my problems, but Evie was there and she's the least judgmental person you can imagine. She invites confidences. She asked me if I took any medications and explained how a lot of drugs, particularly mood stabilizers, can cause anorgasmia.

"I'd been off antidepressants for a couple of years by then, but I'd spent a long, long time on them. No one had told me that they could make masturbation an exercise in frustration. Evie took a lot of time talking me through various things. And then she sold me a vibrator. A little one. Nothing elaborate. She said to come back when I'd tried it a few times and let her know how it went."

She took a deep breath and relaxed against him. *Finally.* "I was supremely skeptical. This little silicone wand with a ring on the end was going to open up a world of pleasure I'd been unable to achieve for years? But she was right.

"I went back. And back again. And I met Benny, and he offered me a job. I'm not kidding when I say he and Evie changed my life. But I still can't have an orgasm with a partner."

"Okay."

"Okay?" She half turned in his arms to examine his face. "Just like that?"

"No." He rubbed his chin against the top of her head. "I'd like to say I'm evolved enough not to take what happens—or doesn't happen—when we're in bed together personally, but I'm not. It's my job, and my pleasure, to give you pleasure. So, yeah, I am going to keep trying to do that."

She turned fully and put her hands on his cheeks. "You do give me pleasure."

"Shh. Let me finish." He pressed a kiss into each of

her palms, then moved her hands down to his chest and leaned his forehead against hers. "I'm going to give you pleasure, and when I go on too long, when you want me to stop, you let me know. Not by faking an orgasm. Just say the words." Her eyes teared up and she buried her face in his neck. He stroked her hair, rough strands catching on his calluses.

"I don't want to ruin this," she mumbled.

"You won't, sweetheart. I swear. But no more lies. I can't take them."

"No more lies." Her face was still hidden against him, but her words found their way into his heart and cracked it open.

Fuck, he was in so much trouble.

CHAPTER 7

WHILE LUKE CHECKED INTO FLIGHTS home, Kai showered and changed into her new pink houndstooth suit. What had possessed her to bare herself to Luke that way? She had been with Rick three months before admitting her issue, and with Darius even longer. In both cases, she'd expected a future with them, had felt it only fair to be honest. But she and Luke were having a fling, for crying out loud. They had no commitment to one another. What if he got drunk and blabbed about it to Joe?

Dude, why'd you hook me up with such a broken chick?

But that wasn't Luke. No matter how disappointed he was, he wouldn't talk behind her back. Her secret was safe.

She combed a shock of pink through the front of her still-purple hair to match the suit and put on her makeup with a light hand. She stepped into the closet and looked at her shoe choices. She was bending over to pick up her chrome-heeled black stilettos when Luke walked up behind her.

"Jesus, woman," he said, running a finger down her butt, "are you trying to kill me?"

She twisted her head, deliberately remaining bent over, and winked at him. "Oh, Sugar, you're no good to me dead."

He groaned, shifted his grip to her hips, and drew her

back, settling her ass into the hard heat of his erection. Damn her choice of a narrow, conservative skirt. She wanted to climb his body, wrap her legs around his waist and take all that throbbing heat inside her. Right here, right now.

She wiggled against him and he groaned again. "For God's sake, stay still."

"Can't." She shimmied again and his big hands slid down and then under the hem of her skirt. Her inner muscles clenched and heat flooded her body. Luke pressed his mouth against the back of her neck and drew the skirt slowly up over her thighs and past her waist. A rough sound escaped him as the movement revealed her garter belt, lacy panties, and thigh-highs.

She reached behind her and grabbed the waistband of his sweats. Fingers splayed on his thighs, she lowered herself into a crouch, pulling the sweats down with her. Luke never let go of her and the movement brought his hands, still caught in the fabric of her skirt, over her breasts. She tried to catch her breath, but her heart was pounding an irregular tattoo and her lungs didn't work properly. She leaned back, rubbing against him as she stood, reveling in his choked growl.

Luke locked his bandaged arm around her waist, slipping his other hand beneath the cotton lace of her panties. The light graze of his fingers over her clit sent a shock through her and she dropped her head back against his shoulder, arching into his touch.

He bit her neck. "If you want those to survive, you'll take them off."

She'd never been the least bit submissive, but she practically tore the panties herself in her haste to remove them.

The second they were gone, he pulled her back against his body. But it wasn't enough. Nothing was ever going to be enough. She spread her legs and arched her back in unmistakable invitation. He entered her in a single, slick plunge, practically lifting her off the floor.

She reached out and laid her hands flat on the wall, using all her strength to push back into him, her feet scrabbling for purchase. But there was no purchase to be had, and it didn't matter, because he was behind her and below her and around her and inside her and her whole body was on fire and oh-so-close to the edge.

But the edge slipped away and as she teetered there, furiously trying to bring it back, she knew Luke could feel it. His body stilled, just for a split second, but she was damned if her dysfunction was going to steal his joy, and she clenched her muscles around him, begging him in silence to finish what he'd begun. He sucked in a harsh breath and then thrust twice deeply inside her before giving in to his own release.

After a few shaky breaths later, he let her go, then—when she pushed away from the wall—gathered her into his arms and carried her to the bed. She tried to pull down her skirt, unaccountably shy, but he stayed her hands.

"Don't want to ruin the material. Let me clean you up first." He headed for the bathroom and came back a moment later with a damp washcloth. With exquisite care, he wiped her clean, then smoothed the skirt back down. Tossing the washcloth into the wastebasket, he lay down beside her and slid his arms around her.

"Sorry. That wasn't part of the plan."

"It wasn't? What plan?"

"I had a plan. It didn't include a quickie in the closet. It was much more civilized. But I find I'm not terribly civilized around you. Which isn't...I like to think of myself as in control."

She laughed. She couldn't help it. "Don't we all. If it's any comfort, I'm decidedly uncivilized around you, too. And I've never had a quickie in a closet in my life. So I can cross that off my bucket list."

"Glad to be of service." He grinned and all her odd embarrassment and anxiety melted away. He wasn't going to make a big production out of her problem. And he didn't even seem intimidated by it. She crawled up his body and kissed him and he kissed her back, slowly and thoroughly.

"You are just flat determined to ruin that cute little suit, aren't you?"

"Cute?" She sat up. "This is cool, sophisticated, a perfect combination of classic and punk—anything but cute."

"I'm a guy. I don't know from classic. I think it looks cute. And knowing what you're wearing underneath, yeah, that steals away the cute. But I hope like hell no one else knows. They can just look at you and go 'oh, what a cute outfit.' Only I get to know how super incredibly hot it really is."

Oh. Well, then. "I guess I can live with that."

"Mmm." He kissed her again, quickly this time, and rolled out of the bed. "Let me take a quick shower and then we can go get some breakfast. Unfortunately, I have to leave around two if I'm going to make my flight. Are you sure you'll be okay?"

"Absolutely."

ONCE LUKE HAD SHOWERED AND Kai had made herself a little more presentable, they headed downstairs to forage for breakfast. When they stepped off the elevator, Kai saw Georgie and Julia in a heated debate in a corner of the lobby. Luke tried to steer them in the opposite direction, but his mother waved them over. Kai straightened her shoulders and resisted the urge to check her clothing. She was pretty sure Luke's family would take one look at them and know exactly what they'd been up to.

"Lucas, talk some sense into your sister. The conference room we were planning to use for the card party tonight has been taken over by the contractors fixing the café, so she wants to switch the party to the casino."

"Not the casino itself. A banquet room inside the casino."

"You know how your father feels about gambling."

"Then he doesn't have to gamble. He doesn't even have to show up if he feels so strongly about it."

"Georgette!"

"This is my wedding, Mother. Not yours. Not Dad's. I get that you'd prefer to forget that Brad owns a casino, but that won't make it go away."

"Lucas—"

But Luke raised his hands to ward her off. "Not my department. In fact, I think when I get married I'll elope, if this is the kind of argument that ensues when one has an actual wedding."

Georgie flicked a glance at Kai. "What if your fiancée wants a big wedding?"

Luke curved an arm around Kai's shoulders and hugged her close. "Then she can hash it out with *her* mother. One of the great things about being a guy is that you get to show up at your wedding dressed in a tux, partake of all the delicious food and high quality booze, and go home with the woman you love without having to do any of the work."

"Is *that* how it works?" Kai asked.

"We're not talking about your wedding," said Julia. "We're talking about your sister's. You're no fan of casinos, either."

"As it happens, I won't be here tonight. One of my clients is having a meltdown so I have to run home this afternoon. I'll be back tomorrow evening."

"Oh, Luke, really?" Georgie sighed. "I did tell you he couldn't take a proper week off," she said to Kai.

"You did. So I was prepared."

"You'll come tonight, won't you?"

"Of course. No matter where you hold it. I even have the perfect outfit for a card party, though I admit I'm not sure what a card party consists of."

"Oh, they're fun. Basically, we set up tables and put out decks of cards. And food and drink, of course. Everyone plays whatever games they like and some don't play at all, they just socialize. There are raffles for spa appointments, bottles of wine, things like that."

"If what you're telling me is that just by showing up I can win another massage, I'll be there with bells on."

"That's exactly what I'm saying. Can't wait to see your bells." Georgie gave her a thumbs-up.

Julia hmmphed. "I guess I'm outvoted. I'll go tell your father."

"I'll make sure notes are delivered to all the rooms," Georgie said.

"Kai and I are on the way to breakfast. Where did they move that to, do you know?" Luke asked.

"The steakhouse. Can I tag along? I haven't eaten, either."

"Sure," said Kai. Luke's arm tightened around her momentarily, then relaxed again. But when she looked up at him, he was smiling serenely.

"So tell me about the landscaping emergency," Georgie said as they headed for the restaurant.

Luke told her about Barrowman's brick walls, ending with how Kai had talked the man around. "You should have heard her," he said. "She was amazing."

Kai shrugged off the praise, though it snuck in and warmed a tiny corner of her heart. "It's just sales psychology. I'm sure Georgie has the same skills."

They took a table against the back wall of the restaurant and ordered.

"Aside from mom being mom, is everything going okay?" Luke asked.

"Sure. Nothing I can't handle. I do wish I hadn't let her talk me into this week-long affair, though. I should have gone simple."

"Why didn't you?" asked Kai.

Georgie rubbed her forehead with two fingers. "I'm not sure, to tell you the truth. My mother said hardly anyone had met Brad, and his family didn't know me all that well, and we had the hotel…It was originally going to be a long weekend. Then five days. Then it became a week. Even knowing that part of mom's insistence on the long lead-up is that she's hoping I'll change my mind, it's still easier to let her have her way."

"She doesn't want you to marry Brad? He seems like a good guy to me. And she can't be concerned that he's after your money—he obviously has plenty of his own."

"He *is* a good guy. The best. But she can't see beyond his lack of pedigree or the fact that he lives in Nevada and owns a casino. It doesn't matter to her that he'd do anything for me, including hosting all my crazy relatives in his hotel for a week."

"Five more days," Luke said "Then you can send her home."

"Believe me, I'm counting down."

The waiter brought their food and Georgie shifted the conversation to Kai's job. "The longer I spend with my mother, the more I wish Luke had told me in advance that he planned to invite you. At this point, I would totally have asked you to bring a few truly outrageous goodies for the raffle tonight."

"Umm, I don't think that's a good idea."

Georgie clapped her hands. "Oh my God! Does that mean you did bring some?"

"I did. Just in case things got too staid."

"Which ones?"

"*No!*" People turned to look at Luke's exclamation and he lowered his voice. "No. Not happening. I am *not* listening to my sister discuss sex toys with my girlfriend."

My girlfriend. Kai almost choked. Here, with Georgie, one of the few people in on the deception, Luke had referred to her as his girlfriend. Her lungs squeezed and her head felt light.

"Spoilsport," Georgie teased, and Kai forced herself to remember what they were talking about.

"Yup. That's me."

Georgie sighed. "Fine. But now you've got me thinking. You're flying in and out of Vegas, right?"

"Yup."

"So if I decide that I need a few goodies for the bachelorette party, you could stop and pick them up on your way back?"

"Oh, hell no."

Kai had never seen a grown man blush the color of a lobster. It was absolutely adorable.

"Aww, come on, Luke. I'll call in the order and they'll have it all bagged up before you get there. You won't even have to look at the receipt."

He glared, but with that deep blush he had going on, it lacked effect. Finally he threw up his hands. "Fine. You win."

Georgie leaned over and hugged him. "You're the best brother ever."

"Like you would know. I'm the only one you have."

"What about you, Kai? Do you have brothers?"

"No. No siblings."

Under the table, Luke laid a hand on her thigh and squeezed gently. "I'm sure there were times growing up Georgie wished she could say the same."

"No way. I loved you even when you decapitated my teddy."

MUCH AS LUKE APPRECIATED THE fact that Georgie got along with Kai, he could have done without the "embarrassing childhood memories" conversation. Kai had already called him immature for his attitude toward Gil, he didn't need Georgie revealing yet more of his stupidity.

"I didn't mean to take his head off. But I have to admit, it was pretty cool when it happened."

"How, may I ask, do you accidentally chop the head

off a stuffed animal?"

"I was only eleven. I tried to make a parachute out of a baggie and I attached it to the bow around the bear's neck and tossed it off the second floor balcony. I guess the drag was too much. There was stuffing everywhere."

"Oh, no!" She snorted, her eyes lighting up.

He put on his most pious tone, hoping to elicit a proper laugh. "It's a brother's job to terrorize his sister."

"Is that what it says in the rulebook?" Georgie asked.

"Yup. You'll see when you have one of your own."

"Oh." She shifted. "Brad and I aren't sure whether we want kids."

"You…*what*?"

"Not everyone has children, Luke."

"No, obviously. But you love kids." *What the hell?* All the warning bells that had rung when he'd received the wedding invitation went off again, and louder. He took a breath but Kai pinched him and he clamped his lips shut.

"I think it's very smart to wait and see what your life holds," Kai said.

Part of him wanted to ask her who she thought she was, giving his sister advice, but he kept his mouth shut, mostly because the greater part of him knew she was right—pushing Georgie would just make her defensive.

"Yes," Georgie said. "That's the thing. It's not like we're ruling it out, we just aren't sure yet." She looked at her watch. "You guys, I should really get going. I need to make sure to send messages to everyone's room about tonight's change of venue."

"Sure thing." Luke stood and hugged his sister. "I love you, Sprout. You know that, right?"

"Of course! What's got into you all of a sudden?"

"Nothing. I haven't told you in a while, that's all."

"Yeah. Well, you're not dying or anything, are you?"

"No!"

"Okay, then. I'll see you when you get back from California." She frowned at him, bussed his cheek, and strode out of the restaurant.

"Fuck. I screwed that up."

"No. You came close, but you pulled it out in the end. I take it the no kids thing came as a shock?"

"Georgie started babysitting when she was fourteen. And she tutored during college and then worked at a day care center for a year. She always wanted a bunch of kids. Always. Something's wrong."

"She'll tell you when she's ready."

"And if it's too late to help?" Acid rose in the back of his throat. Georgie should never be unhappy. She'd spent too long in their cold house. She needed a marriage of love. But he couldn't explain that to Kai without sounding like an utter fool.

"You can't fix the world," Kai said.

No. He couldn't fix anything. Not his business partner. Not his parents. Not his sister.

"Luke." She laid a soft hand over his. "I hate to say it, but in this particular instance, your mother is right. Time, and the stress of all the wedding arrangements and events, will clarify to Georgie what she wants more than anything you could say."

"I guess."

"But?" She bent forward so she could peek up at him. Sweet.

"But will you try to talk to her while I'm gone anyway?"

"Of course. But she's only just met me. She's unlikely to confide in me."

"She likes you. She told me so. And women…share things. Things they wouldn't tell their brothers."

"I'll give it a shot, then. I promise."

KAI THOUGHT ABOUT THAT PROMISE as Luke paid for breakfast and then led her out to walk the grounds of the resort. What did she know about relationships? Or girl talk?

Although they'd explored the grounds the first day, there was still plenty they hadn't gotten to. For a while, they stood by the huge, kidney-shaped infinity pool and watched crazy people baking themselves in the sun.

"Haven't any of them heard of skin cancer?" Luke asked.

"Apparently not. Plus, check the tables...almost every one of them is drinking alcohol. They'd be my favorite kind of customer for the store. Drunk and dehydrated. I could sell them anything."

"Yeah, speaking of sales...can you try to keep Georgie under control when she decides she wants to go nuts on bachelorette party toys?"

"Aww, now where would be the fun in that? Please tell me your mom's invited to the party. I want to put a big, fat dildo in her hand and see what she says."

"Good grief."

"I'm just teasing, Luke."

"I know." He steered her away from the pool and down a little path. After a few minutes, they found the lemon grove which, as Georgie had said, was stunning. The perfect spot for a wedding. A little pang went through Kai as she imagined the scene. What would it be like to promise yourself to another forever? To know that person would be there for you for the rest of your life?

Her thoughts must have shown on her face, because Luke wrapped his arms around her and rubbed his cheek on the top of her head. "What's the matter?"

"Nothing. I guess I'm more of a girl than I thought." She shrugged. "Weddings make me sappy. It's a surprise."

He tightened his grip. "More? Sweetheart you're *all* girl. No question about that. But maybe you're a little more romantic than you like to admit, which doesn't actually surprise me. You have a lot of heart."

"Now *you're* being overly romantic; seeing things

that aren't there."

"Maybe. Maybe not." He cupped her cheek and tilted her head up to drop a kiss on her lips. "I'm pretty sure this is one of those things that's clearer from the outside."

And what did it say about her and all her hard-won independence that she wanted him to be right? That she wanted, in that lemon-scented moment, to be the kind of woman who could give her whole heart to a man. Who even had one to give.

She clung to Luke for a moment, allowing herself the luxury of the dream before pulling away. Rather than letting her go, however, he captured her hand in his, twining their fingers together. Ah, God, giving him up at the end of the week was going to prove the hardest thing she'd ever done.

They wandered that way, hand in hand, talking little, until it was time for Luke to leave. And although she felt slightly ridiculous doing so, Kai stood by the entrance and watched as he drove away. She was still standing there, processing the peculiar sense of loss, when Georgie joined her.

"He'll be back tomorrow," she said.

"He will."

"You know what you need, Kai? You need a mani-pedi."

"What?"

"Come on. It will be fun."

"Aren't you having a manicure party on Saturday?"

"Yup. But a girl can never have too many manicures. They massage your hands and feet, and your skin is all smooth and happy."

"You're too much. But you said the magic word."

"Massage?"

"That's the one." And maybe, while they were at the spa, she'd find a way to keep her promise to Luke.

"Great. Let me run to the front desk and set it up. Can we go by the casino first? I need to be sure the room is organized for tonight."

"Of course." Kai looked down at her shoes. "If someone's doing my toes, I should probably change into sandals so I don't ruin them right away."

"Okay. I'll meet you by the concierge desk."

"Perfect."

In the room, Kai switched to a pair of sandals and checked herself out in the mirror. She looked normal, or as normal as she ever did, but she felt…off-kilter. Out of step.

Five more days and she'd be back in her natural habitat. She considered calling Benny or Celia but didn't want to keep Georgie waiting. She'd do it before the card party. Talking to her friends would ground her.

Downstairs, Georgie was pacing, talking a mile a minute into her cell phone. In that moment, she could have been Luke. Especially when she ran a hand through her hair, tumbling the blonde waves into a messy frenzy. She waved at Kai but kept up her conversation.

"No, I didn't say *Oriental* lilies, I said *Calla* lilies. No. For God's sake, Julian, how many of these have we done together? You can't make a substitution like that. The bride will go through the roof. If you need to switch something up you have to give me time to check." She listened for a few seconds. "It's not the money and you know it. You screwed up. Own it." Another long pause and she nodded. "Okay. Call me back. Bye."

"Business problems?"

"Yup. I guess it's running in the family at the moment."

"I'm surprised you took on another wedding so close to your own."

"Well, my business is still pretty new. I don't like to turn people away. I want a reputation for being able to do whatever's needed. This couple didn't want me there. If they had, I'd have had to say no, but they just wanted me to organize. Julian is supposed to deliver the bride's bouquet tomorrow morning, so I called to be sure everything was on target, only to find he ordered the wrong flowers."

"What can you do?"

"He's going to call me back in an hour when he's had a chance to talk to his supplier. The wedding isn't until tomorrow at one, so I'm betting he can get the Calla lilies. But he'll have to eat the cost of the Orientals unless he can sell them to someone else, and he doesn't want to."

"Gotcha."

Georgie shook herself a bit like a wet dog, and waved away the conversation. "We have almost an hour before the mani-pedi appointments, so let's hit up the casino." She looked down. "Love the sandals. What I wouldn't give for your sense of style."

"You wouldn't want it. You have your own."

"You're sweet."

"Are you kidding? Anything but that!"

Georgie laughed. "I promise not to tell."

They pushed through the big, heavy doors of the casino and even though the space was enormous, the smell of recirculated air, the sound of the dinging machines and the sheer busyness of the place in sharp contrast to the outside peace fell over Kai like a smothering blanket. Oh, right. This was why she didn't spend more time in casinos.

She followed as Georgie wove around the first few machines at the front, past the bar and the poker tables, heading for a door in the back right corner. Before they got there, however, Georgie's eyes went to a television screen in the sports betting area and her steps faltered. Kai followed her gaze and saw two men facing off in a cage. Georgie picked up her pace right away, but it was too late.

Fuck. Kai recognized the sport on the screen. MMA. Which had to remind Georgie of Joe. Which shouldn't matter to a woman who was getting married in less than a week to another man. But it obviously did.

Chapter 8

Luke pulled out his phone and tried to dictate notes to himself on the drive to McCarran Airport, but his mind kept returning to his final sight of Kai in the rearview mirror as he left Oasis Springs. A hollow opened in his heart and instead of the logistics of the new contract with Barrowman, his thoughts focused on how to keep Kai in his life once their week was up.

The Barrowman job was the cornerstone of his future. With that, and maybe two more good-sized installations, Cesar would be able to buy out the business. Then Luke could look into a full-time firefighting career. Maybe even in Las Vegas.

But first he had to straighten out the Barrowman mess. He'd taken the job out of pure greed, because he and Cesar had agreed on a number when all the equipment would be paid off and the accounts were healthy, and until they got there Luke was tied to the company. Even if the San Francisco Fire Department called, Luke would have to find a way to manage both jobs until HomeScapes reached that magic number. So when Barrowman had called, all Luke had considered was how much closer to goal the work would bring them.

And now he was paying for it by losing time with both Kai and his sister.

He called Cesar and filled him in on all the details. Cesar agreed to pick him up on the other end of the flight, but he sounded detached, distracted. The longer they talked, the more the knot in Luke's gut tightened. This was supposed to be a relaxing week. Instead, he was panicking over his sister, the business, and his relationship with a woman who probably didn't even realize they were in a relationship.

He hung up with Cesar as he was pulling in to short-term parking, and began calling stone suppliers. He'd priced the walls in both stone and brick before giving Barrowman a choice, so by the time his flight landed a few hours later he'd pulled together the first draft of a new contract, and he was beginning to breathe properly again.

Cesar's disheveled appearance sent Luke straight back into free fall.

"What's the matter?" he asked as soon as they were on the freeway.

"What makes you think something's the matter?"

"You haven't shaved since I left for the wedding."

"Marta's sister is sick. She's been down there for a week."

"That's all?" Marta had left Cesar once, when he gambled away their mortgage payment. Luke had fronted them the money on the condition that Cesar seek treatment for his gambling addiction. He'd won his wife and kids back, but it had taken him seven long months.

"Yeah, the kids are still with me because she doesn't want them to get sick, too. We're solid."

"You don't *sound* solid."

Cesar glanced at him, then back at the road. "I'm not sure I want to buy you out."

Luke's stomach dropped and bile welled up in his throat. His dreams of freedom fled. He swallowed hard.

"Why not?"

"Because the last time I tried to run a business, I ended up on the edge of bankruptcy."

"You were gambling."

"Running a business *is* gambling. I don't want you to

give up your plans. I just want you to see whether you can't sell to another landscape architect. With you and Marta both out of the picture this week, I realized how much I need grounding in both my personal and business lives. I've gone to meetings every single night because it's the only way to avoid calling a few old friends to come over for poker."

"Oh, hell. I'm sorry."

"Don't be. I'm holding it together. But that first day, if I hadn't called you I would have wrecked the whole Barrowman job. I need a partner who can talk me down from crap like that."

"Understood." But sickness still roiled in Luke's gut. Everything in his life was going south at once, all his careful plans developing fissures and fractures. But Cesar didn't need to carry that weight. "I'll start looking into it when I get back from the wedding. Unless you have ideas already?"

"No one solid. I'll put out feelers. I'm really sorry, Luke. I know this wasn't our agreement."

"You have to do what's right for your mental health. Don't worry, we'll figure it out."

"Thanks. You have no idea what a load off my mind that is."

"It's cool. I'm just glad you said something and didn't let it fester."

But long after Cesar dropped Luke at his house with a promise to pick him up the next morning to go over to Barrowman's, Luke sat in his home office going over the contacts he'd made in the landscaping business, searching for a way out.

AFTER THEIR MANICURES, GEORGIE WANTED to see which Goody's Goodies Kai had brought along, so they went up to Kai's suite. Kai laid the pieces she'd brought—including an assortment of condoms and three different styles of vibrator—on the coffee table. During the mani-pedi session, she'd tried to come up with an opening gambit to discuss what she'd seen at the casino, but nothing had come to her. Subtlety wasn't her strong suit, so she addressed it the only way she could—directly.

"I know this is personal, and you can tell me to buzz off, but why did you and Joe break up?"

Georgie looked up from the goodies, but instead of answering she asked a question of her own.

"Are you in love with my brother?"

Kai's first instinct was to laugh the question off. She and Luke had had a few phone calls and a couple of very intense days at the resort. People didn't fall in love that fast. And yet, they shared more than a simple friendship.

"I care about him."

"Okay, we'll go with that. Has he mentioned to you that he wants to quit landscaping and become a professional firefighter?"

"Yes. I didn't realize he'd mentioned it to his family, though."

"I doubt he planned to until it was a done deal. I confronted him about it one day and he admitted it."

"Ah."

"Would it bother you if he did that? Would you date—or marry—a firefighter? A man who risked his life every single day?"

"I don't know. First, Luke and I are nowhere near that point. I'm not sure I'll ever get married. And if I did, I don't *think* my husband's career would matter, but I just can't say. I hope that if our relationship was strong enough to want to commit to a lifetime together, I could support whatever he wanted to do. But I haven't ever had to consider it."

"Well I have. The fighting…watching Joe get beat up all the time… I couldn't do it. Even when he won, he'd come home bruised and bloody. And then he'd go right back to training, waiting for his next chance in the ring.

Every one of those cuts and bruises, I felt them on my own body. Concussions, broken bones, torn ligaments…they heal, but they have long-term consequences. A kick to the head, a punch to the heart…Guys have died in the ring. I loved him desperately when we were together, but hated him passionately every time he left me to go get the hell beat out of him."

"Oh, Georgie, I'm so sorry." Maybe Luke had been right about Kai having a big heart since her whole chest ached with sympathy. "Did you tell him how you felt?"

"Not all of it, but I did ask him whether there were any other careers he'd enjoy. He said MMA was what he loved."

"So you broke up with him."

"If I'd asked him to quit fighting, he might have done it. But sooner or later he'd have resented me for taking him away from the sport he loved. And I couldn't stand that."

"And Brad?"

"I love Brad. He loves me. It's not a grand passion, but we've both had those and neither of us are interested in going that route again."

"What happened with his?"

"Gina. She was a fashion model he dated while we were in school. She died in a drunk driving accident my junior year. It gutted him."

"But Joe's not dead. Does Brad know you still have feelings for a living, breathing man?"

"I don't. I mean, I *do*. But not those kind of feelings. Not the marrying kind." She pressed her lips together and rubbed her forehead. "Can we stop talking about Joe? Please?"

"Of course. I'm really sorry."

"Let's talk sex toys instead."

"Excellent plan. Tell me about the bachelorette party and we'll come up with a few appropriately inappropriate items for your brother to pick up at

Goody's."

Kai hadn't brought a paper catalog or price list, but they used Georgie's tablet to log into the Goody's website and poke around.

"Penis pops?"

"One of our most popular bachelorette items."

"I didn't plan to even have a bachelorette party, but Brad's cousins want to take him fishing on Lake Mead on Friday and they won't get back until late, by which time they'll be wiped out. And drunk. So Sue convinced me I should have a party as well as the whole manicure thing."

"Who's coming?"

"Everyone? I mean, I'm not planning to restrict it. I don't think my mother will come, but you never know."

"So how many is that? If everyone shows?"

"Maybe twenty? Twenty-six if absolutely everyone comes."

"Wow."

"Yeah. I have five bridesmaids. We were in a sorority together in college. I asked Brad's sister to be my maid of honor because I couldn't choose one of the five without offending the others."

"Are they more prim and proper or more wild and crazy?"

"A mix."

"And where are you having this shindig?"

"In the same room we're having the card party tonight."

"Okay, so will there be tables set up?"

"Yes. A big one and several smaller ones. The girls said they were bringing presents for me, so we figured I'd spend at least a little time at the big table opening stuff."

"Maybe they'll be bringing you some Goodies, too. But one thing I think looks great is to do little penis pop 'bouquets' for the centerpieces. It takes a while for people to realize what they are when they're all dolled up with ribbons in a pretty vase and when they do, it gets quite a reaction."

"Oh, that's a great idea. Cathy and Sarah are arriving tomorrow, but the rest won't be here until Thursday night. Maybe we can spend an afternoon making the bouquets before they get here, so they won't see them until Friday."

"Great. We'll need…oh…thirty or forty, I'd say, if we're doing bouquets for a bunch of tables."

"I'll have Julian send over some greenery and ribbons."

"Now, since you already have tickets for the raffles tonight, you can use them to do raffles at the bachelorette party, too. And the prizes can be much more risqué."

They spent the next half hour picking out items. Then Kai called the store and spoke to Benny himself about placing the order.

"So pretty boy's going to pick it up?" he asked.

"He's not a pretty boy. But yes."

"How are things going there?"

"Well, Georgie and I just finished picking these items out for a party on Friday."

"So she's sitting next to you?"

"Yes. And you know how far ahead I like to plan things, so you can imagine that I'm not at my best."

"Gotcha. You holding up okay, though?"

"Oh, yes."

"Great. Then I'll get these things together and send them up. You want me to throw in anything else?"

"No, I think that will do."

"Okay, I'll bag this up for him."

"Thanks, Benny, you're the best."

"Of course I am."

Kai hung up on a laugh. Benny was the most arrogant man she'd ever met, but ninety percent of it was an act.

Georgie raised her eyebrows. "Is Benny Silver as wild as they say?"

"Maybe even wilder. But he's a really nice guy. And he mother-hens his employees to death. He even went to Tennessee when my former boss had to go help out a relative and he stayed there to be sure she was okay."

"A mensch." Georgie grinned.

"Totally."

"Do you like your job?"

"I do. It's never the same two days in a row. Much like yours, I imagine."

"Absolutely." She checked the time on her phone. "But as much fun as I've had planning Friday's event, I have to go get ready for tonight's. Can't wait to see your outfit! Do you want me to come by and pick you up so we can walk over together?"

"Sure."

"Fab. I know it's stupid, but I hate walking into events by myself."

"Not stupid at all. I feel the same way."

Georgie leaned over and gave her a quick hug. "I'm so glad Luke brought you. I'll see you in about half an hour?"

"Uh, yeah. Perfect."

KAI SAT STUNNED ON THE couch for a full three minutes after Georgie left. The girl had *hugged* her. People didn't do that. Ever since grade school, Kai had been called "intimidating" or "aloof." And mostly, she was okay with that. She wasn't a hugger. But obviously Georgie was. Either that or Kai's aloof and intimidating persona was losing power.

She needed to reset it to full strength before the party, so she took a quick shower and washed an overcoat of bright red over the leftover purple. It came out a dark burgundy, which was just fine for her purposes. A loose black shirt went on underneath her Queen of Hearts bustier, which featured black side panels and a white centerpiece with three red hearts down the center. A black A-line skirt and white tights with tiny hearts running up the back seams finished the outfit. Carefully, she drew a heart-shaped beauty mark just below her left eye in scarlet lipliner.

When Georgie knocked, Kai slipped back into her chrome-heeled shoes and stiffened her spine. She didn't look forward to facing the Clarke clan without Luke's reassuring solidity at her side, but she'd managed more difficult situations, and the outfit would help. *A good offense is the best defense.*

Much to her surprise, Kai got a kick out of the card party. Walt beckoned to her the minute she and Georgie arrived and insisted on teaching her how to play poker. After trouncing her soundly for a good hour, he pronounced her unfit to play with others due to a condition he called "SLOP-F", Severe Lack of Poker Face. She won a bottle of champagne and a deck of cards in the raffles, and both Jenna and Cecily took selfies with her because they liked her outfit.

She managed to avoid the Clarkes for most of the night. Or they avoided her. She wasn't certain which, or whether it even mattered, but twice she saw Julia watching her from another table, a frown etching lines into her smooth skin. So much for accepting her son's girlfriend in the hopes of having him lose interest. A shadow slipped over Kai's enjoyment when she thought about the harm Julia could do if she actually put her mind to it, but she forced her mind away from that consideration. With a little luck, the woman would be too preoccupied with her daughter's wedding to stick her nose into Kai's business.

The party ended at ten, and both Gil and Sue invited Kai out afterward—Sue to join a group playing the slots, Gil to the steakhouse bar. She turned them both down. It wasn't that she was tired, she simply couldn't cope with being social any longer. Her pajamas were calling her name.

She considered popping the champagne she'd won at the party, but settled for a mug of instant cocoa made in the coffee machine. She flipped on the television, found aliens attacking Los Angeles, and settled in for a couple of hours of mindless enjoyment.

Her cell rang at a quarter after eleven.

"I didn't wake you, did I?" Luke asked.

"No." Though, truth be told, she was half-asleep on the couch, She'd avoided the bedroom, not ready to sleep in the big, soft, comfortable bed alone.

"How was the party? Did you win a massage?"

"No, but I won a bottle of champagne." She read him the label.

"Nice. That's probably worth more than a spa trip."

"You think I can trade it in at the front desk?"

He laughed. "I have your number now. You're a massage addict."

"It's your fault. You created a monster."

"Guilty as charged. Everyone treating you okay?"

"Absolutely. Georgie took me for a mani-pedi after you left, so my hands and feet got massaged. And my nails are way nicer than I can do myself."

"Yeah? What color are they? And what color is your hair?"

"The nails are stardust. It's a black base coat with an iridescent finish. And my hair is burgundy, because I rocked a Queen of Hearts outfit for the card party."

"I gotta see that. Will you model it for me when I get back?"

Oh. Muscles clenched low and deep inside her. "The silly sisters, Brad's cousins, took pictures."

"I don't want pictures. I want the real thing."

She swallowed. "Okay."

"Good. Are you in bed yet?"

"No. Watching television."

"Hmm."

"What's up?"

"Remember what we talked about this morning?

Your little battery-operated friend?"

Heat swamped her, embarrassment and desire fighting for supremacy. "I remember."

"Did you bring him with you?"

"No. I figured it might not be appropriate." Actually, she'd judged him too uptight to want to share his bed with a vibrator, but she couldn't very well say so.

"What about the stuff you brought from the shop?"

"What's going on, Luke?"

"My plan."

Right. He'd mentioned a plan after the closet incident. "What plan is that, again?"

His voice went low, seductive. "I told you I wasn't ready to give up on bringing you to orgasm. Step one of that is being close while you take yourself there. I'd rather be watching, but I'll settle for listening. And talking to you. Maybe we can get to a Pavlovian state, where just the sound of my voice turns you on."

They were already there, but he didn't need to know that.

"You still there?" he asked.

"Yes." She cleared her throat, glanced at the items still spread out on the coffee table from when she and Georgie had talked earlier. "And yes, I brought a couple of Goodies that would do the trick."

"Are you up for this? If it makes you uncomfortable…"

"No. It's not that. I just haven't done it before."

"Me, either. So we'll be virgins together."

She reached for the little bullet vibrator that came packaged with a AA battery. "I'll need a minute to get ready."

"We have all the time in the world."

No, they only had a few days. If his plan worked, what then? *Don't get ahead of yourself. This may be an utter disaster and you won't ever be able to look the guy in the eye again.* But that was her brain. Her body was completely on board with Luke's idea, tightening in anticipation as she rinsed the toy, put the battery in, and lay down on the bed.

"Still there?" she asked when she'd propped all the pillows behind her head.

"Damned straight. Are you wearing your striped pajamas?"

"They're the only ones I brought."

"I don't think you should be wearing anything."

Heat shot through her at the low, rough suggestion. "Are you naked?"

"Bet your sweet, round ass I am. I brought the sweats for you."

"Oh. Okay." She put the phone on speaker and wriggled out of her pajamas. If she'd been alone she would already be scrambling for the vibrator. Her body screamed with longing and she was as wet as she'd ever been in her life. "What now?" she asked.

"Now I want you to pet yourself. And tell me how it feels. How *you* feel. Because I'm going to be imagining those are my fingers on you. In you."

She closed her eyes, imagining Luke as he would look on the other end of the call. A whimper escaped her and he answered with a groan.

"Talk to me," he said. "How do you feel?"

"I can't. Oh God, Luke. I'm so close."

"I want to feel your breasts. Touch them for me."

She slid her hand up her body, ran it over her breasts. Her hand was too small, too smooth. She wanted Luke's long, callused fingers, not her own.

"Jesus," he rasped when she told him so. "I'm not going to last much longer here, sweetheart. How you doing?"

"Same," she managed.

"Take us over, then."

She reached for the vibrator and flicked it on. Within seconds she shattered, sobbing out Luke's name. Long moments later, when she pulled herself back together, she could hear Luke's harsh, uneven breathing. It was the only sound in the room.

"Wow," he said at last.

She laughed a little. "Yeah."

"That may be the hottest thing I've ever experienced."

From "frigid" to the hottest thing a man had ever experienced. *Take that, Rick.* "Me, too," she admitted.

"We're definitely doing it again when I get back."

Her whole body tightened in approval. *Yes, please.* "Agreed."

"Sweet dreams, Kai."

"You, too."

But it was a long time before she slept.

THE NEXT MORNING, KAI SLEPT in. She woke relaxed, languid, more refreshed than she'd been even after her spa treatments. On the bed next to her, the little aquamarine bullet tempted her to play, but she ignored it. The orgasm last night had been great, but it wouldn't be as much fun without Luke.

He'll be back tonight. Ten o'clock. She just had to get through…eleven hours. Eleven hours of vacation. Not such a bad thing. And being on vacation, in her book, did not include dealing with people like Julia Clarke or Gil Markham. So she ordered room service and decided to give her hair a hot oil treatment. Not for Luke. Just because it was feeling a bit rough and dry. And because she liked Georgie and wanted to look her best for her wedding.

At two, Georgie called and invited her to play tennis with her, Sue, and Jenna. Kai tried to contain her laughter at the idea of herself on a tennis court, let alone playing doubles. She begged off, explaining that her head was currently wrapped in a hot towel and that it would be at least another hour before she could be seen in public.

"But you're coming to the murder mystery dinner tonight, right? You got the invitation with your role?"

"You know it. I'm a showgirl. Which is absolutely hilarious, since I work with a real showgirl at the shop and my old boss was one, too, before she came to work for Benny. I'm way too short to be Sally Showstopper, but I'll do my best in the role."

"Who was Luke supposed to be?"

"My…how did the description put it? Paramour, I think. Muscles McGee, a weightlifter and gambler who's deeply in debt. He was supposed to try to chase off any men I flirted with." And she was supposed to be crazy in love with him, hoping that he'd propose at the party.

"Damn. It's a shame he won't be back in time."

"I don't suppose you can make me the murderer? I've always wanted to kill someone and I may never get another chance."

"I would if I could. But we have a company putting it on and they manage handing out the cards and everything. They even assigned the roles. They just asked me for things like age, sex, and how outgoing people are."

"Damn."

"If I'd known you were coming, I'd have asked them to theme it so the victim was bludgeoned to death with a…personal device."

Kai choked. "Your mother is attending this, right?"

"Yes. And I'm not exactly happy with her at the moment. But unfortunately I don't get to pick the victim, either."

"It's probably for the best."

"Probably."

Kai finished her hair and spent the rest of the afternoon on the balcony, which faced out over the pool, reading. When the phone rang at four-thirty, she grabbed for it, hoping it was Luke, but it was Celia.

"Hey," Celia said. "I hate to bother you, but Benny's not answering his phone and I can't get the product code lookup to work on the bar code machine. I know there's a trick to it but I don't want to screw up."

"No problem. You have to turn the key all the way to the left. Hard. It likes to stick right before it clicks into place." She waited while Celia tried.

"That worked, thanks! We got in some Big Blues and I need to price them."

"Yeah, they have to stop printing those codes in pretty colors. They never work with the scanners."

"Right? And then you just have to cover up the pretty one with an ugly sticker. We should really talk to Benny about it."

"He knows. He said they're going to black. But the warehouse still has a whole lot of blue and purple."

"Gotcha."

"Hey, Celia, know what I am doing tonight?"

"Having sex with Hottie McHotterson?"

"No! Well, probably." And a little thrill went through her at the admission. She shoved it away. Long distance was one thing—there was no guarantee things would be as good in person. "I'm going to a murder mystery party as a showgirl."

"*Stop*."

"It's true!"

"You should call Evie. She'd get a huge kick out of that."

"I'll call her next week and tell her about it. I intend to give showgirls a *very* bad name."

Celia laughed. "Worse than we already have? Seriously, I can't wait to hear about it. They had those once in a while at the dinner theater I waitressed at before I got my dancing job. They can be a hoot."

"I'm looking forward to it."

"So you're having a good time? Luke's family isn't too awful?"

"His sister is very sweet."

"Ah. Gotcha. Well, try not to kill them in earnest tonight."

"I'll do my best."

CHAPTER 9

THE MURDER MYSTERY PARTY WAS held on the pool deck. Night had drawn a curtain across the sky and the area was lit with a wash of blue from the underwater lights and the purple bulbs in the sconces that lined the stone walls. A fire pit at the deeper end of the pool wafted the scent of smoke and cedar over the party and two tuxedo-clad bartenders manned a bar near the shallow end. Music filtered over the crowd, something quiet and classical that Kai didn't recognize.

It felt surreal, like a set designed for a fairy tale play. A uniformed woman handed her an envelope when she checked in just before stepping outside, and in it she found a "Sally Showstopper" name tag, a bundle of fake money, and some character notes about what Sally was hoping to get out of attending the party. Sally, she learned, was a bit of a flirt, playing Harry Highroller—a married man with more money than brains—against her boyfriend, Muscles McGee, in the hopes of bringing Muscles up to snuff.

She wandered through the pool area, accepting a glass of wine and a few hors d'oeuvres from strolling waiters and looking at name tags.

Walt wore a tag that said simply "Elvis" and when she said hello to him, he responded with a credible Elvis imitation that made his wife, wearing a "Rhonda Reporter" tag, laugh.

"He's supposed to be the hotel's Elvis impersonator,"

she said. "And I'm writing a story about him. But my envelope says that I'm tired of fluff pieces and want to do real journalism, so I'm really investigating a series of burglaries that have taken place while people have been staying at the resort."

"Oh, my."

Marion whipped out a notebook. "So tell me, Sally, have you noticed nefarious-looking people about while you've been between shows?"

Kai shook her head. "I'm afraid not, Rhonda. I'm too busy trying to remember my choreography and fending off the advances of every high roller in the casino."

Brad and Georgie joined them, wearing "Max Martini" and "Donna Daiquiri" tags.

"Brad's a bartender and I'm a cocktail waitress."

"I don't think your skirt is short enough," Kai teased. "And your blouse is definitely not cut low enough. You'll never make good tips dressed like that. But the heels are good."

"I should have borrowed from you," Georgie said. Then she clapped a hand across her mouth. "Oh! That came out wrong!"

"No worries. My wardrobe is absolutely better suited to a cocktail waitress than yours is."

Gil strolled up. "Harry Highroller, at your service," he said.

Ugh. Of course it would be Gil she was supposed to flirt with. She smiled. "Sally Showstopper."

"Ah. My wife, Henrietta, is very jealous of you."

"And where is your wife?"

Henrietta turned out to be Jenna, who took Gil's hand and glared with passable menace at Kai. "You're not taking my husband," she said, but then ruined it by bursting into a fit of the giggles. They mingled for the next half hour or so. Kai even managed to be civil to Julia and John, who'd been assigned the roles of casino owners, Mr. and Mrs. Bigbucks.

She was standing and chatting with Jenna and Cecily,

along with Sharla Markham, Gil and Sue's mother, when the "murder" occurred. With much waving of arms, choking, gasping and generally making an ass of himself, Gil staggered through the crowd to die at her feet.

"Oh, no!" shrieked Jenna. "My husband! This is terrible! He must have had a heart attack!"

"Make way, make way," said an older man Kai vaguely remembered as being related to the Clarkes. "Detective Digdirt on the scene!" He poked Gil a few times until Kai heard Gil tell him to lay off, then turned to the crowd. "This was not a heart attack. This was murder. His drink has been *poisoned*!"

A pair of arms came around Kai from behind and she looked up in surprise to see Luke. Her heart jumped and she tilted her head all the way back to kiss his chin.

"Luke!"

"Not Luke," he said with a smile that barely lightened the exhausted shadows beneath his eyes. "Didn't you read my name tag? Muscles McGee, steroid-enraged jealous boyfriend here to keep an eye on his woman."

She wanted to ask how his meetings had gone, but he looked so tired that she went for humor instead. "Muscles takes *steroids*? Sally disapproves. They interfere with some of her favorite things."

"Shhh," said Cecily, stepping away from them. "Detective Digdirt is explaining the evidence."

"Did you murder Harry Highroller for flirting with Sally?" she whispered.

"Nope. Did you kill him because he wouldn't leave his wife and take you away from your miserable life with your steroid-addled boyfriend?"

"Afraid not."

"Excellent. Since neither of us poisoned my cousin, we can leave early, right?"

Oh, how she wanted to say yes. But she owed Georgie.

"I wish. But we have to stick around so the others can question us. And then there's the big reveal."

"Damn."

"Muscles McGee?" said Julia, walking up to stand next to them. "Is everything all right in the world of gardening?"

"I'm not a gardener, Mrs. Bigbucks," he said. He was smiling, but Kai saw his eye twitch slightly. *A gardener? What the actual fuck?* Luke was a successful landscape architect with his own business. What kind of mother talked like that? Hers had, but she'd been a screw-up, so at least her mother had some excuse. Julia had none. Kai faced Luke and wrapped her arms around his waist and he linked his hands behind her back. "In case we haven't been properly introduced, Mrs. Bigbucks, I'm a bodybuilder and inveterate gambler."

Julia waved away the comment. "This is a ridiculous event. I don't even know what your sister was thinking."

"I think it's great," said Kai. "Of course, if it were me, I'd have assigned roles before people even left home and insisted everyone come in costume." She ran a hand slowly, deliberately up Luke's dress shirt under his jacket. "This, for example, is completely out of character. Muscles always wears tank tops to show off his sculpted body."

Luke grabbed her hand and brought it to his mouth to press a kiss into the palm. His eyes shone with unholy glee and hot desire, all signs of exhaustion gone. "Now, now, Sally. How many times do I have to tell you to keep your hands to yourself?"

Cecily chose that moment to join them. "Hi, Mrs. Clarke. I mean, Mrs. Bigbucks. Hey, Kai, I talked to Gil before the murder and he said Harry and Sally were having an affair."

"In his dreams," Kai replied. "Sally's a flirt, but she's faithful to her one true love, Muscles."

"Damned straight," said Luke.

With an audible huff, Julia moved away.

"Maybe Sally killed Harry because he misinterpreted her flirting, then." Cecily raised her eyebrows.

"I'll never tell," said Kai.

Marion joined them. "I don't think Sally did it. Didn't you see what the detective found in Harry's pockets? He'd been stealing from the casino. My money's on the casino owners or maybe Sam Stud, the poker dealer. Harry always sits at Sam's table, and Sam's in trouble because he's not making enough for the casino."

"Wow, you're really getting into the investigative reporter thing," Kai said. "You'll be off the fluff beat in no time."

"This is so much fun," said Marion. "I admit, when Brad told us about it, I was leery, but I'm having a ball." She peered around the shadow-dappled pool deck. "Oh, look. There's Sam Stud. I'm going to go question him. You want to come with me, Cecily?"

"Sure, Aunt— er, Rhonda. See you guys!" The two struck out toward the bar, leaving Kai and Luke alone again. He checked over one shoulder, then backed up a few steps until they were near the wall, obscured by a pair of potted palms.

"Hi, Sally," he murmured.

"Hi, Muscles."

He slid a hand into her hair. "It's too dark out here. I can't see the color."

"It's still burgundy."

"Good. I want to see every color." His thumb stroked her cheekbone. "I missed you."

Oh. Her heart cracked. She couldn't even meet his eyes because she was afraid hers might tear up. "I missed you, too." She swallowed. "How did it go in California?"

He rubbed a bristled cheek over the top of her head. "Rough. Barrowman agreed to the contract, thanks to you, but other issues came up."

"Is there anything I can do?"

"No. Yes. You're doing it."

She pressed a kiss to the patch of skin revealed by his open collar, "You're an easy man to please."

"Actually, I'm not. Ask any of the firefighters in my company. Or the guys who work for me. I just have a soft spot for you."

She did look up at him then, and the warmth and affection in his baby-blue eyes shredded her. In her whole life, she didn't remember anyone ever looking at her that way.

"Luke—"

"Shh." He kissed her, a gentle, sweet touch that tore through her like a hurricane and left her shaken and utterly lost. She buried her face in his shoulder and he swayed slightly. "What are you thinking about?"

"Wishing we had more than three days."

"We have all the time we want. It's just a short commuter flight to Vegas. I did it today. I can do it again."

KAI LOOKED UP AT HIM, her eyes huge in the darkness. Had he scared her? He'd surprised himself, but once the words were out, a profound relief settled over him. He didn't want to give her up. Not yet.

"Really?"

He slid his hands down her spine to cup her butt and press her lower body into his. She was more comfortable with sex than commitment, so sex was what he'd give her. At least for the moment.

"Really, Cuz." Gil's voice broke in before Luke had a chance to take things any further. "Groping girls in the corner? Aren't you a little past that?"

"Go away, Gil. You're dead."

"I'm a ghost. And you will be, too, if you don't participate in the party instead of cuddling with your mother's least favorite person in the corner."

"Mother is going to have to get used to Kai."

Gil stared at him. "I do believe you mean that. How strange. When I saw you that first night, I would have sworn—no offense, Kai—but I would have sworn your date was nothing more than a woman deliberately chosen to piss off Julia and John."

And of course, she had been. Maybe it was all the years of competition, but his cousin read him surprisingly well.

"Julia can't always get what she wants," he said. "It's time she learned that."

"A word of warning, Luke. When my mother decided I needed a political career because I was useless at anything else, she sent me to Aunt Julia for training and I learned a great deal. My mother is a pain in the ass, but yours is—how do I put this?—a vindictive, scary bitch. You've defied her for years and she's let you, but you never showed her anything you cared about. It's like…showing your soft underbelly to a wild dog. She will not take this lying down."

In his arms, Kai shivered.

"Laying it on a bit thick, aren't you? What can she do? She's already tried to buy Kai off. It's not as if she's going to hire an assassin."

"No, I suppose not. But I wouldn't turn my back on her. And I wouldn't rub her nose in the fact that she's not getting her way."

"You make her sound like a monster," said Kai, pulling away from him so she could face Gil. Instantly, he wanted to wrap himself around her again. He settled for taking her hand.

"She's not a monster." Gil was more serious than Luke had ever seen him. "She's a woman who's rarely been thwarted. The one thing she wants, the thing she feels she doesn't have, is power. The kind money can't easily buy. And she aims to get that through her son, since she failed to get it through her husband. If she has a motto, it's 'whatever it takes.' So a word of friendly warning—watch your back."

With that, Gil was gone, as was the romantic moment he'd interrupted.

For the next hour, Luke pushed away all his concerns and played Muscles to the hilt. He had to admit it was fun, and Georgie was in her element pretending to be a ditzy cocktail waitress. His father unbent enough to flash some of Mr. Bigbucks's fake wad of cash, promising a reward to whoever made his casino safe from murderers.

In the end the killer was revealed to be Sam Stud, the poker dealer, who had been helping Harry steal from the casino until Harry double-crossed him. The minute Detective Digdirt made his announcement, Luke leaned down and whispered in Kai's ear. "Can we leave now?"

The smile she turned on him was bright and full of mischief and sent a shaft of longing though him, though he couldn't put a name to what it was he wanted.

"Yes, please," she said.

In the elevator on the way up to their room, Kai asked him about his trip. "Did you go to your firehouse?"

"I did. How did you guess?"

"I'd like to say I'm psychic, but actually your sister said you didn't have it in you to take a week off. And it seems to me you're the kind of person who takes his responsibilities very seriously. What's it like in a volunteer company? Is there anyone there when there's not an emergency going on?"

"Depends. No one *has* to be there, but we've got a bar, a pool table, a weight room, and a big-screen TV upstairs at the house. About half the guys work locally, either for the town or as business owners like me, so they often stop in to eat lunch. The younger ones, well, real estate is ridiculously overpriced, so they mostly live with their parents and hang out at the firehouse to watch sports or whatever."

"And what's the point of dropping by there in the middle of your vacation?"

"Certain things are supposed to happen after every call, and it's my job as captain to make sure they do. Trucks wiped down, hoses packed properly, air tanks topped off. Next year Mike, my first lieutenant, becomes captain. In my absence, he's responsible for the checklist. The engines have been out on five calls since we've been gone. Two fires, one MVA, two commercial alarms."

"MVA?"

"Sorry. Motor vehicle accident."

"Ah." She nodded. "I didn't realize fire engines got called out to those, but I suppose it makes sense."

"You really find this interesting?"

"Of course. Why not?"

"Most people glaze over when I talk about the day-to-day operations, the paperwork, the boredom calls. They're happy to hear about the fires, but the rest of it, not so much."

"I would imagine the fires are the smallest part of the job."

"They are. But they're the only part many people—even many of my own guys—care about. It's a constant struggle to motivate guys to show up to babysit a downed power line until PG&E shows up."

"I can see that. They sign up for the excitement. But I want to know how the job affects *you*, which means understanding all of it, not just the exciting bits."

I love you. Such a strange time to have that revelation, stepping out of an elevator into the hallway of a hotel faintly scented with industrial cleaner. But nothing about this relationship had gone according to plan, or followed a normal pattern.

"So, two fires, two alarms, and a car accident—five calls in about three or four days. Is that normal?"

He had to get his head back into the conversation. "Pretty much. We average between four and five hundred calls a year. Of course, not every man makes every call."

"Still, that's a serious volunteer commitment. So what did you find at the firehouse? Were they keeping it together while you were gone?"

"Yup. Trucks looked good, tools were clean. Mike'll be a good captain when it's his turn."

"That should ease your mind a little. What happens to you then? When you're no longer captain?"

"I could run for chief if I wanted. Or I could go back into the officer's line down near the bottom. Or just become a regular firefighter again. Officer's line positions generally last a year, but this is my second year as captain because the guy who should have succeeded me broke his leg in three places and had to take an extended leave."

They stopped in front of their door and she leaned into him and wrapped her arms around his neck. "Chief Hottie. I like it."

"I like *you*." He speared a hand through her hair and backed her up against the wall for a long kiss while he fumbled with the room key. Her mouth was hot and sweet and he lost himself in her taste. When he came up for air, she took the key card from his hand and let them into the suite.

"Did I mention that I missed you?" he asked.

"You did. And I can tell." Her hands slid beneath his jacket and she eased it off his shoulders, laid it over the back of a chair, then went to work on his shirt buttons. "Way too many clothes."

"When you said that in front of my mother… It's a memory I'll treasure as long as I live."

She hummed approvingly. "Only fair. You gave me one last night."

"That one I'll remember long after I'm dead."

She chuckled as she pulled his shirt out of his pants and stripped it off him. "Let's make more."

"Hell, yes." On impulse, he swung her up into his arms and carried her into the bedroom. She kicked off her shoes and shrieked with laughter, sparking a bright flame deep inside him. She should laugh all the time. He wanted to hear that sound every day for the rest of his life.

He laid her on the bed and she rolled onto her side and reached over to shut off the light.

"Don't," he said. "Let me look at you."

LET ME LOOK AT YOU. Why did the request send a shiver through her? Men looked at her all the time. Her wardrobe attracted attention, and though she didn't choose her outfits to please anyone but herself, nor did she shy away from the reactions they inspired. But Luke saw too much already. And she was so very vulnerable to him.

He touched a finger to the hollow of her throat, then slid it down to the top of the black, stretch-lace shirt she wore over her navy and black bustier.

"Now who's wearing too many clothes?"

She sat up and pulled off the shirt, stretching her arms high above her head so that her breasts rose, threatening to pop free of the bustier. Luke growled and reached for her.

"How do you get this thing off?"

"See all those little hooks? Every one of them has to be undone." She leaned back on her elbows. "Start at the top and bottom, and work your way to the middle."

Luke worked diligently, his long fingers sure and nimble, sliding against her skin as they pulled and twisted, unlocking each hook. Men had undressed her before, but never with such care, and never while she was wearing a corset. Those she undid herself—they were too expensive, too finicky to leave to impatient male fingers.

But Luke showed no impatience. He revealed her inch by inch, as if he were unwrapping a particularly delicate piece of china, and when he was done he smoothed the bustier open on either side of her and ran his finger down the impression one of the stays had left along her ribcage.

"Why do you put yourself through this?"

"Don't you like the way they look?"

"Do you even have to ask?"

"Well, I like it, too. Plus, I know the marks aren't attractive, but they're temporary and they don't hurt. The support actually feels good when you're on your feet all day like I am at the store. It's like wearing a back brace."

He bent his head and traced his tongue down the indentation on the left side of her body, then back up the right. He never touched her breasts and she still wore her skirt, his mouth touched no piece of skin that could be considered an erogenous zone, but heat flooded through her at the contact. She fisted her fingers in his hair and dragged him up for a kiss.

His mouth plundered hers, seeking, sucking, nibbling, until the world narrowed to that one point of contact. She ran her hands over his back, desperate to pull him down on her, to feel his weight. His hand found her breast and she pushed herself into him like a cat. He rolled her nipple between one rough thumb and forefinger and she whimpered her desire into his mouth.

With a groan, he pulled away from her, kicked off his shoes, and stripped out of the rest of his clothes. Good grief, the man was a work of art. A turned on work of art.

He tugged at her skirt. "Please tell me this doesn't have a hundred tiny hooks, too."

How did he manage to be so cute, so sweet, and so hot all at the same time? It was killing her.

"No, just one." She undid the skirt and shimmied out of both it and her stretch lace, thigh-length, shapewear panties, leaving her in thigh-highs. He made a sound deep in the back of his throat that sent a shaft of white-hot desire like lightning through her blood.

"You are the sexiest thing I have ever seen," he said.

"Right back atcha." She reached down and cupped his balls in her hand, liking the way his cock jumped to attention and his breath hitched in that very fine chest.

He dipped his head and swiped a rough tongue across her breast, then drew her nipple into his mouth. Muscles clenched low and deep in her body and she squirmed beneath him. His hand stroked her belly, her thighs, touching her everywhere except where she needed him. She tangled her fingers in his and drew them toward her center, and he chuckled against her breast, a deep, thrumming vibration that weakened her muscles and turned her bones to liquid.

Instead of following her implicit direction, Luke grabbed her other hand and spread both arms out, away from her body. He urged her fingers to grasp the sheets, silently telling her not to move, then returned to his worship. He cupped her breasts and thumbed her nipples, the rough pads of his fingers bringing them to almost painful sensitivity. His mouth nibbled a trail down her body, between her breasts, pausing just below her bellybutton.

She growled and he grinned up at her, blue eyes sparkling. His hands held her hips firmly to the bed and slowly, far too slowly, lowered his mouth over her. The first touch of his tongue to her clit had her bucking against his grip and grabbing at his shoulders to pull him up her body. Who cared whether she actually climaxed? She wanted him inside her. Now. *Yesterday.*

"Luke, please."

He ignored her request, slipping one long finger inside her as he sucked her clit between his teeth. Her whole body was a writing mass of fiery nerves. She clutched at his hair, dragged him up so they were face to face. "Now," she said.

"I'm not coming without you. Not again. Get the vibrator."

For a moment, her mind was completely blank. Where the hell had she even put it? *Nightstand.* She grabbed it from the drawer.

"Show me," he ordered.

She was drunk with heat, trembling, burning, melting with it. Her hand shook so hard she could barely press the little button on the end of the bullet. And then her nerve failed.

"I don't think I can do this."

"You can. You're halfway there already."

"The easy half." Just the words were pulling her away from that delicious cliff. Luke took the bullet from her fingers and lightly, so lightly, ran it over her breast, just grazing her nipple. He followed it with his mouth, scraping the already tender flesh gently between his teeth. *Okay, maybe more than half.*

He hummed quietly against her, his own personal vibration colliding with the electronically inspired ones rippling over her skin as he skimmed a light, skipping path across her body with the bullet. Tension wound her in knots, but Luke moved slowly, patiently, despite the insistent throb of his cock against her thigh.

In Luke's fingers, the vibrator traced a circle around her belly button, then spiraled out…and out. With each circle, her muscles tightened further, her lungs constricted until she could barely draw a breath. Her heart raced as the vibrator passed over her pubic bone, then dipped, dancing lightly over her clit.

A whimper escaped her.

"Good?"

There were no words. Her hand covered his, guiding him into her rhythm, her force. She closed her eyes, concentrating on the sensation, the buzz, the heat, the build. It would take her. She was past the point of no return, even with Luke watching, with his hand beneath hers on the vibrator.

"Please," she gasped out. "Luke, come with me."

"Next time," he whispered, then rubbed his stubbled cheek over one breast. The sharp pinch and scrape sent her over the edge and her hand twisted in his hair, holding him to her as if he might run.

And indeed, when he could put a coherent thought together at all, he might. What was the matter with her, anyway? She loosed her hold on him and he eased up on one elbow.

"Wow." There was amusement in his voice, but there was desire, too. He wasn't laughing at her, he was inviting her to play.

She swallowed. "So sex toys aren't so bad after all?"

"Not if they can do that. You keep taking me places I've never been, and each one is hotter than the last."

"Can't have been that hot," she said, reaching out and running a finger along his erection to gather a tiny drop of liquid from the tip. She sucked it off her finger and his cock twitched. "Your turn."

CHAPTER 10

"My TURN?" LUKE CHOKED STUPIDLY. There was a good chance he wouldn't survive the night. But he'd die happy. Kai's eyes had been closed when she came, but his had been open, and he'd never in his life seen anything so beautiful. It was like stepping into a burning building. Awe-inspiring, frightening, and enthralling. What was it she'd said to him? *Sex is a journey, orgasm is just a destination.* Well, he might not have made it to the destination, but that was a hell of a journey.

And that habit she had of tasting him on her fingers. It was like watching porn. Only…not. Because there wasn't an ounce of artifice in it. It wasn't learned behavior; he'd bet his life on that.

She pushed him back onto the bed and plucked the vibrator, still humming along, from his fingers. With a twist, she turned it off. "I don't think we need any more of that tonight."

Her fingers caught a few of his chest hairs and she tugged, sending a sharp bolt of desire arrowing down to his already thoroughly erect cock. He reached for her to pull her hips over him, but she scooted out of the way.

"Uh-uh. I said it was your turn and I meant it. Besides, my legs are shot. No way they're going to drive the action." She knelt between his knees and took him in her mouth and his whole body contracted. Jesus. He was going to go off like a fucking rocket. He tried to hold back, but the sight of her there, those flaming wings tattooed on her shoulders fluttering with her movements, shredded his restraint.

"Kai, baby, I don't want to—" But he couldn't finish the thought. She sucked him hard and his control splintered and it was all he could do not to slam himself down her throat as his orgasm ripped through him. And even as far gone as he was, he could feel her swallow, feel her little hum of pleasure reverberating up his body. It sent an extra shot of heat through him.

She unfolded herself and slid up his body, coming to rest with her head on his shoulder. With his last ounce of energy, he smoothed a hand up and down her spine.

"Amazing," he said.

"Yeah. I guess I'm not so bad at sex after all."

His heart broke a little despite the lightness of her tone. "Oh, honey, that wasn't sex. That was way more. And you aren't bad at *any* of it."

"No?"

He cupped her face in one hand and covered her lips with his own. "No."

FOR ONCE, KAI WOKE BEFORE Luke. In the sunlight peeking around the edges of the curtains, she watched him sleep. He lay on his back, one arm flung out to the side, the other curved beneath her head. Even at peace, his muscles remained defined, smooth, heavy ridges under the skin. Shadows peeked through the golden fans of his lashes—the trip home had worn him out, and she wished she could ask him what had happened. But she wasn't part of his life, not really.

She tried to ease away, to let him sleep, but as soon as she shifted he rolled to his side and curled his body around her.

"Don't go," he murmured.

"You need to sleep."

"Mmm. Better when you're here."

Her breath caught. He was doing it again, turning her into someone bigger, better, more important. She wasn't the kind of woman who made anything better. In fact, she was the queen of making things worse. Nonetheless, she settled back into his embrace. He slid a hand through her hair, sighed, and sank back into sleep. Eventually, Kai followed.

The next time she woke, her phone's alarm was buzzing. Ten o'clock. How had it gotten so late?

"It's totally uncalled for to organize daytime events when people are supposed to be on vacation," Luke grumbled. "Georgie should know better."

"I suspect she wanted a day away from your parents. Nothing on earth could persuade them to get on a bus for a field trip to Vegas and an amusement park."

"True that," Luke said. "I can't say I'm particularly fond of the idea myself. I just made that drive and getting on a bus doesn't thrill me. Getting away from Julia, on the other hand…"

"I'm sure Georgie would understand if we begged off."

"Do you want to go?"

She did. Not because she cared about roller coasters, but because she wanted to spend a day with Luke away from the resort, away from his responsibilities.

"I live in Vegas. I can go to the Adventuredome any time."

"You *do* want to. So we will."

"No. You need to relax. You've spent too much time traveling and stressing."

"How about a deal? If the bus my sister hired looks comfortable, we go. If it's some sort of reno'd school bus or dollar drive, we stay here."

"Sounds like a plan."

They hit the lobby at a quarter to twelve to find it teeming with wedding guests. Apparently, at least a few more had arrived the night before. They found Gil, drink already in hand, and asked him whether the bus had arrived yet.

"It's parked in the lot. I checked it out. I'll give your sister's fiancé this, he knows how to do it up right. I've seen luxury liners less well-appointed. Full bar, leather seats, the whole nine yards."

"I guess we're going, then." Luke ran a finger down her cheek and she wished the bus had turned out to be junk.

"You were considering skipping?" Gil tsked, wagging his finger. "Shame on you. But I admit I don't plan to play in the kiddie park. I'm going to hit a couple of casinos."

"You don't have to go to Vegas to do that," Kai pointed out.

"True, but if I stay here, I'll also be gambling on not running into the family. I don't mind losing money, but I believe I have already mentioned my fear of Julia. And we all know how she feels about casinos."

The idea of a grown man running away from his aunt should have diminished Gil in her eyes. Instead, it made Julia loom larger, a cold, dark shadow over the festivities.

As usual, Luke sensed her emotions. He laced his fingers through hers, his big hand warm and comforting.

Georgie danced up to them. "You guys ready? I can't wait. I haven't been on a roller coaster since college." She focused on Kai. "Are the Adventuredome coasters as much fun as they look in the ads?"

"I don't know. I've never been."

"Really? How come?"

"I'm not sure. When I first moved to Vegas, I went to the Stratosphere. After that, I guess I got busy." Plus, the Adventuredome had been built for tourists and families, not cash-strapped locals without a big group of pals to run with.

Luke sliced one of his indecipherable glances down at her and she wondered what she'd inadvertently revealed. Clearly, Walt had been right to tell her to stay away from the poker tables.

"I'm not much of a coaster guy," Luke said. "I hope that doesn't mean I have to turn in my man card."

"Not as long as you'll ride the spider-type things with me," Kai teased.

"Great. Whirl and hurl."

She choked. "Never mind, I won't make you ride with me."

KAI FOUND THE ADVENTUREDOME BOTH fascinating and strangely repellant. The noise and crowds reminded her of being inside a casino. Having a floor beneath her feet rather than dirt or grass, combined with the pink-orange light filtering through the giant dome, gave the whole place a surreal atmosphere. She felt as if she'd stepped into an episode of *Doctor Who* on a plane with a dying sun flaming out in the distance.

"Wow," said Luke. "This feels all kinds of wrong."

The group had split up when they got off the bus. True to his word, Gil hadn't even bothered to venture inside the dome. Nor was he alone. The boyfriends of the two bridesmaids Kai had met on the bus had gone with him. The bridesmaids, Andrea and Missy, ran off with Georgie the minute they got into the park. Others headed out in ones and twos.

"You want to ride the whirl and hurl?" Luke asked.

"Nah. It's not fun without the wind in your face."

"I did wonder about the subdued hair and makeup. I hadn't thought about how the rides would affect them."

"Always dress for the occasion," she said, cocking a hip and throwing her arms out to show off her hand-painted jeans and cut-off Black Flag T-shirt. "Even I don't wear miniskirts and heels to an amusement park."

Just then, three young women in miniskirts sashayed by. Two of them glared and a giggle bubbled up in Kai's throat.

"Oops."

"That was perfect," Luke said.

"How are they going to manage the Canyon Blaster in those outfits?"

"I sincerely doubt that's the kind of ride those women are looking for."

The girls met up with three guys, all wearing backwards Yankees caps and T-shirts with the sleeves cut out.

"See what I mean?"

"The three stooges," Kai said.

"Maybe they're triplets."

"Even if they are, that's no excuse for dressing alike. That should stop by the time you hit middle school."

"Not everyone has their own sense of style. Some people are happier not standing out from the crowd."

"They should find a better-dressed crowd not to stand out from." But she winked as she said it. Being around Luke lightened her mood.

"What shall we do first?" he asked.

"Let's just walk."

"Sounds like a plan." He took her hand, bringing it to his mouth to press a kiss in her palm before leading her down the corridor. In a few steps, he dragged her into a photo booth.

"Luke!"

"Come on, it's a midway staple. You can't do an amusement park without a photo booth." Laughing, she mugged while the flash went off twice, and then Luke captured her in a surprisingly hot, deep kiss.

"I'm keeping these," he said when the pictures printed. He tucked them in his wallet without even letting her see them.

They wandered through the dome for the next hour. Luke soundly trounced her in a videogame motorcycle race, but she creamed him in laser tag. He bought her cotton candy and laughed when she accidentally got the sticky fluff caught in her hair. And over a lunch of hot dogs—a radical departure from their elegant room service breakfast—Kai found the courage to ask Luke about his trip home.

"I know he's right," he said, after explaining Cesar's reluctance to buy him out. "He lost a business before I knew him, and he almost lost his family. But I always assumed gambling was the issue. I figured if he quit, went to meetings, he'd be fine. It didn't occur to me that the gambling was just a symptom."

"What are you going to do?"

He ran a hand through his hair and three pieces stood straight up. "Try to find someone to take my place. The best option is to look for a landscape architect hoping to leave a large firm. You don't want one fresh out of school. But it's a delicate balance. Cesar is great to work with for the most part, but not everyone's cut out to own their own business. A lot of guys want to stick with the big firms, where their lives are secure."

"What made you want to sell the business in the first place?"

KAI WAS LEANING OVER THE table, chin in hand, watching him. He'd avoided talking about the mess with Cesar earlier, because he knew it made him sound whiny. He had a good job, made the type of money most people would love to make, and had few commitments or responsibilities other than those he'd chosen himself. Complaining because he couldn't simply ditch his business partner smacked of privilege and immaturity.

Kai, however, seemed to think there was more to it than that, so he took his time answering her. Even when he'd gone to Cesar with his proposal, he hadn't had to explain why he wanted out, so he'd never worked through it himself.

"When I started out, every project excited me.

Changing a plot of unstructured earth into a landscape that people would enjoy, structuring the land in a particular way that enhanced its beauty—it felt meaningful. But for the past few years, we've had more clients like Barrow-man. We've been designing and installing spaces for workaholics who more than likely will barely even notice them. It pays well and there's still a certain satisfaction in creating a landscape from a lawn, but it's not what I signed on for. For Cesar, working with the land is its own reward. That's not enough for me anymore."

"I'm sorry. It's not easy when things have to end."

"No. I thought I was going to get off easy, but it never works that way."

She cocked her head, studying him. "And once you sell the business, you'll become a full-time firefighter?"

"I hope so. I've applied in San Francisco, but there are a lot of politics in fire department jobs. It's not just qualifications, it's family history. I've passed the test and have my EMT certificate from the state. Because I'm a volly, I've also taken Firefighter One, which gives me a minuscule advantage. But I'll take any advantage I can get."

"If they're smart, they'll take you."

"Are you going to recommend me based on one fire? A fire, might I remind you, that I injured myself in because I acted like an idiot?" He held up his bandaged arm.

"No. I'd recommend you because you take your responsibilities seriously, even when you don't want to. Like the way you're thinking through who would be the best type of person to sell your business to, instead of just closing it down and leaving Cesar to find work as an installer for any random landscaper. You're a born leader."

"Please don't say things like that. Next, you'll be trying to convince me that my mother's right and I should run for office."

"Good grief, no."

He huffed in mock offense. "Why not? You just said I was a responsible leader."

"Yes. Because you're a people person. You'd hate a job that was all paperwork except for the election cycle where you had to go out and press the flesh."

Four days together, and she already knew him better than his mother did.

She touched his chest. "Besides, it would be an enormous waste to hide this behind suits and ties. As a firefighter, you'd have to work out, and letting women ogle you would be a public service."

He choked on a laugh.

"Come on, smart-mouth. Let's go see what else this joint has to offer." He pulled her from her seat, planted a kiss on her lips, and slung an arm across her shoulders.

They played a round of miniature golf, during which Luke laughed more than he could remember doing in possibly forever. He thought about asking if Kai wanted to ride the Chaos, mostly because it was a two-seater and he could hold her hand, but he figured throwing up his hot dog onto her wouldn't win him any points, so he settled for the Inverter. Being upside down had never caused him any problems. When they rounded the corner into the midway area, Kai's hand twitched in his and he followed her gaze to what had to be the world's ugliest plush purple unicorns hanging on the walls of a basketball game.

"You want one?" he asked.

"What would I do with a two-foot-tall purple unicorn?"

"C'mon. I'll win you one."

Of course, being a carnival game, that was easier said than done. The balls weren't regulation size or weight and the baskets were the wrong size and a different height than he was used to. But after three tries, he got it right and won her the purple unicorn.

"Thank you," she said, cuddling the ridiculous

creature to her cheek. "I love it."

"I love you." The words popped out and she froze, brandy eyes huge, a perfect center of stillness in the mass of movement under the dome. *Fuck. Too soon.*

"Luke, I—"

He touched her lips with his finger. "Shh. Don't worry about it. I don't expect you to say anything. I just wanted you to know. Now, we have half an hour left before we have to meet the bus. What shall we do?"

KAI HAD NO IDEA HOW the rest of the day passed. Luke's words rang in her head on an endless loop, drowning out everything else. *I love you.* Why had he said it? What did he mean? Was he the kind of guy who told women he loved them every day? He didn't seem to be, but you never knew with men.

And what was she supposed to do about it? His behavior hadn't changed in the slightest. He held her hand in the park, looped an arm around her neck on the bus, continued to touch her constantly, but he'd done that since the beginning.

When they got back to the room, she begged off dinner with the family. "I've had too much today," she told him. "Too many people. Too many crowds. I need downtime."

"Totally understandable. Don't worry about it." He frowned. "I never even asked you...did you get a chance to talk to Georgie while I was gone?"

The question yanked her out of her obsession with those three little words. How was she going to explain Georgie's decision without giving away the secret?

"I...did."

"What did she say?"

"She said she loves Brad."

"You don't sound very sure."

"I think...I think everyone has to decide for

themselves what they want out of life. Your sister has made her decision."

"Do you think she'll be happy with it in the long run?"

"Only time will tell. This isn't something you get to control."

"Have I mentioned that I hate not controlling things?"

She wrapped her arms around him and tucked her head against his chest, offering the only comfort she knew how. "I can relate. But she's a grown woman."

"Yeah." He sighed, rubbing her back. "Thanks for giving it a shot."

"Of course."

"I should take a shower. I smell like…well, I'm not sure what. But whatever it is, it's not appropriate for dinner with the family."

Once Luke had gone, Kai finally let herself unwind. She took a long hot shower to loosen the muscles that had tensed up at Luke's assertion and had never relaxed. She ordered a light dinner from room service, pulled out her book on punk culture, and settled on the couch, determined to ignore both Luke's crazy outburst and her own reaction to it.

The words on the screen gave way to ideas and Kai unpacked her full kit of pencils, markers, and large and small pads, then settled on the floor where she had the space to spread out. The next few items she made were going to be '80s-inspired. There had been a lot of studded leather, which she could neither afford nor stitch herself, but she could design around that. Most of her clothing customers hadn't even been born until 1990, but '80s culture still sold. She sketched out three outfits, losing herself in the designs, before the click of the lock jerked her back to the present.

CHAPTER 11

S HE LOOKED LIKE A FAIRy, a sprite, a garden nymph, Luke thought. Sitting cross-legged on the floor, in a circle of pens and paper, all big eyes and spiky hair, she was not entirely human. If she were a statue, he'd install her as a fountain, a fey creature rising from the water, surrounded by lily pads.

"Hey," she said, looking up at him. "How was dinner?"

"About what you'd expect. Good food, stiff conversation." He yawned. "Damn. Sorry. Long day. Walt and Marion asked after you."

"They're very nice. That's one thing you don't have to worry about. They love Georgie."

"Yeah. She'll definitely win in the new family department."

Kai began to gather up her pens, sliding them into a slotted case. He reached for one of the sketchbooks but paused before he could lay a hand on it. "May I?"

"Sure. I wouldn't think fashion is really your thing."

"Ordinarily, no. But this is different. It's something you created, which means I want to see it." He ignored her little twitch. The strength of his feelings for her made her uncomfortable, but the only way he could change that was to desensitize her. He didn't know what to expect from the sketchbook she passed him, but the fact that it was so professionally drawn surprised him. "This is really good. Very artistic looking."

"I promise you, they're not. What looks artistic to you is standard fashion sketch style. I took online courses to learn how to draw that way. I'm sure you took similar ones so you could lay out a landscape with trees and flowers and brick and rock walls."

"I did. I never realized fashion design worked the same way, though it makes perfect sense." She really had no idea how amazing she was. He tried to remember what she'd told him about her education. Community college, she'd said. While working at a big box store. She'd never mentioned online fashion drawing classes. Of course, he hadn't asked her, then, about her dreams and ambitions.

He helped her up off the floor and she did a little dance to shake out her legs.

"Oh, my knees." She bent over, laying her hands flat on the floor to stretch her hamstrings.

Holy fuck. Every drop of exhaustion fled in the face of roaring desire. He'd managed to forget, in the rush of more tender feelings, just how sexy Kai was. Even in those ridiculous sailor-stripe pajamas, her body called to his. She straightened up, caught his eye, and grinned.

"Maybe I shouldn't have done that."

"Oh, no. Please continue. Just let me get some popcorn so I can watch properly. Or maybe I can help?"

"Hmm. It's always good to have a partner when you're stretching."

"Your wish is my command."

She looked him over critically. "I don't think you're really dressed for exercise."

"No?" He looked down at his button-down shirt, jeans, and deck shoes. "What's wrong with my clothes?"

"There are too many of them." She ran a hand up his chest and popped the top button of his shirt open. He reached for her, but she backed away, cocking her head to the side. "Better. But not enough." She darted closer and slipped another button free.

The next time she sprang toward him, Luke was

prepared. He clamped his arms shut, holding her against him. "Oh, no you don't. You're not getting away again."

"Oooh, very macho," she teased.

"You want macho? How's this?" He bent his knees and lifted her to toss her over his shoulder like a sack of grain, one hand on her ass.

"Stop," she said, but the word was drowned in a fit of laughter that reverberated against his shoulder, neck, and back. "Oh my god, Luke, this is ridiculous."

With a growl, he tossed her onto the bed. "Now you're mine."

"Oh, yeah?"

He knelt on the bed, his knees on either side of her hips. "Yeah."

"Ooh," she said, throwing an arm across her eyes in a Victorian fainting pose. "I'm terrified."

"Right. Like there's anything that scares you."

She stilled, then dropped her arm and met his eyes. "You're kidding, right?"

"I was, sort of. But honestly, if you consider facing down my mother a fun puzzle, I can't think much scares you. So tell me what does?"

"Are you sure you wouldn't rather just have sex?"

Well, yeah. But he wanted her heart even more than he wanted her body and he'd never get that without her trust. "Can't we do both? Pretty please?"

That brought a little smile and a roll of her gorgeous eyes. She squirmed a bit and he moved to the side, setting her free to prop herself up on the pillows.

"Despite what your cousin says, your mother's not really *that* scary, you know."

"You're stalling."

"Tell me something you're afraid of first."

He paused and she laughed. "Not so much fun, is it?"

"I haven't ever really thought about it. Not in years. I remember very clearly what scared me when I was little, though. Maybe we should start there. Do you remember being five years old?"

"Of course. Kindergarten, first grade, thereabouts. Right?"

"Yeah. Well, when I was five, I was terrified of my uncle Rupert. He liked to jump out from behind corners and shout and wave his arms around. The first time he did it to me, I wet myself, which he thought was hilarious, so he kept it up for years. I dreaded his visits."

"What an asshole."

"Pretty much. He was my mother's brother. He died when I was twelve and I'm not ashamed to admit that the only thing I felt was relief."

"I don't blame you."

"So, your turn. What scared five-year-old Kai?"

"The creature under the bed. I was that kid who needed her parents to run a flashlight under there before she could go to sleep."

He nodded. "I used to have to do that with Georgie's closet. She developed a terror of it at about six that lasted a couple of years. The door had to be shut and a chair propped under the handle."

"You're a good brother. When you're not decapitating teddy bears."

He laughed. "I'm never going to live that down. Let's go for age ten. That's fifth grade, right? In fifth grade I was super short and skinny and miserably afraid I'd never fit in. You've heard the expression 'you're ugly and your mother dresses you funny?' That was me."

"No way."

"Way. I had a growth spurt when I was fourteen, but until then I was one of the shortest kids in my class. I was too small for any of the prestige sports at my school—football and basketball called for height and weight, baseball required strength, and tennis, which my parents insisted I learn, didn't earn me any points with the other kids."

"Poor little Luke.

"Yeah, well. When I grew I got my own back. What about you? What was fourth grade like?"

"Oh, geez. In fourth grade I was afraid of everything. After my dad died, my mother moved us from this little town where I'd spend my whole life to Dallas. There weren't many opportunities, either social or economic, for her where we lived. So when I was ten, I entered a much, much bigger school. I was afraid of never making friends, of getting lost, of public transportation…you name it."

"That must have been really tough."

"It was one of those situations where the fight or flight response saves your ass. I was furious at my mother—at ten, mortgages and life insurance policies aren't part of your mental landscape—and that fury spilled over onto all the things I was afraid of. I got in trouble a lot. I didn't really get over my resentment until I spent time in therapy, and by then my nonconformist attitude was too deeply ingrained."

"Which, I would imagine only got worse as a teen-ager?"

"Well, yeah." She sat up and looked him over. "Did you ever rebel? I mean, I know you're not following your parents' plans now, but did you go through that phase?"

"Not really. In my teen years, I realized I wouldn't be stuck in that house forever. As soon as I realized that, my greatest fear became *getting* stuck in that house forever. I learned to get along, to at least pretend on the surface that I was trying to please them. Rebellion would have been a tactical error. But I think the strategy of trying to please them made that fear worse in many ways. It's the only time in my life I ever had panic dreams. I regularly dreamed of being smothered."

"That's a pretty horrible nightmare to endure. No one in your house thought that was worth getting help for?"

"You think I told them? Weakness might have meant they wouldn't let me go away to school."

"Oh yeah."

"But it didn't last. I did get away. Even if I'm still

fighting the same damn fight twenty years later." He shook his head. "What about you? What scared you as a teenager?"

"Pinecrest." Her voice was completely flat and it took him a minute to place the name. When it came to him, he cursed himself for an ass.

"Shit. I'm sorry, Kai. Of course it did. I'm sorry."

"Don't be. I'm over it. And in a way it's…nice…to be able to talk about it with someone. I don't usually. None of my Vegas friends know. Well, Benny does. Benny knows everything. But between thirteen and eighteen, the idea of being locked up again hung over every choice I made. For the most part, I lived very carefully because of it. It…cramped my style."

"For the most part?"

"I made mistakes. Acted out when I shouldn't have. But even when I did, I was always aware of the stakes."

"That sucks."

"Like I said, it ended when I was eighteen. Once I gained my independence, moved away, started my own life on my own terms, the fear went away. Just like yours must have when you moved out of your parents' house."

He didn't think it had been that easy for her, but he let it go when she asked what he'd feared at twenty.

"Nothing," he replied.

"Oh, please."

"No, really. At twenty I thought I was invincible. I was still in school, so I hadn't had to look for a job. I was getting good grades, had a big group of friends, generally thought pretty well of myself. What about you?"

"Not being able to pay the rent. Not being able to support myself. When I first moved to Vegas, I had a little money. My dad had started a savings account for me and by the time I turned eighteen it had grown to about seven thousand dollars. That's a fair chunk of cash, but I was working for minimum wage and I was very aware that I was using up my savings. I rented a room from one of the women who worked in the same store I did and then switched to waitressing as soon as I could."

His life had been so damned easy compared to hers. He couldn't imagine her working in some behemoth box store, wearing a uniform every day, worrying that her paycheck wouldn't cover the rent. It tore him up inside.

"And now?"

"Now Benny pays me well and I like my apartment and I'm slowly replenishing my savings. I can afford to splurge every once in a while—though I don't foresee a huge number of massages in my future—and I have a financial safety net."

"Then I guess we're at the present again."

"I guess so. Have you come up with an answer?"

"I don't know if it's so much a fear. But they say we hate the things we fear, so maybe it is. I hate disappointing people. Letting them down. I'll do almost anything to avoid it. Maybe I fear it. Maybe it's leftover from those years trying to figure out how to avoid doing what my parents wanted without pissing them off."

Which made him sound like a wimp. Fuck. But it was true.

"It's okay to disappoint people once in a while, you know. In fact, it's pretty much inevitable. Have you ever pushed that to 'what will happen if I do disappoint this person'?"

"Not really."

"My therapist used to make me do that. See everything out to its logical conclusion."

"Huh. Well, I suppose the end result would be that fifth grade fear of being friendless."

"You know that wouldn't happen, right?"

"It's not in the nature of fear to be logical. I fear…"

She raised her eyebrows. "You fear?"

"I've known you such a short time, but I'm afraid of losing you."

"Luke—"

"Don't. You'll say it's not rational. I get that. You'll say I can't possibly feel this way. You're wrong. I do understand that *you* can't feel the same way. Not yet. But if I want you to trust me with your fears, I have to trust you with mine. Okay?"

She nodded and her chin wobbled a bit.

"So. What scares you?"

YOU. BUT THERE WAS NO way Kai could tell him that. He threatened her in ways she didn't even understand. She wanted him to stay. She wanted him to go. Above all, she wanted him to stop making foolish statements about love and loss.

But she could give him some truth, if not all of it. "I guess the thing that still keeps me up nights is that old fear of failure. Of being in a position where I'm forced to rely on other people. If you're stuck at age ten, I'm stuck at age twenty."

He curled his arms around her and drew her against him. "I could tell from the very beginning that you were twice as mature as I was."

"Oh, sure."

"No, really. I went back to my hotel the night after I invited you to this mess and immediately started freaking out."

"Why?"

"Because you were so damned sure of yourself. I thought you'd see right through me, probably make fun of me for not properly standing up to my parents. Your level of self-confidence made quite an impression."

"Really?"

"Of course. Why?"

"Because I thought that same thing about you. Oh, not the parental aspect, but that it would be nice to be as sure of myself as you were."

"A ten out of ten on the 'fooling the world' scale, then." He grinned, but she remained serious.

"Here's the thing, though… If that's who you have feelings for—the secure, self-assured person you met at Goody's—then you're going to be disappointed when you figure out that she isn't real."

"She *is* real. It's just that she's only a small piece of who you are."

"She's the piece you like. The piece you're attracted to."

"Actually, I'm far more selfish than that. What I like is that you—all of you, from the tiniest fragment to the overwhelming whole—make me feel good. When I'm around you, I feel…better. I wish I had more eloquent words. It's not that my problems disappear. They're still there, they just…weigh on me less. They feel like hurdles instead of brick walls."

"I do that?"

"You do."

"How?"

"If I knew that, I'd bottle it and make a fortune."

She shoved his shoulder, but an air of melancholy still hung in the air around him, reflected in his next words. "I wish I could do the same thing for you."

"You know, you promised to do something *else* for me. Or at least to try."

The left side of his mouth kicked up in a grin. "Is that a challenge?"

"No, not at all."

"Uh-huh." He trailed his fingers up her body. "If I'm going to work on fulfilling that promise, you're going to have to take these pajamas off, sexy as they are."

"If I'm the pot, you're the kettle." She tugged on his shirt. "There's no doubt you look good in a suit, but much better out of it, Captain Hottie."

He groaned at the nickname, pulled back and shrugged out of his shirt, then grabbed the hem of her pajama top and tugged it off over her head. His eyes dropped to her breasts and he touched the crest of one nipple with his forefinger. She'd begun the flirtation to distract him from the too-personal discussion, but his hands on her skin took her from zero to sixty in an instant.

He shifted off the bed and stripped out of his pants and she shimmied out of her pajama bottoms. He ran a finger along the twists of the coral snake that wound its way up her arm.

"When did you get this one?"

"Eighteen. My first legal tat. One of the guys I worked with had a brother in the business. It's not a complicated design, so he did it for a good price."

"Why?"

"Why the design or why the placement or why a tat at all?"

"All of the above, I suppose."

His hand still stroked her, sweeping up and down from her hip to her breast and back, making it hard for her to concentrate, but she tried to give him an honest answer anyway. "I'm not sure. I was making a statement, so I didn't want it hidden like my phoenix. It was mine. Something not generic, but chosen. I knew eventually I would get the wings because they've been in my head forever, but I couldn't afford them. And they wouldn't show. This…marked my transition. As to why the design, well, I liked the colors and I liked what it said about me. And it wasn't complicated, so I could afford it."

"Do you think you'll get more?"

"I don't know. Maybe. If I need to commemorate an event. But I've actually backed off on some of my body mods. I've let several of my piercings close up, mostly out of sheer laziness."

He ran a finger over the two barbells in her eyebrow. "What do they feel like?"

"They don't, really. It's sort of a tug. I had a tongue piercing for a while, and that one changed the way my whole mouth felt. But the eyebrows are more like ears, not particularly sensitive. You don't even really notice them."

"I notice them." He pressed his lips to her eyebrow, licked gently at the barbells, then blew on them. Heat swept through her. Okay, she'd lied—her eyebrows were suddenly incredibly sensitive. "I noticed them right away."

She swallowed. "What did you think?"

"I thought you were probably not like most women I'd met. I was right."

The rasp in his voice raised goosebumps all over her skin and she pushed him onto his back, impatient with the slow seduction. She pressed her mouth to his neck and touched the tip of her tongue to the pulsing skin where his collarbone split. She ran her hand down the flat strength of his chest and belly, then trailed her fingers up his erection. His hips jerked and she raised her pierced brow.

"You scare me when you look at me that way," he said.

"I think I like that." She worked her way down his body, her eyes never leaving his, using her hands to guide her, until she knelt between his legs, her mouth hovering over the head of his cock. "I sort of wish I hadn't gotten rid of that tongue piercing now."

She let her tongue learn him, around and around, base to tip and back again. Taste and texture and heat and strength, she lost herself in him until his fingers tangled in her hair and he pulled her back up his body.

"Not again," he insisted. "Together this time." He flipped their positions and reached out for the nightstand, scrabbling in the drawer for the bullet. In an instant he was inside her, the bullet buzzing between them. He held perfectly still, pressing the vibrator just where she liked, his eyes on her face as the heat and pressure and motion made her squirm against him.

Everything inside her clenched and she felt her

control slipping. She dug her fingers into his butt, urging him to move, but he held back until finally, finally, he gave in, thrusting against her, pushing her up and over that last hurdle into free fall. She convulsed beneath him, around him, and when he spilled into her, sending a second shockwave through her, it was utterly unlike any other experience of her life.

When he at last slipped from her body, she felt the loss deeply, though he was back in only a minute with a warm washcloth. He smoothed it gently over her, then pressed a hot, open-mouthed kiss to her still-throbbing core and a little squeak escaped her. She felt his grin against her skin and pulled him up for a kiss.

"Look at that," he murmured against her lips. "We did it."

"You mean *you* did. You don't have to beg for compliments."

"Nope. Much as I've told you I don't like to disappoint people, I can't take credit here. We did that together."

A warmth that had nothing to do with desire slipped through her. "Yeah, I guess we did."

He wrapped his arms around her, settled her cheek against his shoulder, and rubbed his chin over her head. "Let me get some sleep and we can try again."

CHAPTER 12

Friday morning, Luke had to go off with the guys for the bachelor party day of fishing. The alarm woke Kai, but she didn't bother to get out of bed, settling for a quick kiss goodbye before snuggling back under the covers. When she emerged again, it was nearly eleven. Since the cafe hadn't yet re-opened and she wasn't in the mood for any of the fancier restaurants, she ordered room service and forced herself to do a stretch routine while waiting for it to arrive, though she really didn't feel like it.

At noon, Georgie called and asked whether Kai was free to help set up for the bachelorette party. Kai agreed to meet her at the conference room with the bags of goodies Luke had brought from Vegas.

"Good news, bad news," Georgie said when Kai arrived. "Julian got the flowers and greenery, as you can see. That's the good. The bad is that my mother decided she should be here. I told her it was unnecessary and she wouldn't be happy, but she insisted."

Kai looked down at the two large bags of penis pops, novelty condoms, creams, lotions, and raffle vibrators and then back to Georgie. "Are we changing the theme?"

"Nope. It's a bachelorette party. She's had her fingers in every other part of this trip, she's not getting this one."

"You know, your cousin Gil warned me about your mother. He's scared of her."

"I imagine he is. She helped with his election and she's made no bones about the fact that without her he's nothing."

"Nice."

Georgie pulled out a seat and began to fill a vase with penis pops and cut greenery, turning it into a tiny phallic bouquet. Kai sat beside her to help.

"It's funny," Georgie said after a few seconds, without looking up from her task, "she wanted me to have this whole build-up to the wedding so I'd figure out I didn't want to marry Brad, but what I've really figured out is that I don't care to be around *her*, and that my father is just a puppet she bends to her will."

"Ouch. Well, the week's almost over. And then you'll be married and they'll go back to California and you'll only have to see them at holidays."

"Is that what you do with your family?"

"I don't have family."

"Oh, no!" Georgie focused on Kai, her eyes wide. "I'm so sorry."

"It's no big deal. My dad died when I was a kid and I haven't spoken to my mother in years. We never did get along. For things like Thanksgiving and Christmas, I go to Benny's. He invites a ton of people. Anyone who needs a place to crash or a family to eat with is welcome."

"That sounds great. Of course, you could have holidays with my family. You know, with Luke."

"Subtle."

"I'm trying to be braver. Say what I think more. And that's what I think."

"That I should spend the holidays with your family? Thanks, but no thanks."

"No. That you're good for my brother. He laughs with you. And even if he did invite you to my wedding as a joke, I can tell he really cares about you."

"And you care about him. It's very sweet."

"And you don't?"

Why did the Clarkes never ask the easy questions?

"I do. But we certainly aren't at the family-holiday-dinner stage yet."

Georgie tied a big pink bow around the first vase and set it aside to work on another. "We'll see."

An hour passed as they changed the room from a dull, conventional meeting room to a riot of pink, purple, and blue decorations, toys and games. They wrapped vibrators, lotions, and silly sexy games in brightly colored cellophane and tucked them into a large basket to pull from for the raffle. Sexy dice games, card games, and accessories surrounded the penis pop centerpieces.

Kai had asked Benny to throw in some costume essentials—cuffs, a flogger, a tickler, some leather and lace—and they were setting up a separate display in a corner for anyone who wanted to take risqué selfies when Julia arrived.

"That's disgusting," she said flatly. "And entirely inappropriate."

"Oh, please. It's just for fun," said Kai.

"My friends will not consider this fun."

"No," agreed Georgie, "but *mine* will. I told you you didn't have to come. My friends will get a good laugh out of dressing up. And they'll think the bouquets are a hoot."

"You didn't conceive such an offensive display until you met *her*."

Kai stiffened. Julia's constant snipes and insults ate at her. And worse, her reaction to them brought home to her just how much she was beginning to feel for Luke.

"This wasn't Kai's idea. It was mine. The girls wanted a bachelorette party and this is exactly what a bachelorette party should be. The guys are all off getting drunk on boats—excuse me, *fishing*—so why shouldn't we have a good time on our own?"

Julia sniffed, glared at Kai, and stalked out.

"Oh, this is going to be *so* much fun," Kai said.

"Now that she's seen it, I bet she doesn't show."

"We can only hope."

As they'd suspected, Julia didn't show up for the bachelorette party, which started at five. Marion did, however, and she was the life of the party. She insisted on being the one to describe the raffle items and she had Kai in hysterics by putting on a ring announcer voice to pull the winning tickets.

"In this hand," she said into the microphone, "wearing a grass-green cellophane wrapper, we have a lovely silicone vibrator with a turtle on it. Ladies, I can assure you I have *no idea* why anyone would put a turtle on a vibrator, but there it is. And in this hand"—she reached into a bucket—"ticket number 10135. Who's going to come claim this fabulous be-turtled toy?"

The hotel had supplied a female bartender for the evening, and Georgie insisted the woman take some raffle tickets so that she could get in on the action as well. Everyone took selfies with the toys and the accessories. Two of the bridesmaids tweeted their pictures, causing a huge storm of social media hilarity that bred even more photo-taking, and pretty soon flashes were going off everywhere.

Sue texted a picture of herself sucking one of the penis pops to her boyfriend, who'd arrived that morning and was out on the fishing trip. His response was immediate.

— We're almost back at the hotel. I'm holding you to the promise in that picture.

Sue cracked up and passed her phone around so everyone could see the text. Plenty of crude suggestions were made as to what she ought to reply, and Kai found herself laughing with the rest of them. She'd never understood the appeal of bachelorette parties before, but this one was fun.

They played a game of "Pin the Penis on Paulie," which won Elaine a purple glass dildo.

"I don't think I've ever been so proud to have an unerring sense of direction," she said.

"You only won because you haven't had as much to drink as the rest of us," Georgie retorted, dragging her over to get another glass of wine.

The party broke up at ten, and Kai went back up to her room, carrying three penis pops, a pair of sex suggestion dice, and a pair of pink fuzzy handcuffs. She shared the elevator with an elderly couple. The man examined her haul with raised eyebrows, but his wife winked and said, "You go, girl."

She was still giggling when she entered the suite. Luke was stretched out on the sofa in his sweatpants and a T-shirt, his hair wet, and she took a flying leap to land on top of him. He caught her, as she'd known he would.

"Nice party favors," he said. "Is that what I brought back from the store?"

"It is." She dropped the dice and one came up *tickle* and the other *breasts*.

"I think I love your job," Luke said, taking the dice's suggestion.

"Stop that." She pushed his hands away and he slid them down to slide beneath her skirt and cup her butt.

"I have an idea," he said.

"Yeah?"

"Yeah. How about you rinse out your hair so it doesn't run and we go swimming? I saw a suit in your bag. The pool's open all night, and no one's using it. Or at least they weren't a few minutes ago when I was out on the balcony."

"Ooh, swimming. That does sound good." Actually, what sounded good was Luke half-naked and wet. But she did enjoy swimming. "Did you bring trunks?"

"I did. Let's do it."

THE POOL WAS STILL DESERTED when they got downstairs. Underwater lights lit it in some places, leaving others dark. Luke dropped their towels on a chair while

Kai dove in at the deep end. The water was slightly cool but not cold.

"Come on in," she called to Luke.

"You won't believe who I see heading our way."

She looked into the hotel and saw his mother hurrying through the lobby, Georgie hard on her heels.

"Ugh. Come in. She can't yell at us if we're underwater."

He bent and dropped a kiss on her wet lips. "Nah, let me get rid of her. I don't want her to ruin our night. I have plans."

She laughed. "You and your plans."

"They've worked out well so far, right?"

"They have indeed. Okay. Go head off the wicked witch at the pass."

Luke cupped her cheek and stole another kiss before rising to stride away from the pool toward the door his mother was exiting.

Kai swam through the dappled water, coming up for breath occasionally to see Luke and Julia arguing. It seemed to last forever, but she couldn't hear what they were saying over the rush of the waterfall that dumped into the pool at one end. Georgie had come out, too, and was trying to drag her mother inside. But Julia pulled away and shoved a piece of paper at Luke and he glanced down and froze. What the hell was going on? She swam over to the steps and climbed out, shivering slightly in the cool night air.

"Luke? Is everything okay?"

Even in the darkness, she could see the bleakness in his blue eyes. All the heat had gone out of them, all the joy, and they were dull gray ice blocks in his frozen face. His expression stopped her in her tracks. Water dripped from her body, but she was paralyzed, she couldn't even reach for a towel.

"Don't do this," Georgie said. "Don't, Luke."

"Go inside. Both of you."

"Please, Luke, think about this," Georgie begged.

"Go. Inside. *Now*."

Georgie turned on her mother. "I hate you. I will hate you for the rest of my life."

"Don't be a child. Your brother understands."

"No he doesn't. But trust me, when he does, he'll hate you, too."

"Please." Luke rubbed his hand over his head. "Please. Go inside."

"No," said Georgie. "Not this time." But instead of remaining with Luke, she strode over and took Kai's hand.

And Kai knew. Somehow, Luke's mother had found out about her past. All of it. And now she'd pay for wanting to keep her mistakes to herself. For trying to grow beyond them.

Julia walked toward her. "I told you you would be better off accepting my deal."

"And I told you that I would keep my self-respect." Kai leaned in close to Julia's face. "And you should have listened to me. Because nobody dumps all over me without consequences." She didn't think, didn't consider what might happen, she just reached out with the hand Georgie wasn't hanging on to and shoved Julia backward into the pool.

Julia came up sputtering and furious. "I will have you arrested! You'll go to jail for assault! And this one you won't be able to wipe away by changing your name!"

"Try it," said Georgie in a voice as cold as Luke's eyes. "I'll say you fell. You have to be drunk to do what you've done, so maybe that's why you overbalanced."

"How dare you!"

Through it all, Kai felt Luke's icy gaze on them, though he never spoke. As Julia pulled herself from the water, Kai shook free of Georgie's grasp and stepped over to him. When she was close enough to touch him, she put a hand on his cheek, feeling the stubble of a long day.

"I'm sorry."

"All I asked for was the truth."

"I gave it to you. Every word, every action, it was all true."

"Bullshit. You didn't even give me your name."

"I did. My name is Kai Tyler."

"Then who's this?" He bent over and picked up the piece of paper that had fluttered to the ground during his argument with his mother. A printout of her mug shot, her name scrawled in red over the top—Karen Redmond.

"I had it changed. Because Kai sounded more interesting than boring old Karen with stepfather problems and a history of insanity, and because there was an amazing woman on television named Rose Tyler and I wanted to be her instead of me. But that's not the true problem."

"Really? You lying to me about who you were wasn't the problem? It sure sounds like a problem to me."

Anger overrode the pain cleaving her in two, gave her the strength to speak in spite of it. "No. The problem is that I fell off the fucking pedestal you put me on. I'm not perfect. I tried to tell you. I tried to tell you that I was fucked up and broken and you should leave me alone, but you didn't listen. All you saw was a tiny, minor dysfunction that you could fix and make yourself feel good about. And because *you* didn't listen, it's *my* fault."

He didn't say anything. Didn't move.

"So, yeah, I'm sorry for not detailing every event of my life for you so you could pass judgment on it before you slept with me. But that's not how it works in the real world." She turned to Georgie. "And I'm really, really sorry I won't be here for your wedding. I wish you everything good."

And then, because if she stayed one second longer she was going to break down and cry an ocean of tears and lose every tiny bit of self-respect she'd hung on to, she walked away. Her legs were stiff, her eyes burning, but she refused to run.

She made it up to the room before the tears won out.

She tossed all her clothes into a bag, determined to get out as soon as possible and worry about cleaning and ironing later.

You're such a fucking idiot. You never learn.

But recriminations wouldn't help. She'd dared to hope, dared to count on someone, and she'd taken the fall. As usual. Which meant there was still only one person outside herself she could count on. She made the call, then stood at the window, arms wrapped around herself, gazing at the now-empty pool deck.

"Kai." She hadn't even heard Luke come in, and she would not, could not face him. "Where are you going?"

"Home."

"How? It's two in the morning."

"I've called Benny. Don't worry, I won't steal any of the guest's cars. I haven't been hauled in for grand theft auto since I was sixteen. I have friends now, you see." At least one. Probably even two or three. If Celia had a car, she would have come, too.

"That's not what I was thinking."

"Well, I'd understand if you did. I mean, why should you think I would have changed just because it's been more than a *decade*?"

"Kai." He came up behind her and touched her on the shoulder and she flinched. She couldn't help it. His touch burned and a sob caught in her throat.

"Please leave me alone. I'll be out of your hair as soon as Benny gets here. Just do that one last thing for me."

He stayed there behind her, close enough for her to feel his breath, close enough that if she turned the slightest bit she could lean into him and shore up her own weakness with his strength, but she did no such thing. She held herself together, sucked in the hurt and hollowness and pain, and refused to budge. And after a long, long moment, he left.

And she cried.

LUKE STOOD OUT IN THE hallway and listened to the choked sobs coming from the room he had shared with…Karen? *No*, Kai.

Sixteen.

He hadn't even considered looking at the date on the arrest report. She could have been twenty, even twenty-five in the picture, with her hair a tangled mess and dyed a cheap matte black. He should have thought about the fact that the Kai he knew now took far better care of herself. But he'd been so fucking poleaxed by his mother's ambush.

Plus, he'd been waiting for the relationship to go bust. Had expected it. Anticipated it. Because he was *that* guy, the one people took advantage of, lied to, cheated on. He was the guy whose girlfriend had taken money from his mother to change him and whose business partner had backed out of a deal at the last minute. And he'd dumped all that baggage on Kai.

He didn't know how to make it right. That twitch, that flinch away from his touch had sent a fucking sword through his heart. She'd been hurt so often, let down over and over. And he'd done the same damned thing. Even if he walked back into that room and told her that he didn't care about her past, it wouldn't erase the fact that the instant things got tough, he'd deserted her. He hadn't even stuck around long enough to find out the facts, just ripped away the support he'd promised her, both implicitly and explicitly. How did he come back from that?

He leaned against the door, pressing his hands against the wood, wishing he could go to her, but knowing she was better off without him.

At least she had Benny. She wouldn't be alone. And while the idea of Kai turning to another man for solace—even one as paternal as Benny—spilled acid through his gut and tore his heart in two, it was a hundred, a thousand times better than the alternative—that he'd left her with no one.

The elevator doors opened and Georgie stepped out, faltering when she saw him standing there.

"She kicked you out?"

"Do you blame her?"

"Not really, no."

He shook his head. "I need to go find mom. It's time for some home truths."

A wistful smile passed over his sister's face. "You know how many times I've wanted to shove that woman into a pool?"

"You're not kidding."

Georgie hugged him tightly, then touched two fingers to his cheek. "She'll forgive you, Luke. She loves you."

"God, Sprout, I hope so. Benny's coming to pick her up. Will you stay with her until he does? I don't think she should be alone."

"Of course." Luke slipped his key through the lock and Georgie pushed the door open. With a little wave, she disappeared inside.

Luke waited another minute, then touched his fingers to his lips and to the door. It was as close as he could get. For now. He leaned against the door for a moment gathering his strength, then went to face a confrontation he'd avoided most of his life.

He banged on the door of his parents' room with no regard for the sleep of other guests on the floor. After a minute, his father answered, dressed in his pajamas.

"Lucas. What's going on?"

"Don't. Don't pretend she didn't tell you."

"Your mother only wants what's best for you."

"Bullshit."

"Lucas!" Julia stepped out of the bathroom. She had removed her makeup, but still wore her suit and heels. "You know I don't care for coarse language."

He fixed his eyes on her. "Then you won't like this. You've fucked with my life for the last time. I should have put a stop to it years ago, but I didn't. That's on me, and I'll own it. I didn't put my foot down then, but I am now. It's over. I am never going into politics. Ever. In fact, I am planning to quit my landscape architecture job and become a full-time firefighter. And there's not a damned thing you can do to stop me."

"Lucas—"

"No." He held up a hand. "You don't get a say in my life anymore. You have no respect for me. You lie to me and manipulate me and try to pay people I care about to do the same. And the worst part of it is that you don't even see anything wrong with treating your own son that way.

"Kai…" His throat clogged and he had to swallow hard to clear it. "Kai makes me a better person. I'm lucky as hell to have met her. And if I am far, far luckier than I deserve, she'll take me back. But whether she does or doesn't, it won't affect my relationship with you. I'll be here for the next two days. The rehearsal dinner and the wedding. I'll be polite. But you will leave me the fuck alone."

Julia sucked in a breath, but Luke didn't stick around to hear what she had to say. Benny wouldn't have had time to pick Kai up yet, so he went down to the bar, settled into a dark corner, and proceeded to get roaring drunk.

THE SOUND OF THE DOOR set Kai's nerves aflutter, but it wasn't Luke. Only Georgie.

"Sorry," she said, as if reading Kai's mind.

"Don't be. I'm happy to see you." Even if looking at Georgie's blonde hair and blue eyes squeezed her heart even harder.

"I wanted to tell you…" Georgie sat on the sofa, her hands clasped between her knees. "I wanted to say I'm sorry. For how things turned out. If I'd known she hired a PI, I would have warned you."

"A PI? Wow. I didn't realize I ranked so high on her shitlist."

"Yeah." Georgie patted the sofa. "You want to talk about it?"

"Not particularly, no. But I suppose it's better if someone in your family knows the truth."

"Kai—"

Kai held up a hand. "Don't, okay? Just let it be. I'll tell you about the car, but I don't want to talk about Luke."

Georgie nodded, pressing her lips together, and Kai sat with a sigh.

"I had some issues when I was a kid. Your brother knows. You can ask him. Anyway, when I was sixteen, my stepfather moved us out to California. It didn't make all that much difference at first—I'd been in boarding school for two years already—but it was awkward. I came home for summer break and I didn't have a place. No friends, nothing familiar. I got into it a couple of times with my stepfather and one day he shoved me down the stairs."

"Oh my God."

"It sounds worse than it was. Seriously. It was the first time he'd ever laid a hand on me, but it freaked me the fuck out and I ran. Hit the garage, where his fancy new BMW was sitting with the keys in the ignition, and took off."

"And he pressed charges? Wasn't he afraid of what you'd say?"

"It was *he said, she said*. And I had a history of mental instability. He said I was lying. He dropped the charges after forty-eight hours, saying he thought maybe I was just having a breakdown. That was that. There was an arrest, but no conviction. My record is clean, so your mother must have really dug deep."

"You pissed her off, telling her you had too much self-respect to take her money."

"In retrospect, that might have been a mistake." She tried to smile, but her lips didn't work.

"How did you get so brave? A guy pushes you down the stairs when you're a kid and you're still standing up to people. I never had anything like that happen to me, and I'm terrified of confrontation."

"It's not bravery."

"It is. You went away for a week with a guy you'd only just met."

"And look how well that turned out. Stupidity, not bravery."

"It wasn't stupid. Seriously. I know you don't want to talk about Luke, but don't count him out yet, okay? You're the best thing that ever happened to him and he knows it. Just…leave the possibility open?"

Kai couldn't answer. "Look, I need to take a shower and get the chlorine off me before Benny gets here. He drives a fancy car and he won't want me damaging the leather."

"How about I pour us a drink while you shower?"

"Yeah, that sounds good. In fact, how about you pop that champagne I won the other night? It's in the fridge." She'd almost taken it down to the pool earlier, but she hadn't been sure about the hotel's policy toward such things. She'd planned to have a single glass with Luke, but using it to drown out her misery now seemed like a good plan. She could go back to abstinence in the morning. And easily would, if her recollection of the misery of a champagne hangover was correct.

She stepped into the shower in her bathing suit, cranked the water to hot, and let it sluice over her for a couple of minutes. Georgie hadn't mentioned her red, swollen eyes, but she knew she looked a wreck. Her entire body hurt, from the soles of her feet to the tightly clenched fist of her heart and straight up to her tear-clogged throat. Even the very follicles of her hair ached. The hot water didn't help much, but it gave her a few minutes to get herself under control without having to kick Georgie out. The girl was only trying to help.

When she felt capable of facing Georgie again, she stepped out, dried herself off and pulled on a pair of leggings and a Ramones T-shirt. Avoiding the mirror, she went out and took the glass of champagne Georgie handed her.

"Cheers," she said. "May you and Brad live happily ever after."

They drank until a banging on the door signified Benny's arrival. She ran over and opened it before considering the fact that Georgie—with her history with Joe—might prefer to be elsewhere.

Benny swept into the room, arms outstretched, and pulled her into a hug. "Where's the dickhead?"

"He's not a dickhead. And I asked him to disappear until we're gone."

Benny put a finger under her chin and tilted her head up so he could see her eyes. "He made you cry. In my book, that makes him an asshole."

"He was an asshole," Georgie chimed in. "But it's not his natural state. He'll come around."

"And you are?"

"I'm Georgie." She held out a hand, but Benny—in the only act of downright rudeness Kai had seen in all the years she'd known him—made no move to take it.

"Great. The other Clarke destruction engine. Of course you'd defend him."

"Benny, leave Georgie alone."

"No, it's okay. I get it."

Georgie headed for the door, but Kai extricated herself from Benny and hugged her. "I'm sorry I screwed up your week. Be happy, Georgie. You deserve it."

"So do you." Georgie patted her on the back and left with a last, troubled glance at Benny.

"Give me your bags and let's get the hell out of here," Benny said. "This place is so stuffy I don't know how you could even breathe."

"It's not so bad. But I'm definitely ready to leave." She went into the bedroom for her suitcases and found herself stuck, paralyzed by the sight of the bed and the covers and the memories she and Luke had created there.

"Don't," said Benny, coming up behind her and plucking the luggage from the bed. "Put it out of your mind."

Only when they were safely away from the hotel did Kai begin to relax. She melted into the soft leather seats of Benny's Mercedes and closed her eyes. Hollow and heavy and hurt, she wanted to hide away and not see another living being. Maybe ever.

But Benny wasn't the quiet type. "You want to talk about it?" he asked.

"I got above myself. Thought I could have it all. Same old, same old." Benny was the one person in her life who knew her entire past. He'd explained before he hired her that he always did background checks and had asked if there was anything she wanted to tell him before he did. They'd discussed what he would find—changing her name didn't change her social security number, and although the charges against her had been dropped, she wasn't one hundred percent sure a dedicated researcher couldn't uncover them. Benny had glowered at the story and she'd counted the job as lost until he asked why she hadn't crashed the damned car instead of letting her stepfather have it back undamaged.

He'd always backed her. Right from the beginning. She didn't need fair-weather friends like Luke Clarke. Or biological family like her mother. She had Benny. And Celia. And Joe. She hadn't appreciated them enough, but that was going to change.

"Celia said you probably fell in love."

I don't think love is supposed to hurt like this. "Celia reads too many romance novels."

"You'll get no argument from me on that."

Kai closed her eyes, pretending to sleep. Not that she was fooling Benny, but she couldn't deal with talking.

The sun was peeking over the horizon when they pulled up in front of Benny's huge, hacienda-style home.

"I know it's out of the way, but do you mind driving me home?"

"Yes."

"Oh. Okay. No worries, I'll call a cab."

"No you will *not.* You're family, Kai. You'll stay with me for a couple of days until you're better." Benny climbed from the car and grabbed her suitcases from the trunk, leaving her no choice but to follow him.

"Really, Benny, I'm fine."

"No, you're not. You look exhausted. I made up the guest room for you and you can stay as long as you like."

"I do need to sleep." For maybe a month. Or the rest of her life. "But tomorrow—I mean, this afternoon—I'm going home."

Benny shook his head. "We'll talk when you wake up."

"Thanks, Benny."

"Anytime, kiddo."

Kai crawled into the big, fluffy bed in Benny's guest room without even taking off her clothes. The beginnings of a headache throbbed behind her eyes.

CHAPTER 13

L UKE FINALLY WENT UPSTAIRS AFTER the bar closed at four, but even drunk he couldn't sleep. The bed smelled like Kai and the room was too goddamned empty. Everywhere he looked, even in the closet, he was reminded of her. He'd betrayed her in the worst possible way. How was he going to make it up to her? Because it was inconceivable that he should live the rest of his life without her.

At some point, the exhaustion and booze dragged him under. He woke to the piercing ring of his cell phone but by the time he found where it had fallen under the couch, he'd missed the call. Georgie. A second later, a text popped up.

℈ Are you going after her?

Damned straight. But not today. He had things to do first.

℈ Later. I'll be here for the rehearsal dinner and the wedding. Don't worry.

He glanced at the clock. 1:10. Almost six free hours,

all of which he could use to take the first steps toward a new life. But first, he needed a shower and a gallon of coffee.

THE DUELING SMELLS OF COFFEE and bacon greeted Kai when she woke. Her head still pounded and her stomach revolted at even the thought of bacon—one of her all-time favorite foods—testifying to the quantity of champagne she'd consumed at the hotel. Coffee, though. Coffee would be helpful. But first she had to do something about her desert-dry sour mouth, so she dug around in her makeup bag for her toothbrush. The lights in the bathroom stabbed at her swollen, gritty eyes and she avoided the mirror as she brushed her teeth and tongue and splashed water over her face.

Still wearing the clothes she'd slept in, Kai trudged downstairs to the kitchen. Benny stood at the stove turning the bacon. He turned when Kai came in.

"Coffee's over there." He tilted his head toward the counter.

Kai filled a mug and sipped at it cautiously. She'd had Benny's coffee before and in general it reminded her of tar pits, but that wasn't such a bad thing just at the moment.

The doorbell rang, echoing through Kai's skull. "Watch the bacon," Benny said as he dashed out of the kitchen.

He returned a moment later and when Kai saw who was following him, her eyes filled with tears.

"Evie! What are you doing here?" But of course, she knew. Benny always tried to give people what they needed.

"*Someone* called me at a ridiculous hour and told me he'd bought me a ticket on the seven a.m. flight out of Knoxville." She glared at Benny. "There'd better be coffee."

"There is," he assured her, "and bacon. And English muffins. And you didn't *have* to come. I didn't pay for the ticket until you agreed."

"Of course I did. You said you needed me. When do you ever need anyone?"

"I said no such thing," Benny grumbled. "I merely mentioned that Kai was upset and I wasn't precisely sure what to do about it."

"Uh-huh." Evie poured herself a mug of coffee, took a deep draught, and sighed happily. "Oh, that's better." She used one foot to push out the chair opposite her at the table. "Sit, Kai, and tell me what's going on. Let Benny finish making breakfast."

Kai sat. "I wish Benny hadn't called you. I feel like an idiot."

Evie patted her hand. "I'm familiar with that feeling. I think that's why they call it falling in love—you feel clumsy, foolish, always tripping over your emotions."

"It's not love."

"Mmm."

"I've known him less than a week!"

"Time didn't make a lot of difference to me and Griff."

"But you're not me. You're…"

Evie raised her eyebrows. "I can't wait to hear this."

Benny plunked a big platter of bacon and another of English muffins down on the table then pulled out a chair and sat down. "Me, either."

"You have your shit together. You're open, easy to get along with. People like you. They take one look and know they can trust you. I certainly did."

"Honey, they trust you, too."

Kai thought about how quickly Luke had turned on her. Yes, he'd come upstairs afterward to try to apologize, but if he'd really trusted her, if he'd really loved her the way he said he did, would he have pulled away so quickly?

"It doesn't matter. Whatever happened, whatever

might have been…I just want to get my life back."

"Are you sure?" Evie asked. "I'm not asking you to share anything you're not comfortable with, but if it was just an argument, well, they happen. He hurt you. I can see that. But that doesn't have to be the end of the relationship. If he didn't mean to, and you want to save it, you could fight for him."

She could. He wanted her back. But how much worse would the pain be the next time he turned on her?

She shook her head. She couldn't talk about Luke. Not even with Evie. "Who's on the schedule tomorrow?" she asked Benny.

"Like I would know? I'm not the manager."

"No, but you're a total control freak. I don't remember the schedule off the top of my head, though I have it on my phone so I can go look if I have to, but you can't pretend with me. I'm about ninety percent sure you've been in every day that I've been gone, and I'm absolutely positive you've already checked the schedule for both today and tomorrow."

Evie snorted. "Busted."

Benny shrugged. "So maybe I'm a little bit compulsive. Is that necessarily a bad thing? Why do you want to know, anyway? You thinking of going in tomorrow?"

She swallowed the lump in her throat. "Yeah. I could use the time to start putting together next month's schedule. Celia wants more hours, but she's hard to schedule around the dancing. I need to talk to her about what her shows look like and I have to see when Joe's training and fighting."

"Uh-huh. And you can't do that the next day you're scheduled?"

"I *can*. But I can also do it tomorrow, when I won't be distracted by helping customers and stuff because I won't have to be out front."

"As it happens, both Celia and Joe are working tomorrow. They're opening."

"Great. I'll head in midday then." With a little luck, by one o'clock she would be deeply immersed in scheduling and wouldn't think about the wedding. "Do you have time to take me home when we're done eating? If not, I'll catch a cab. I need to do laundry and unpack."

And she needed some alone time. By the time she went back to work she'd be able to smile and greet shoppers and play the cheeky extrovert again, but for the moment she craved the quiet comfort of her tiny apartment.

The rehearsal dinner was in a private room behind the resort's steakhouse. Luke arrived five minutes late to minimize any forced mingling or awkward questions—everyone liked Kai, they'd wonder where she was. He slipped into the room and found his designated seat at one of the round center tables facing the head table which, to his surprise, was set for only four people.

Sue came up next to him. "Georgie's been down here all afternoon rearranging like a madwoman. She had them yank the long table and reset for four, then moved your parents and mine to a table over there"—she pointed to the left side of the room—"along with the other aunts and uncles. Brad's family is on the other side."

I will hate you for the rest of my life. His sister hadn't been kidding. "Does Julia know?"

"Oh, yeah." Sue bared her teeth. "Elaine and I helped Georgie with the new seating plans and your mother arrived just as we were putting out the place cards. She tried to get Georgie to put it back the way it was, but Georgie told her—oh my God, Luke, I couldn't believe it—Georgie told her to 'butt the fuck out or go the fuck home.'"

Holy hell. For a moment, he almost felt sorry for his mother. She'd sown the wind, not expecting the whirlwind. He shook off the moment of pity. "Is she here? Georgie, I mean."

"Not yet. I guess she and Brad are waiting to make a grand entrance."

Sue's boyfriend came up and handed her a drink. "Hey, Luke. Can I get you anything?"

"No, thanks." His head still ached from the night before, and he missed Kai. If she were beside him, she would know precisely how to navigate this crowd, how to make the best of an evening he dreaded. Of course, if she were beside him, he wouldn't dread the evening to start with.

From the corner of his eye, Luke saw Brad and Georgie enter the restaurant. Holding hands, they headed straight for the front table, where they sat with Elaine and the best man, who Luke had met on the fishing trip. Taking the hint, everyone else shuffled around and found their seats. When conversation began to die down, Brad and Georgie rose.

"We'd like to thank you all so much for coming," Brad said. "It hasn't been the week we expected, but Georgie and I feel privileged and lucky to have such good friends to share both good times and bad." He smiled down at Georgie and she took up the speech.

"On your invitations, this was called the rehearsal dinner. But we deliberately planned our wedding to be fairly straightforward so that we wouldn't need a rehearsal and, as it turns out, we *really* didn't need one, because we're not getting married."

At the collective indrawn breath of the crowd, Luke cursed himself. He'd been so caught up in the clusterfuck of his own relationship that he'd lost track of his whole purpose in spending a whole week at this fiasco. He had forgotten that his sister might need him. But when he focused on Georgie, Brad had his arm around her shoulders. Her own arm was around his waist. Whatever had happened between them, it clearly wasn't a tragedy that would ruin her life.

As if she could feel his thoughts, Georgie looked directly at him before she spoke again. "Brad and I have a great deal in common. One big characteristic we share is that we've both tried to avoid risk in personal relationships. We're both confrontation-averse. We are best friends and for both of us, getting married was an easy decision. A partner who cares about you is worth a lot. But what both of us have realized over the course of this week is that to get real love, the kind that changes your life, you have to be brave. You have to make the hard decisions instead of the easy ones." A tear slipped down her cheek. "And we deserve that. You deserve that." The others might think she meant the last three words generically, but Luke understood—she was talking to him.

"This week was supposed to be a celebration of a new phase of life," Georgie continued. "We hope that tomorrow, even though there won't be a wedding, you will help us celebrate that new phase with cake, champagne, a band, and plenty of love to go around."

A fierce pride swept through Luke. Georgie had grown up. Better, stronger than he'd ever expected. Her life was in order and she'd let him know in no uncertain terms that it was time for him to put his to rights, too.

He waited until some of the commotion died down, then made his way up to the head table and leaned over to kiss her cheek. "I won't ask if you're okay. I can see you are. Maybe more than you've been since we got here. I'll just tell you that I love you. So much. And I am sorry if I don't tell you that often enough."

"Love you right back, big brother. Now, get out of here."

He got.

BEING IN HER OWN SPACE helped Kai get her equilibrium back, but by the time Sunday morning rolled around she was more than ready to get out. Her hangover had abated after generous applications of coffee, but her body still weighed more than it should and it was hard to breathe past the boulder in her throat. Even a two-mile run hadn't eased the constriction in her chest, and she hadn't slept at all. Her double bed—more than adequate most of the time—felt simultaneously too small and cavernously empty.

Before leaving, she applied a bright blue swath at the front of her currently black hair to draw attention away from her face, and matched it with oversized blue earrings. Still, she applied her makeup with a heavier than usual hand to hide the shadows and redness that persisted around her eyes and conceal the pastiness of her skin.

At the shop, things were blessedly normal. When she walked in, Joe was showing off cock rings to a tall, thin man in his late thirties or early forties with all the authority of one who had tried them—which she knew for a fact he had not. Celia had two women in the hosiery section discussing the pros and cons of fishnets as party wear.

Kai slipped into the back room and put her purse away, then pulled out the scheduling book. A couple of minutes later, Celia stuck her head through the curtain.

"I thought I saw you sneaking in. You doing okay?"

"Yup. Working on next month's schedule. You have a minute to go over your hours?"

"Sure." But before she sat down, her eyes went to the screen over Kai's shoulder. "Uh, there might be a problem."

Kai spun on her chair and glanced at the television. Joe was standing, hands on hips, upper body tilted slightly forward in unmistakable threat. His head blocked her view of his adversary's face, but she didn't need to see it to recognize him.

Luke.

Her stomach dropped and a wave of bile rose up her

throat. Though she was sitting down, she put a hand out to steady herself. Celia squatted in front of her. "Are you all right? What can I do?"

"Nothing. Get out there and make sure Joe doesn't kill him. It's bad for business. I'll be there in a minute." Celia waffled until Kai forcibly shooed her away.

She allowed herself three deep breaths to quell the nausea and dizziness, then composed her face and walked out into the shop. Thank goodness they had no customers.

"You need to leave," Joe was saying.

"Just tell me—" Luke spotted her. "Kai."

"What are you doing here, Luke?"

"I tried your apartment and you weren't there. So I called Benny. Evie—your old boss?—told me you'd be at the shop."

Kai made a production of looking at her wrist, though her vision was far too fogged to see. She swallowed hard. "Shouldn't you be at your sister's wedding?"

"She's not getting married." Luke shot a glance at Joe. "They announced it last night at the rehearsal dinner."

"Why not?" Joe's question was low, but it rang loud in the heavy silence.

"They said they loved each other, and that the decision to get married had been easy, but that they had talked it over and maybe easy wasn't the answer. Anything else you'll have to get from Georgie."

"Thanks for the news," Joe said. "You can go now."

Luke fixed his gaze on Kai. "Take a walk with me."

"Why?"

"Because I don't want to do this here. I'm pretty sure you don't, either."

"Luke, there's nothing left to do."

"Yeah, there is. And if you don't care whether your coworkers and customers hear it, that's fine with me. I figure I owe you whatever humiliation you want."

"Oh," said Celia. "You're planning to humiliate

yourself? Then you can stay."

"No, he can't," said Joe.

And just when Kai thought it couldn't get worse, Benny walked in and said, "I agree." He stepped around the counter and put a hand on her shoulder. "Out, Clarke. You're not wanted here."

Still, Luke watched her and when she had the strength to meet his steady gaze, the emotions burning there seared through her. She shook her head and patted Benny's hand.

"Say what you need to say."

"I'm sorry. You were right. But you were also wrong. It's not you who's broken. It's me. I'm fucked up and broken and I hurt the ones I love."

"No—"

"*Yes*. Listen to me. What happened, it was entirely on me. I blamed you because it was easier than admitting that you scared the hell out of me. What I feel for you, it has no precedent. I told you at the beginning that I wasn't sure I was cut out for love. And it turns out I suck at it. But I want to try. I don't have the right to ask you to forgive me, but I'm going to do it anyway. Because you have the biggest heart of anyone I've ever met and if I get really lucky, you might cut me a break I don't deserve at all."

Tears slid down her face. "I don't know what you want from me."

"I want a chance. A chance to make it right. To start over and try to make you half as happy as you make me."

"I don't fit into your world, Luke."

"Then I'll remake my world from the ground up so you do. Because none of the rest of it matters."

"Oh God, Luke. What am I supposed to say to that?"

"Say yes. Please. At least, don't say no. Give me one more shot."

"I don't know if I can."

He took a single step forward. "Sweetheart, you can

do anything. That should never be in doubt. If you don't want to, I get it. But you *can.* If you believe nothing else I've ever said to you, believe that."

Oh, how she wanted to trust him. She had no doubt at all that he believed his own words. But maybe he still wasn't seeing the real her. Did she have it in her to give him another chance to carve her heart into pieces?

He nodded. "I don't blame you. I wouldn't trust me, either. But if you change your mind, you have my number." He stepped forward and put a piece of paper on the counter, bringing him so close she could touch him. And she almost did. "That's my address. And email. And Georgie's information. She wanted you to have it.

"Anyway, I'll go. But one thing you need to know before I do. In case I haven't been clear—I love you. I always will. So when you get to thinking maybe you screwed up in some way and you don't have anyone you can count on, remember me. I won't make the same mistake again. I'll always be there for you."

He turned to leave, his shoulders sagging, and she finally broke.

"Luke."

He spun so fast he almost smacked into her as she came around the counter. She stood right in front of him, studying those bright, sky-blue eyes. He waited, perfectly still, until she wiped the tears off her face and nodded. "Yes."

"Yes? Like, yes, you'll give me another chance?"

"If you're sure."

"I've never been surer of anything. Ever." He opened his arms and she stepped into them. Pressed against him, his hand cradling the back of her head and his body rocking slightly, she felt the rise of his chest as he sucked in an enormous breath. The muscles of his body relaxed one by one as he let it out, and for the first time she believed down to her toes that he'd suffered their separation as acutely as she had.

"Thank you," he whispered and her heart cracked. Who *said* that? He might be broken, but he worked harder at being good than anyone she'd ever met. So she gave him the words she'd planned to give him at the pool.

"I love you."

Behind her, Benny coughed. "You two want to take it somewhere else? Kai, you're on vacation. And you're a mess. Get out of my store."

She managed a watery laugh and Luke squeezed her tight before loosening his grip so she could face Benny. "Yes, boss."

"Treat her right," Joe warned.

"I intend to." Luke handed Joe the slip of paper from the counter. "If I don't, here's my address. Feel free to come beat the living hell out of me. I'll deserve it."

Joe's eyes flicked to the paper and Kai remembered that it also had Georgie's information. Was that why Luke wanted Joe to have it? Neither man said anything about the second address.

"Here," said Celia, handing Kai her purse. "And don't let me forget to say I told you so."

"As if you'd forget a thing like that."

"Yeah, I suppose it's not likely."

And holding tight to Luke's hand, Kai stepped out of the shop into the bright afternoon sun.

Epilogue

Six months later.

Kai was still sleeping when Luke got home, but the minute he slipped into bed, she knew. No matter how quiet he was, even in sleep she felt him. She rolled over, buried her face in his chest, and sniffed.

"You had a fire."

"I took a shower."

"I can still smell it."

He'd been with Las Vegas Fire & Rescue for two months. Because it would give him a better chance of getting a job, he'd stuck it out in California for the first four months they'd been together so he could remain with his volunteer company.

At the three month mark, they agreed that he'd take whichever firefighting job he could get—California or Las Vegas. Benny had a shop in Sacramento, so Luke had applied there as well as San Francisco. But the Clark County job came through first and he'd moved immediately.

She worried about him when he was on shift, which he knew without her ever telling him. During the day, he texted periodically and she answered when things were slow in the store. He assured her that most of his calls weren't fires, which she knew to be true, but it was an adjustment. Caring about someone was harder than she'd imagined, and she was beginning to understand why Georgie had been so reluctant to stay with Joe.

Not that they were been any good at staying apart, either. Georgie had called Kai two weeks after her aborted wedding and asked for Joe's number. Months later, they were still working through their issues, but both of them seemed committed to doing so. And even when he was bitching about "overly emotional women," Joe was happier than Kai had ever seen him.

"Whatcha thinking about?" Luke asked.

"Your sister. Your job. Our lives."

"Mmm. I think our life is pretty good. Though we ought to look for a bigger place." They hadn't managed to move out of Kai's apartment, mostly because she was still hesitant to take on a house payment. Luke didn't push, but he didn't back off, either.

"Maybe your next off day we can look for a place."

"I've got twenty-four hours off now."

"Yeah, but I have to work. In fact, I have to be at work in five hours and I didn't get much sleep. So make like a pillow." She patted his chest and rested her cheek against his shoulder.

"I don't want to be a pillow. I'd much rather be a Goody."

She choked on a laugh. "Luke!"

"You have five hours. Sleep for the last four."

She peered up at him. "Are you promising me a full hour of fun and games?"

"Hell, no. I'm not nineteen. I'd never last an hour. I *am* promising you at least one orgasm and then a massage."

He ran a finger down her cheek and her body tightened. He was more than capable of fulfilling the first part of the promise, and he wasn't half bad at the second, either. Her life was infinitely better with him in it, both in and out of bed. And after two solid months, she was finally accepting that it might stay that way.

She slid her fingers through his hair and pulled his

mouth down to hers. "You know I can't resist a massage."

Turn the page for an excerpt of

Toying with His Affections

Excerpt of TOYING WITH HIS AFFECTIONS

CHAPTER 1

THE PALE, PINK LIGHT OF dawn should have made the familiar house with its weathered grey clapboard and neat white trim appear charming. Welcoming, even. But it didn't. All Evie felt as she pulled into the driveway was dread, and all she noticed was the darkness of the shadows hiding the deep front porch.

No welcome home light here, though her aunt had known Evie would be arriving overnight.

Maybe the bulb's out. Or she wants you to know you don't have to bother stopping at the main house yet.

Or maybe Patricia was no happier to have her than Evie was to be here. Though she'd spent most of her childhood living with her aunt, Evie had never been able to read the woman. And it hadn't been Patricia herself who had called. No, that had been left to Evie's cousin, Candace. No matter, Patricia needed her, and Evie owed her far too much to deny her anything. So here she was and here she'd stay.

She turned her attention to the detached garage. In the ten years she'd been away, an apartment had been built atop it, precisely matching the style of the house. Candace had sent her the key, so at least she could shower and change out of the sweats she had worn for the long drive from Vegas before facing her aunt.

As she slid from the car and stretched, joints popping and cracking, her eye caught the boxes in the back seat with their prominent markings. She didn't feel like hauling them up the stairs to the apartment—especially as they would likely remain unopened the entire time she was there—but unless she wanted the whole town talking about how she sold sex toys for a living in Las Vegas, she had to get them out of sight.

The garage would do fine. With her broken leg, Patricia wasn't apt to be driving any time soon. After all, that's what she had Evie for.

The boxes weren't huge, but they were heavy. Her boss and best friend, Benny, had slid them into the back of her Civic as they said goodbye. "You never know," he'd said with a wink, bussing her on the cheek, "they just might come in handy."

Right. Like the upright citizens of Fairview, Tennessee, would be so eager to be seen buying sex toys from the prodigal daughter. Or prodigal niece. Or whatever.

Shake it off. You're here. They'll just have to deal with it.

With a sigh, she opened the garage. No fancy electronics here, just twist the handle and raise the door. Beside Patricia's ancient, maroon convertible Chevy there was plenty of room in the two-car space to store the cartons. Evie dragged them out of the car and plopped them down behind the various gardening implements Patricia's injury would prevent her from using.

That project complete, she pulled the suitcase from her trunk and climbed the stairs to the apartment where she'd be staying for the next several months.

A multicolored area rug covered most of the floor in the single, large room. Along the right side, beneath the windows that looked toward the main house, a built-in counter functioned as a desk. A big fireplace took up the far wall, with doors on either side that turned out to lead into a bathroom that had been divided into two sections, each tucked into a corner under the eaves. One held a tub and vanity, the other a toilet and sink.

On the left wall was a full-sized bed, hidden behind a needlepoint screen. A memory assailed her of her mother sitting on the couch in their little Nashville apartment stitching a canvas of a ballerina. "All the women in my family do some form of needlework," she'd said. "It may be the only thing I actually have in common with them." Evie had been seven or eight at the time, and that ballerina, framed the minute she could afford to do so, was now packed away with some of her most precious possessions. A well-worn loveseat provided the sole place to sit in the room, and a closet-sized kitchen just left of the entry contained a dorm-room refrigerator, a toaster oven, a two-burner electric stove, and a sink.

But no coffeemaker that she could see. That was going to be a problem. *Think about it tomorrow. Just get through today.*

She put her clothes away in the built-in drawers on the back wall of the closet and hung up her lone dress and two nice shirts.

The sun was fully up now, streaming through the windows, hurting her tired eyes. She dropped the matchstick shades to dim the light and give herself a bit of privacy. Her aunt would be expecting her. Time to clean up and face the day.

Because of the slope of the roof, there was no shower in the bathtub under the eaves, and Evie's long hair slid down the drain when she tucked her head beneath the faucet to rinse out the shampoo. By the time she'd gotten most of the conditioner out, she'd resolved to spend a few of her remaining dollars on a hand shower.

She wound her damp, wavy tresses into a loose knot and stuck a pair of chopsticks into it. She'd left her blow dryer in Vegas, knowing she had no one in Fairview to impress. The dress she'd hung in the closet was more than a bit wrinkled, but Evie didn't own an iron, let alone an ironing board, so she pulled it on and hoped her aunt wouldn't ride her too badly over her sloppy appearance. At least the dress gave her self-confidence a bit of a boost.

As she walked from the garage to the main house, her eye caught on the masses of roses on both sides of the birch steps. She'd planted those bushes with her uncle half a lifetime ago, in the first days after she'd come to live in Fairview after her mother's death. They'd searched nursery after nursery for the perfect color. Patricia had suggested yellow because Emma, Evie's mother, had been so cheerful, but when Evie actually saw the flowers she'd burst into tears. They were too happy, too bright. And pink were too girly. Red too somber. Finally, they'd found what the nursery owner called a "Tracey Wickham" rose with pale yellow petals that darkened to deep pink at the tips.

In the six years Evie had lived with her aunt and uncle, the roses had been her responsibility. Harry had taught her how and when to prune and fertilize the bushes, what to look for when it came to deciding whether insects were good or bad. At the memory, a sick pang went through her.

"I'm so sorry, Harry," she whispered, touching one of the flowers and inhaling its rich, sweet scent. "I wish I could have been here for you."

Shaking off the melancholy, she climbed the porch steps and rang the doorbell. She heard the thump of crutches approaching from the other side and reflexively stood straighter.

The close-cropped curls of the woman who opened the door had grayed slightly since Evie had last seen her, but the intervening years had left few other marks. Evie straightened even further, well aware the same could not be said for her.

"Hello, Aunt Patricia."

"You're a little old to be calling me Aunt these days. Patricia will do fine."

"Oh. Okay." Evie stilled her fidgeting fingers. "May I come in?"

Excerpt of TOYING WITH HIS AFFECTIONS

Patricia winced—either at the boldness of the question or at the reminder of her own lack of hospitality, Evie couldn't be sure—and swung the door wider. "Of course. Please. I was just taking you in. You haven't changed much despite the years."

Really? Evie certainly felt different. Or she had, until she found herself fidgeting under her aunt's scrutiny. "I told Candace I'd be here last night or this morning. And the apartment was all set up. I needed a few days to get my things together and contact my boss about a replacement at work." Benny had been in New York dealing with an issue in his Times Square store when Evie had called. He was none too pleased to have to return to look after the Vegas shop which, under Evie's supervision, usually "took care of itself."

"But all that foolishness is over now. You're back home where you belong. Let me make tea and we can discuss the plan for the day."

Evie shoved away her immediate, defensive reaction to Patricia's dismissal of her job as "foolishness," focusing instead on the second half of the statement. Tea. Good grief, she'd have to drink a gallon of the stuff to come even half-awake.

"I can make the tea, Au— I mean, Patricia. I'm here to help until your cast comes off." And not a moment longer. No matter that Patricia seemed to take for granted Evie had returned for good.

"I'm not an invalid, despite what my daughter may have told you. I can make my own tea. We'll drink it in the kitchen so we don't need a tray."

Evie dutifully followed her aunt through the swinging door into the kitchen. This, too, was both familiar and new. They'd eaten at the miniature trestle table in the center of the room every night. Strange how small the table seemed to her now. The bare oak cabinets remained, but they'd been whitewashed and distressed, and the Formica countertops replaced with gleaming green composite stone.

ABOUT THE AUTHOR

Laura K. Curtis has always done everything backward. As a child, she was extremely serious, so now that she's chronologically an adult, she feels perfectly justified in acting the fool. She started teaching at age fifteen, then decided to go back to school herself at thirty. And she wrote her first book in first grade. It was released in (notebook) paperback to rave reviews, and she's been trying to achieve the same level of acclaim ever since. She lives in Westchester County, New York, with her husband and a pack of wild Irish terriers, which has taught her how easily love can coexist with the desire to kill.

To find out more about Laura and her books, please visit her online:

Website: laurakcurtis.com.
Twitter: @laurakcurtis

my half of the apartment furnished so I didn't have to sell everything before coming back here, but I only had a week to find someone, so she's not paying my full share. I still owe a bit on that, and I have ongoing bills." She didn't want to talk about the biggest, so she waved a hand vaguely. "Cell phone, stuff like that."

"Don't you have savings? How could I raise a child who lives paycheck to paycheck? Candace—"

"Don't go there. I don't need a big salary. I can manage on a couple hundred a week."

"You expect me to pay you two hundred dollars a week? I could hire someone for that!"

"You could try, but even kids don't work that cheap these days. You're stuck with me."

"And what if I don't happen to have a spare few hundred a week to donate to the cause?"

The question might have been rhetorical, merely another way for Patricia to express her disgust at being asked to pay for something she considered her due, but a hint of desperation lurked beneath the words. It resonated with a dreadful familiarity, sending a shiver down Evie's spine. Patricia wouldn't appreciate being confronted, however, so Evie kept her tone as light as possible while privately resolving to examine her aunt's finances as soon as possible.

"If you don't, then my job will include making the store more profitable, won't it? So why don't you finish your sandwich, and we'll get started."

get it at the café in the mornings when we go into the store." Patricia thumped over to the table and set a plate in front of Evie, then got her own.

"I'll buy a machine. They're cheap, and I'll want caffeine before I see anyone in the mornings. But that brings up a subject we haven't had a chance to talk about." Evie took a deep breath. "Salary."

For the first time in her life, Evie saw Patricia's jaw literally drop. Her facial muscles seemed completely frozen, her mouth unable to close. It lasted only a moment, however.

"I'm not planning on paying you. I don't need an employee. As I said to Candace, I only need a hand here and there. I'm supplying you with room and board; what else do you need money for?"

"It's not here and there, Patricia. I'll be driving you everywhere you need to go, working in the shop, helping out around here. It's a full-time position, even if only a temporary one."

"The cast comes off in a month. Surely you can help me out for a *month*."

"A month until your cast comes off, and then at least another of physical therapy before you can drive. I've known dancers with breaks like yours. It's not an easy recovery." And Patricia, unlike most of Evie's friends, was of an age where bones were starting to become brittle anyway.

"Two months is nothing. You'll be staying in the apartment. I'll stock the kitchen up there and you know you can always come down here and get anything you want."

"It's not just food. I have bills. I have a *life*." And a pile of debt. But she refused to confirm the beliefs of all those who'd whispered about her feckless mother. They'd expect her to fail, expect her to go broke. They wouldn't care about the reasons.

"A life?"

"Back in Vegas. Yes, I found a sub-letter who'd take

that."

"I don't like your egg salad. I adore it. I can't believe you remember my favorite foods."

"Of course I do. I'm not senile." Patricia peeled off her gloves and handed them to Evie along with her hat. "Before you change, please put these back where you found them, will you?"

"Of course."

Evie laid the gloves and hat back on the bureau, then gave in to temptation and walked down the hall to peek into the room she'd shared with Candace as a child. The pale mauve walls had been repainted sky blue, and denim covers, rather than the floral prints of her memory, encased the fluffy duvets on the twin beds. A big box of toys and trucks held pride of place in the far corner. It had clearly become a boys' space, and Evie wondered how often Candace's children spent the night with Grandma.

Closing the door on her past, she headed back to the garage apartment. It took her only a couple of minutes to change out of the sundress and into jeans, a tee shirt, and a pair of scarlet high-top sneakers, but by the time she was done Patricia already had sandwiches on the table. She'd even bought Evie's favorite vegetable chips to go with them, and Evie found herself forced to blink away tears. She really hadn't gotten enough sleep. She shouldn't be reacting so strongly to such a small thing. Her reserved aunt wouldn't thank her for such sentimentality.

So she swallowed the lump in her throat and, at Patricia's instruction, grabbed the pitcher of iced tea from the refrigerator. Which reminded her of something she'd forgotten to check while changing.

"Is there a coffee maker in the apartment? I didn't see one when I looked."

"No. We built the studio over the garage for Harry's father when he came to live with us after Martha died, and he didn't drink coffee. If you want coffee, you can

Excerpt of TOYING WITH HIS AFFECTIONS

been ancient and doddering. His sermons had been gentle, if exceedingly boring. Reverend Masters took a different tack, exhorting his congregation in a harsh and booming tone against the evils of pride. By the time the sermon was over, Evie's jaw ached from gritting her teeth.

They made their way outside—slowly, because of Patricia's crutches and the crowd in front of them—and Patricia began to urge Evie toward the minister.

"You don't want to do that," Evie muttered, trying not to draw attention.

"Don't be ridiculous. You have to meet Reverend Masters."

"No, I don't. And, honestly, Patricia, you don't want me to. Because I'm likely to remind him about stones and glass houses." She heard a gasp behind her, but didn't bother looking to see who she'd offended.

Rescue came from an unlikely corner. "I must admit, Miz Patricia," Griff interjected, flashing that killer grin, "today's wasn't one of the Reverend's more inspiring sermons. Perhaps Evie should wait until next week."

Evie very much doubted the smug minister would improve in a week's time, but she did appreciate the reprieve. She gave Griff a warm smile and he blinked a couple of times like a rabbit caught in the beam of a flashlight.

"I'll just take you ladies home," he continued at last, as if Patricia had agreed. He took one of her crutches and held out an arm, and Patricia conceded with more grace than Evie would have expected.

WHEN THEY ARRIVED AT THE house, Patricia recommended Evie change clothes. "It's dusty in the bookstore these days. I couldn't very well ask Leah to clean for me, so we'll do it today. You run up and change, and I'll get lunch started. I made egg salad. I hope you still like

Excerpt of TOYING WITH HIS AFFECTIONS

With a little mental prod, she joined the others as they passed through the doors. She felt a bit like a bride, slowly making her way up the aisle while those seated in the pews watched her every step. She met their stares with her own, daring them to pity her now. Unfortunately, no handsome prince of a groom awaited her at the end of the procession. Just Candace, her husband Jim, and their twin boys, Billy and Teddy, age five.

"Are you our aunt?" asked Teddy in a loud whisper.

"I am," Evie replied, holding out her hand. "And you must be Teddy. Your grandmother sent me pictures of you."

"She didn't show us any of *you*," Teddy said with an accusatory scowl at Patricia. "We only found out about you after her accident." Both boys solemnly shook her hand.

"Well, I live very far away. I doubt she thought it mattered you had an aunt until we were going to meet."

"Are you Mommy's sister? My teacher says an aunt is Mommy or Daddy's sister." Teddy was obviously the talker of the two.

"That's true," Candace said, "but Evie is *not* my sister. She's my cousin. Which makes her your cousin once removed, but that's hard to say, so we call her your aunt."

Billy wrinkled his forehead at the explanation, but Teddy forged ahead.

"You can't be our cousin. You're too old."

"Teddy!" Patricia glared, but for the first time since leaving Vegas, Evie laughed aloud. Of course, church wasn't precisely the best place for such a thing, even if the service hadn't yet begun.

"It's okay, Teddy," she assured him. "I *am* too old. That's why I'm a cousin once removed instead of a regular one."

"Now, hush," said Patricia, rapping once on the pew. "Here comes Reverend Masters."

The minister in Evie's youth, Reverend French, had

the drying rack. "I'm going to be the talk of the town this week with two such lovely ladies on my arm."

"You're coming to church with us?"

"'Course. I always bring Miz Patricia. Gotta keep my hand in with the Ladies' Auxiliary if I hope to be elected in a couple of months."

Evie looked to her aunt for an explanation. "When Griffin's daddy had his heart attack, the County Commissioner appointed Griffin to the position. But come November, he'll be elected without any problem."

A grimace Evie couldn't interpret flashed across Griff's features before he grinned once more. "Your aunt's one of my biggest supporters."

"Griffin's really made something of himself," said Patricia, and Evie's stomach muscles clenched at the obvious implication.

"Well, we should get a move on," said Mr. Made-Something-Of-Himself into the increasingly awkward silence. "Being late to church won't help my reputation, especially since Candace and Jim will be holding seats for us in a pew near the front."

Of course they would. The knots in Evie's stomach tightened and twisted as the big, black Suburban with SHERIFF painted on the side rolled through town. Just as well she hadn't had any coffee that morning. She'd probably have puked all over the nice, clean leather.

Griff assisted Patricia up the stairs to the church door, and Evie hesitated for a moment below them, dreading what was to come. As a child, she'd sensed the town's pity, a palpable force every Sunday for at least a year. They'd sat in the front then, too, and she'd practically heard the whispers of "poor child" echo at their backs. Evie had always felt herself shrinking, becoming tinier and tinier as she trailed her aunt and uncle up the aisle until by the time they slid into their pew, she was a mere speck, a mote floating in the air. Apparently, Candace had stepped right into her mother's low-heeled pumps, but this time Evie refused to disappear.

woman said. "Run up and get them so we can get moving. We don't want to be late for church."

Griff watched with interest as Evie flinched, then controlled herself. Round two to the pro. This could be more entertaining than anything that had happened since his return to Fairview.

EVIE COULDN'T BELIEVE SHE'D FORGOTTEN her aunt's insistence on Sunday services. It had constituted one of the major changes in her life when she'd moved to Fairview. Before her mother's death, she'd never been to a formal religious service of any kind, but Harry and Patricia attended church every Sunday, and Candace and Evie were expected to dress accordingly, in frilly dresses, fancy bonnets, and white gloves that prevented Evie from chewing her fingernails. As she gathered her aunt's sophisticated straw bowler with white lace trim and white gloves from the dresser, she caught sight of the nails that had so offended her aunt. No longer shredded and torn below the raw tips of her fingers, they were now long, strong, and painted a bright, carnelian red.

Patricia almost certainly didn't approve of the color any more than she had the gnawed remnants, but Evie couldn't afford to care. Literally. If she didn't make some money, she wouldn't be able to pay for a simple manicure, let alone the complicated highlights she'd taken to wearing in her hair. And what, she wondered, did Griff think of her new look? Not that it mattered. She was who she was, after all, but the question of how others—especially her teen self's ideal—would see her transformation was irresistible.

When she returned to the kitchen, Griff stood at the sink rinsing the tea cups. *Some rebel.* He turned and flashed that killer smile again.

"Perfect timing." He laid the final piece of china in

her own right, he wasn't ready to settle down yet, and he wouldn't lead her on.

"Now that Evie's home, you don't need to worry so much. She'll take me to the store in the mornings, and you can get your breakfast there if you still feel the need to check up on me."

Patricia, he knew, considered Beth Ann a perfect match for him. Her invitations to the store had more to do with his unacceptable marital status than the state of his sweet tooth. Not that she'd ever admit it. Patricia maintained an absolutely unruffled, stoic exterior and would be mortified to know he saw through to her good-hearted matchmaking.

"In fact, Evie and I are going in this afternoon and regular hours will resume tomorrow." She plunked a pot of tea in the center of the table, where a plate of scones already lay. Three delicate cups designated the spots where each of them was intended to sit, and Griff helped Patricia lower herself into her seat before taking his own.

"Beth Ann's cousin Leah has been keeping the store open eleven to three while her son is in school, but I need to get back to my normal schedule before people in town forget about me entirely and start going to the chain store in Greeneville." She aimed a pointed glare at Evie, filled with condemnation for not stepping up as quickly as Leah.

Not exactly polite, but Patricia had her reasons. After all, Evie hadn't showed up for her uncle's funeral, nor any time in the four years since.

"We can't have that," Evie replied with a shark-like smile. "The retail gods would never forgive me if I let a big box store swallow you whole. Especially not with my retail experience."

Huh. He didn't understand the return swipe, but Patricia's lips thinned. Round one to the newcomer, which was pretty impressive given Patricia Bell Stewart's legendary poise.

"My gloves and hat are on my dresser," the older

Excerpt of TOYING WITH HIS AFFECTIONS

He grasped her fingers, and the rough slide of his flesh over her own sent such a surprising shock through her that for a moment she entirely missed his words.

"My father had a heart attack four months ago. I was appointed to fill his position."

"Oh, no! I had no idea! I'm so sorry."

"I'd hardly expect you to have heard. I know you and your aunt don't talk much." The censure in his tone erased any lingering frisson of pleasure from his touch, and Evie spun away to lead him toward the kitchen.

"Patricia said to invite you in for a scone and some tea," she tossed over her shoulder, not waiting to see whether he would follow.

WELL. PUT HIM IN HIS place. Griff admired Evie's take-no-prisoners attitude almost as much as the sway of her lithe figure beneath the filmy sundress as he trailed her into the kitchen. He didn't remember her as a particularly attractive girl, but then it had been a long time since he'd seen her, and in those days he'd been more interested in Candace, whose wildness had almost matched his own. And now, Candace was an attorney while good-girl Evie had become a showgirl. Of course, who'd have believed, given his own reputation, that he would take his father's place as sheriff?

"Good morning, Patricia," he said as he entered the kitchen on Evie's heels. "What have you cooked up for me today?"

"Blueberry scones. And you know Beth Ann does all the baking."

"Yes, but they're your recipes. And she doesn't give me freebies." Not that she wouldn't. Beth Ann Wheeler had set her sights on him the minute he'd moved back to Fairview, and while she embodied everything he'd eventually want in a wife, being a quiet woman, diplomatic, conservative, and a force in the community in

Excerpt of TOYING WITH HIS AFFECTIONS

No sooner had Evie settled into one of the well-worn ladder-back chairs and allowed herself to get comfortable, however, than the doorbell rang.

"That'll be Sheriff Barstow," said Patricia. "He stops by in the mornings to check on me. Invite him in for a scone."

The words brought to mind the picture of the scowling, bejowled man who'd issued Evie her first and only speeding ticket. She'd gotten it on her way out of Fairview at age eighteen. Hard to believe he was still sheriff.

She braced herself for an unpleasant blast from her past and got…something else entirely. Not Bertram Barstow at all, though it took her a minute to identify the stunning specimen behind the crisply starched khaki shirt with the badge pinned to its pocket.

Griff Barstow had been all angry young rebel the last time she'd seen him. He'd worn his chestnut hair too long, his jeans too baggy, and his leather jacket like armor. His every muscle, ligament, and tendon had virtually vibrated with defiance. Evie had idealized him. More than that, she'd wanted to *be* him, to crawl inside his skin and find out how it felt to break every rule, to shrug off every expectation.

And he'd gotten out. Two years her senior, Griff had disappeared one day the summer after he graduated high school. Rumors abounded, but the sheriff refused to confirm any of them. By the time Evie herself escaped, people had even stopped talking about him.

So what had happened to turn the rebellious hero of her teenage fantasies into this buttoned-down, buttoned-up, crew-cut cop?

"You must be Evangeline," he said, a smile cutting deep grooves in tan cheeks. Dammit, even his teeth were perfect!

"Call me Evie." She thrust out her hand. "When Patricia said the sheriff was coming by, I expected your father."